RETRIBUTION

L.A. BURCH

BOOK ONE OF THE
MASTERMINDS SERIES

L. A. BURCH

Retribution: The dispensing or receiving of reward or punishment.

L. A. BURCH

Kindle Direct Publishing
Cover Design: A. K. Covers
Typist/Content Editor: Lisa McPhaul

ISBN: 9798990247208

Dedication

This book is dedicated to my Big Brother, Walter Keith Rogers. Sadly, he was taken from us too soon. In defense of his country until the day he died, we all lost more than a soldier when God called him home. Love you Big Bro, and know that this is not a goodbye, but an "I'll see you again soon."

Acknowledgments

First and foremost, I want to give thanks and honor to my Higher Power. Without Your blessings and mercy, I wouldn't be alive and well today.

Next, I want to give thanks to my family, who shows me love and support on a daily basis. Thank you for believing in me and encouraging me to always pursue my dreams. I couldn't ask for a better support system to help me navigate the mountains and valleys that we call life.

Thank you to my CAP brothers, most of whom I grew up with. You guys taught me that when you are away from your family, you don't fill the void with friends, you fill it with more family. Charles P, 50, Matt, BG, KB, John G, Rob, Ride By, Brian, Ghost, Black Ops, Oliver, Steve, JB, Eli, Tuck, Mike Mike, BJ, Lee, TK, Joseph T, Bobby F, Mike M, (If I didn't name you personally, sorry, I am getting old). All of you, thank you so much for putting up with me and becoming closer to me than some of my family. And thanks for some of you becoming either cops or cannon fodder for my killer.

Last but not least, I'd like to thank my author family for leading, helping, and criticizing me until I could produce something at least readable. The Author (Wilford), my mentor, thank you for challenging me and showing me how to pull myself out of the trenches. We are going on tour one day, and we are going to leave our legacy all over this world.

RETRIBUTION

L. A. BURCH

RETRIBUTION

**BOOK ONE OF
THE MASTERMINDS SERIES**

PROLOGUE

"Alright ladies, next 10," yelled Cpt. Dennis. The last of the previous 10 inmates had just vacated the 20 x 15-foot room the officers at Maury Correctional Institution in North Carolina called the shakedown room.

The room had a tile floor, so it was easy to clean up the blood left behind if an inmate got out of line. It was brightly lit, so the officers conducting the searches didn't miss anything. There are no cameras in this room for many reasons. None are good news for the inmates.

"I can't stand these racist bastards," one of the inmates remarked. MCI has always been a tough prison to be housed in. Officers and inmates alike are airlifted to Pitt County Memorial Hospital on a daily basis. From simple assaults, to rapes, to murders, it all happens at the notorious 1500-man, maximum-security facility. Unfortunately, it happens more to the black inmates than anyone else.

"Don't be shy, girls," mouthed the captain. "Make sure you strip all the way down and bend deep before you spread them cheeks."

Even though the Department of Corrections policy states that anyone not participating in the search should not be present, you couldn't drag Cpt. Dennis away with a pack of wild horses. He lives to humiliate and degrade inmates. For the past 25 years, that has been the joy of his life. As a long-standing member of the KKK, to kick a nigger's ass and get paid for it, what more could a white man in the South ask for?

"Hey man, isn't it against policy for you to do all of us in the same room like this?" asked another inmate.

The captain's head whipped around. "Shut the fuck up, inmate!" he shouted, as he stalked towards the man. "Who do you think you are to question me, boy? I will fuck up your whole life."

1

The smart thing to do would be for the inmate to back down and act cowed to appease the captain, but even though this particular inmate is smart, being a coward isn't in him.

"Yeah, you can do a whole lot when all your minions around," he stated, stepping up just like the captain did. "Catch me by yourself and call me a boy, cracker."

Blows came from every direction before the inmate could say another word. The minions he spoke about were ruthless with their punches and kicks until the inmate was in the fetal position on the tiled floor.

"How did that feel, boy?" asked the captain. "Run your mouth to me boy, and you might never make it home."

The room fell silent. Only the hard breathing of the officers and the moans of the downed inmate could be heard. Not one inmate even had a thought to help him, for they knew it was room on the floor for them to lay moaning also.

"Listen up, you pussy motherfuckers," yelled Cpt. Dennis. "Let this be a lesson for everyone in this room." He paused dramatically, looking around. "I decide whether you live or die." He kicked the injured inmate once more to prove his point.

"I decide when you talk, when you sleep, and when you eat," he bellowed with the eyes of a fanatic who believed every word he said. "In other words, I own you."

He then spit on the inmate who was still curled up on the floor. "I say whether you go home or not."

The downed inmate whispered, "All of us don't have life."

Captain Dennis leaned down and asked, "What did you say, inmate? Speak up."

See, there was a lot the captain didn't know about this particular inmate. He had just been granted clemency after serving 10 years of a 26-year sentence. This was the last week he would spend in the North Carolina Department of Corrections.

A little louder this time, the killer said, "All of us don't have life."

CHAPTER 1

"God, this motherfucker is really starting to piss me off," said Sergeant Detective Walter Rogers. Standing at 5-foot 10-inches, with 230 pounds of solid muscles, he could be quite intimidating if he wanted to be.

Det. Rogers had been a force of nature his whole life. As a kid, he was always the fastest and the strongest. By 9th grade, he was the starting running back for one of the best football schools in Philadelphia. Grades had always been a problem, not because of his intelligence, but because he hated going to school.

So, even with scholarship offers coming in from all over the country, he decided to join the Army. He was an MP for 12 years, where he earned the rank of Staff Sergeant. Now, after 15 years with the North Carolina State Bureau of Investigations, he is the sergeant over all detectives.

"When is this guy going to make a mistake?"

The handsome, 48-year-old Det. Rogers, with his caramel skin, and low haircut, was as angry as he had ever been in his life. Even though he is in excellent shape, as a black man with high blood pressure, he had to always control his anger. Before this case, he was doing a pretty good job.

"Don't worry Sarge," said Det. Grace. "He's good, but no way is he better than us."

Det. Ann Grace still had her youthful confidence, even after 13 years in law enforcement. Her beautiful skin betrayed her mixed European and Cherokee heritage. Standing at 5-foot 8-inches, 130 pounds, with long blue-black hair down to her waist, many suspects have underestimated her.

After 5 years of working for the Charlotte/Mecklenburg Police Department, and another 8 years working for the NC SBI, this 35-year-old was anything but a pushover.

"We know his M.O., we just have to get in front of this thing."

As Det. Grace talked to her senior partner, they were standing in front of a sight that was becoming all too familiar. This time, the corrections officer was a young, white female.

You couldn't tell it now, but her driver's license showed a beautiful young lady with dark hair, green eyes, and a perfect olive-colored skin tone. The bullets to her face and head changed all of that.

The two detectives stood in the driveway of a single-story house. It was small with just one bedroom, a kitchen, living room, and one bathroom. With small yards in the front and back, it was a perfect starter home for a young professional. The home was painted Carolina blue with a white door and white shutters.

The house was shielded on each side by 10-foot hedges, which gave it all the privacy a young woman could ask for. This time, that privacy might have worked against her.

Being the SBI means you're always the last to the party. Because the Bureau had sent out an urgent request for information on any crimes against any prison officials or former inmates, they had been called in early on this one. The victim still had her uniform on, so the detectives actually got to see the crime scene with the body still in place.

"Well, at least we got a full night's sleep before they called us," murmured Det. Rogers.

The detective felt he had earned the right to wear whatever he wanted. After wearing uniforms his whole life, he felt like a suit was just another uniform. So, because they were enjoying a spell of good weather for February, he wore blue jeans with an Army sweatshirt and a pair of Air Force Ones.

On the other hand, Det. Grace was as elegant as always. With a dark blue, designer pant suit, and a canary yellow blouse that perfectly complimented her doe-like, brown eyes, she was ready to face any situation. She did have on low-heeled pumps, but knew no suspect would ever outrun her partner, so she was ok with them.

All the looky-loos had gone about their business and the two detectives were waiting on the Swan Quarter police detective to tell them what was up. Not that they couldn't see, with the blown in glass and the body slumped over onto the passenger seat with half her brains on the passenger door. All they knew for certain was that the 11th victim had been claimed. At least by their calculations, the killer was only on number 11.

"Hello, Det. Grace and Sgt. Det. Rogers, I'm Det. Gray. I'm the one who called you guys." Like any heterosexual male, his eyes lingered on Det. Grace for a few seconds. Even with the conservative, business attire on, she still could cause a man to lose his train of thought.

Det. Gray fit his name to the letter. With a gray suit and gray hair, he was medium or average in every way physically. And even though he was over 50, he still had the alert eyes of a cop.

"Nice to meet you," said Det. Rogers, as the detectives both shook his hand. "Fill us in on what you have so far."

"None of the lab work is done yet, obviously. And as per your instructions, the M.E. has held off on moving the body." This last part was said with an air of exasperation.

"Anyway," continued Detective Gray, flipping through a pocket-sized notebook. "Officer Darby Lewis, single white female, 24 years old, lives alone. Worked at Hyde Correctional for the last 2 years. Drove a cherry red 2022 Ford Mustang, which appears to be where the murder occurred. Multiple gunshot wounds to the face and head. No witnesses."

He gestured around with hands held high, to include the neighborhood. "No one heard a gunshot. From what I can gather, just based on my initial investigation, the victim comes home from work, puts the car in park, cuts the engine, and before she can get out of the car, is shot through the driver's side window. She is hit at least 3 times in the head with a 9MM handgun, or something about that size. Time of death is approximately 6:30pm last night, according to initial M.E. onsite evaluation." He paused and looked around to make sure no one was in hearing range.

Leaning in closer, he said, "The fucker walked in, probably hid on the other side of the house. Waited until she pulled in. Walked right up to the car, without a care in the world, and shot this young lady in the face. Then he walked the fuck out of here and probably went and got something to eat. And nobody saw or heard shit. I'd bet my pension that it was some inmate who she turned down, he couldn't take it, so when he got out, he killed her."

Det. Rogers didn't say that if that was the case, the inmate would have taken her in the house and raped her first.

"Who found the body?" asked Det. Grace, glancing around.

"Neighbor, 4 doors down was walking his dog at 4:30 this morning. Noticed the window down and wanted to get a look at the interior. Says victim just got the car 3 days ago. Soon as he got close, he saw the blood and the body. He backed off, whipped his phone out and called 911."

"How did she pay for the car?" asked Det. Rogers. "Did she inherit some money? Because, last time I checked, a corrections officer after only 2 years makes $38,000 a year. And that is an $80,000 car."

Det Gray, looking pained, said, "Come on man, it's only 9:30 in the morning. Give me a little time." Getting worked up now, he said, "I know the SBI normally gets their reports weeks after the initial crime, not hours. Don't bust my balls with all these questions. You're the one who told me to hold up the crime scene."

"Hey, listen, we're all on the same side here," stated Det. Grace, patting her hands in a calming manner. She knew how and when to play up the little woman routine to calm a man down. "We just really want to catch this guy. If it is confirmed, then this will be the 11th victim, that we know of.

This guy is a serial killer, and we all need to work together to stop him."

All the anger drained out of him. With slumped shoulders, he asked, "What do you need me to do?"

It was almost funny how the soft words of a beautiful woman could cause even a hurricane to change directions.

"All of the other victims, except two who we think were just innocent bystanders, have been connected to some shady practices at the prisons. Find out how she paid for the car and if she has money or drugs stashed somewhere."

Det. Rogers paused for a minute, thinking how to say his next line without angering the older detective. "I need you to look beyond what people will say because she was a beautiful, young woman. I need you to investigate her like she is a suspect and not a victim."

The storm he expected didn't come. Instead, the detective, looking resigned, said, "You got it, as fast as I can. Just do me a favor. When you catch up to this piece of shit, do to him what he's been doing to these officers, shoot him in his fucking face."

With that said, Det. Gray turned and walked towards the M.E. The only thing that was on Sgt. Det. Roger's mind was one word; [**IF** we catch this piece of shit.]

CHAPTER 2

"So, you like to abuse inmates?" the killer asked. "You like to beat on inmates while they're handcuffed and helpless?"

The man the killer was talking to didn't have much to say at this point. He was tied to a chair in his own shed. He didn't remember how he got there. The last he remembered, he was cooking on the grill on his back deck, then woke up here.

The man was overweight, to say the least. Although, with all the blood and tissue coming out of him, he had to be losing some weight. The fact that he was thinking about losing weight probably meant most of his mind was gone already.

The killer was just standing in front of him, still clutching the knife he had been using on the man for the last 3 hours.

He was 6-foot 1-inch tall. He was a bald, black man with light-brown skin and was in extremely good shape, with 200 pounds of solid muscles. Right now, he had a smirk on his very handsome face.

"Cat got your tongue, fat motherfucker?" the killer taunted. "No…wait, sorry, I already cut that out didn't I, HAHAHAHA."

When Officer Ford first regained consciousness after being knocked out by a massive blow to the head, he wanted to test the killer to see how serious he was. Talking trash had led to the knife being used to cut out his tongue.

Officer Mario Ford was a short, fat, 48-year-old black man who worked at Piedmont Correctional in Salisbury, North Carolina. He was a 24-year veteran who loved to beat on inmates when they were shackled down.

Fast as lightning, the killer struck again, digging the knife deep into the officer's right hand. The hand that was said to have knocked out over 100 inmates.

"Ahhh!" the officer yelled. "Op, plea, Op. Orry, I'm sorry," the officer cried and begged for the pain to stop, at least as good as he could with his ruined mouth.

"You stink, you pig ass piece of shit," the killer said. "Oh, I found this gas and oil mixture. Let me see if it will make you smell better," he said, as he heaved the mixture all over the officer.

This time, the pain was so great, the officer didn't even make a sound. As the gas and oil mixture hit all his open wounds, it sent his body into convulsions.

"HaHaHaHa, look at your fat ass dance," the killer teased him. "Don't die yet, I have a couple more surprises for you."

The killer would have loved to cut his dick off and shove it in his mouth but knew the officer would die before the grand finale if he did.

"Okay, fat boy," said the killer. "I can see you're tired so I'm going to wrap this up, if it's okay with you."

The officer was so hurt and tired, it took all his strength just to hold his head up. Since he had been punched and kicked in the face for the first hour after he woke up, he could barely see out of his swollen eyes. But what he saw was the most terrifying thing yet.

The shed door was open, so even though it was a cold and dark night, the moonlight provided all the illumination one would need. Seems the decision to take that vacation to his isolated cabin in the woods didn't work out so well for old Officer Ford.

The killer was dumping the remaining gas and oil mixture all over the small shed. He then laid a trail leading about 6 feet outside.

"Anything you want to say to help me make this choice." The killer had pulled out a handgun with his right hand and had a lighter in his left. "Make it good, you have 30 seconds," the killer remarked as he looked at his watch.

Officer Ford knew death had come for him. He was begging in his head, but his body was too exhausted to cooperate.

"Well, sir, on behalf of all the prisoners at Piedmont Correctional, I hereby sentence you to death by fire. I will serve as the witness to your death."

With that, the killer flicked the lighter, bent down and touched it to the mix. With a smile on his face, he watched the fire climb up to claim its victim.

The killer thought it was funny how the fat son of a bitch didn't have the energy to plead for his life but screamed bloody murder as soon as the fire hit him.

After the screams stopped, the fire blazed as the wooden shed fed its flames.

"Damn," said the killer. "He had enough left for me to cut his dick off and still set his ass on fire." He was kind of impressed but also felt robbed of the satisfaction.

"You wasn't the first, you pussy motherfucker, and you won't be the last. But I need a little vacation."

Walking slowly backwards, so he could take in the spectacle, the killer once again faded away into the night, finishing up another perfect murder.

CHAPTER 3

"Okay, fuck this bullshit. Serial killers don't just stop. It's been a year since we found Mario Ford up at his cabin. We're missing something."

Sgt. Det. Rogers was all but yelling as he talked to his partner, Det. Grace. He had on his customary non-uniform consisting of jeans, sweatshirt, and sneakers. His boss had given up years ago on trying to put a dress code on him. Det. Rogers had looked him in his eyes and said, "If you can make me put a suit on then I'll wear one. If not, shut the fuck up and let me make your career." His closure rate was so high, his boss chose to shut the fuck up.

"Listen partner, you need to calm down before you have a stroke," Det. Grace said, reminding her partner of his high blood pressure.

They were in Det. Rogers's office on the third floor of the Justice Building in Raleigh, North Carolina. This is where the State Bureau of Investigations has its offices.

It was a beautiful May morning, but the detectives didn't care about the sun shining. Nor did they care about the view out of the corner office windows. They didn't care that the office looked out on a room full of detectives hard at work on whatever case they were working on.

"This guy has been hurting and killing officers and inmates for over 3 years now, and we don't have shit. You're not embarrassed? I am." Det. Grace knew Walter was just venting, so she kept quiet.

Ann was wearing a knee-length, khaki skirt with a teal blouse that was simple but also stylish. She added white tennis shoes to complete the casual, but work approved, look.

"Come on Ann, talk to me. What are you thinking? Is he done and gone forever? You know if he quits now, he will get away with all of it."

11

"I don't think he is done," said Ann. "He killed eight people and completely destroyed the lives of 4 more." She paused to gather her thoughts. "I know we have made list after list of inmates, but I do think we are missing something. He did all of this over a 2-year span, and I really think we have his name in a file in this office right now. We just have to keep whittling down the list."

When they started those lists 3 years ago, the names numbered in the thousands. The numbers kept rising with each victim. After the 8th victim, the number of names actually started to go down. At one time, they thought they had their man based on survivor's statements and the changes they were able to make to the parameters of the list. The name was a dead end.

Unfortunately, the guy they were chasing was extremely smart. They soon figured out that some of the victims were not really personal to the killer. They were just hurt or killed to muck up the investigation. Genius really, because it left the cops with nowhere to start or stop. Maybe he only wanted one or two personally and the other 10 or 11 were just smoke. The problem was, all of them except 2 had a lot of enemies.

The two officers, the 5th and 6th victims, driving inmate Jamar Edmond, the 4th victim, to the foot doctor, were stellar upstanding officers. Even the inmates mourned them. Nothing in either of their pasts led investigators to believe that they were anything except innocent bystanders of the real target.

Which led investigators to feel that Jamar Edmond was the one victim they knew to be personal to the killer. Then again, he could be the only one who was the smoke screen and the 3 lives lost meant nothing compared to the killer's ultimate goal. Or it was unrelated to their killer in any way.

"Okay, let's go back to the first case for a bit. Get the file and give me the highlights." As Ann got up to get the file Walter asked for, they both felt the frustration that comes from doing the same thing over and over again.

"Alright, here we go," Ann said, retaking her seat. "Officer Trevor Jones. A 50-year-old, black male, buried alive with an air tube but no food or water. Worked at Foothills Youth Center in Morganton. Under investigation for two years before he was fired for starving inmates in Restrictive Housing."

"Sounds like a little payback to me. Kill him the same way he used to torture the inmates." Det. Rogers felt all men, whether incarcerated or not, should be treated like people. "It didn't give this guy the right to kill him, but I would've wanted a little payback myself if someone tried to starve me to death."

He sat back and thought for a minute, then asked, "Which years did he work in the hole?"

Ann did the math and responded, "March 2001 to January 2006, which is when he was fired." She looked back at the file for a minute. "So, we don't know if he was starving them the whole time. The first complaint came in December 2003. They kept coming in, until in March 2004, they put him under investigation, but continued to let him work because they were short of staff. He worked right up to the day he was found guilty of misconduct and fired."

"Alright, so how many on our list, who were out to commit the murder, but was in the hole at FCI from, let's say December 2003 to January 2006? He might not have felt comfortable at first to torture inmates. So, let's go with after the first complaint."

Ann knew that Walter was super smart and probably already knew all the information that he had her researching, but she knew he was still training her, even after all these years together.

"I know what you're doing Walter, but I'll play along," Ann responded. "Let's see, I'm coming up with a grand total of 763 inmates."

Since she had switched to her laptop, it was really fast and easy to just use the database they had created to narrow down any list they wished to make.

"Okay, cross reference that list with the list of inmates who did time with Bruce Battle."

Walter was referring to the inmate, Bruce Battle, who had been deemed the 3rd victim of their killer. He was a 33-year-old, black male. He was a known Blood gang member who was serving time for Armed Robbery. In prison, he was known for using gang intimidation to take other inmates' property. He was shot with a sniper rifle while out for recreation at Pasquotank Prison. He lived, but the damage was so severe to his shoulder, he had to get his arm amputated.

"That doesn't really help us. He has been in so often, that it only takes 200 names off the list. So now we're down to 563," voiced Ann, with her face still glued to the screen.

"Let's add an age requirement to this thing. Say, at the time that the 1st victim, Trevor Jones, was killed, our perp had to be under 50. Put that in and see what we have," instructed Det. Rogers. "Also, we know from survivors that he is black and over six feet."

"Adding all of that, and our new number is 251. But I still feel that Officer Ford was personal too," added Ann.

"Put that one up there and see what you get." Officer Ford had worked at Piedmont for 24 years, so chances were, if the killer had been to Piedmont, their paths had crossed.

"Damn, Piedmont is a processing center, so it only dropped us down to 238."

"Okay, I know we have done this numerous times before, but put all 12 incidents in the parameters and tell me what you think."

Ann did as Walter asked her to do. The results came out to 22 names. When she added the race, size, and age, it came out to 1 name; Carlton Porter.

This was a name that they had researched extensively in the past. She had some thoughts on the subject and now was the time to voice them.

"Carlton Porter, age 40, black male, 6-foot 2-inches tall, 240 pounds. Locked up at 18, served 18 years, and was released 4 years ago. Completely off the grid, hasn't been seen since his reintroduction to society." Ann read a little of his prison record.

Chuckling, she said, "He has a problem with the ladies. The only thing I can see here is that he likes women, and they like him back. A couple of minor things but all the major infractions involve a female officer."

Walter waited to see if she would add anymore. When she didn't, he said, "Here's the thing, we're giving this guy all the credit in the world for being smart. Don't you think that he knew if we looked at all these details, that we would come up with that name? So, if Carlton is our killer, then he's not smart at all. What do you think, is he the killer or is the killer setting him up?"

Before either of them could voice one way or another, the door was flung open by one of the junior detectives in Walter's group. "Sarge," he said, out of breath. He had tried to call but knew Det. Rogers always turns his phone off when he and Ann are brainstorming. "You won't believe this, but we got another one."

Det. Grace and Sgt. Det. Rogers looked at each other and froze for a second. Then they both sprung out of their chairs. Det. Rogers, hyped up and running, yelled to the detective as he passed him, "Send the info to my phone, NOW!" Then they were gone.

CHAPTER 4

"There are a few facts that every single person on this earth should know. You want to hear them?" asked Captain Robert Dennis. He was speaking to his wife, Mary, who sat in the passenger seat of his 1996 Ford Explorer.

"Why do you ask if no matter what I say, you're going to tell me anyway?" replied Mary. She was getting sick and tired of hearing her husband's bullshit. She would have divorced his ass long ago but knew he would kill her before letting her go.

"Well, even though I don't like your fucking attitude, I'm going to educate your ass with a little knowledge about this world. One, the world is round. Two, the sky is fucking blue. Last but not least, Robert Dennis is nobody's pussy. Do you understand those facts?"

They were sitting outside waiting to pick up their daughter from the airport. Her plane had landed 15 minutes ago, so they knew she would be out any minute now.

"Thank you for those crown jewels, worthy gems you just dropped on me. I wonder how I did 12 years of college without your help," Mary said. An explosion of pain in her stomach made her gasp for breath and caused her eyes to water.

"Don't you fucking sass me bitch," Robert said after punching his wife in the stomach. "If Ivory wasn't on her way out, I would beat your fat ass."

Mary was a doctor at Pitt Memorial in Greenville, N.C. She was also a very pretty woman. At 46 years old, she could easily pass for 30. She is thin, but voluptuous, with blond hair down to the center of her back, and bright blue eyes. Even with all the abuse and having a 24-year-old daughter, she worked out and took great care of herself. Her husband tries to make her feel bad by calling her fat, but it doesn't work.

Calling her husband fat would be the understatement of the year. Robert Dennis is 5-foot 10-inches and 400 pounds of pure fat. Any muscle definition from his Army days has been M.I.A. for years. He is a 51-year-old, racist, abusive asshole who she thought was cool, when she was young and dumb. But for the last 20 years, she's come to see him as just sad.

Mary could remember the 175 pound, 24-year-old Army vet who had swept her off her feet and had been the sweetest guy she had ever known. She was only 19 when they met. A year later, they were married. Then he started working in the prison and he changed, just as much on the inside as he did on the outside. She got pregnant and had Ivory 2 years into the marriage. She thought that would bring Robert back to the person she knew, but he kept getting worse. There were never any big events that happened where you could point and say, that's what it was. Over time, he just got really angry and started being very abusive.

"Robert, I am telling you this, and I hope you know how serious I am. If you ever put your hands on me again, I will start the divorce that very second. I will also call the cops and report you. You would have to kill me to stop me, and I would really rather die than to be with you, when you don't mind beating on your wife like you do those inmates." Mary was crying now, and she wished that she could just get out and walk away.

Before Robert could say anything else, Ivory came out of the automatic doors and spotted them at the curb. Thank God for miracles, she was the spitting image of her mother. Except where her mother was 5-foot 5-inches and liked to dress classy, Ivory was 5-foot 9-inches and leaned towards slutty. She was young, tanned, and firm, with legs that seemed a mile long. Ivory could have been a super model but, like her mother, she wanted to make it off of her brain and not her body.

When Ivory got to the car, rolling her luggage behind her, she was halfway into greeting her mother when she saw her face.

"Dad, you are such a dick. Mom, get out, we're taking a cab, or I'll call an UBER."

She was well aware of who and what her father was. Sometimes he tried to hide it from her, but other times, he didn't give a fuck who saw it.

Ivory hated her father, and to get away from him, she went to college at Temple University in Philadelphia, Pennsylvania. She loved black boys growing up because, if all white boys turned into her dad, she wanted to stay as far away from them as possible. She was currently living with a black man in Philly, where she worked as a paralegal while in Grad School to become a lawyer. Her mother had come up 3 months ago and met him, but her dad had said, "No way am I gonna have some nigger smirk in my face because he's fucking my daughter." If her mom would just leave the piece of shit, she would never come back down here again.

"Hi sweetheart, no greeting for your dear old Dad? Where's the nigger at?"

"Mom, if you don't get out right now and come with me, I am jumping right back on the next flight out of here."

When Mary went to get out of the SUV, Robert grabbed her arm. His mouth started to open, but before he could form a word, Ivory was screaming at the top of her lungs.

"Get your fucking hands off her right now. Help, help, police!"

Robert jerked his hand back. He saw an airport security guard on his way over, so as soon as Mary cleared the door, he started the SUV and said, "You better be at home tonight or both of you little bitches will be sorry." With that said, he pulled off and left them.

The security guard asked the women, "Are you both okay? What's going on?"

Mary answered, "We're fine officer, just a little family dispute."

The man didn't look convinced but turned and walked away. They noticed that he didn't go far, and he stood in a way that he could keep an eye on them.

"Listen mom, let's go out and catch up while we eat. Then, just to keep the peace between you two, we will go to the house. But I'm telling you now, I'm not letting you out of my sight."

"Ivory," Mary said with feeling, "I love you so much, and I miss you like crazy."

She hugged her daughter with all her strength. By the time she let go, they both had tears running down their faces.

. . . .

Ivory knew her mother was stressed out, so she took her to Marco's Place. It was an Italian restaurant that didn't have a dress code, but you could get good food and good wine. It was crowded, but they wanted a table, so they waited the 15 minutes to be seated.

"Mom, you look so beautiful." Mary had on a white sundress with sunflowers all over it. She matched it with green, open-toed, high-heeled sandals that matched perfectly with the stems on the sunflowers. Her lack of makeup only made it clear to the world that she was a natural beauty who didn't need any. She fit in with the nicely dressed crowd.

"Honestly, you know that you are beautiful, I just wish you wouldn't show everybody your goodies. Make them earn that right."

Ivory just couldn't help herself. She was a perfect 10 and she knew it. She was beautiful, smart, sexy, and loyal to the man who had won her heart. She was wearing a cut-off wife beater with no bra. It was cut off about an inch above her naval, so her whole mid-riff was bare. If the shirt had been white, you would have been able to see her whole chest. She also had on, what the old folks called daisy dukes. They were tight enough and small enough that some swimsuits were more decent. She wore a pair of black Chuck Taylors to round off her outfit. And just like her mom, she wore no makeup at all.

After they were seated with drinks in hand and food on the way, Ivory made her pitch one more time.

"Mom, come live up north close to me, and divorce that son of a bitch." Mary started to protest but Ivory cut her off. "No, listen to me. You have no friends down here because no one can stand to be around Dad. You are a highly successful doctor, who can get a job anywhere. You're beautiful and young, and you deserve a man who will love and honor you with every breath he takes. You have money and most of all, you are loved by me. And I need you. I don't want to get the call that that bastard has killed you."

Mary had fought to keep her composure because they were in public, but the pain and fear in Ivory's voice finally broke through her shell. "I'm sorry baby, I can't leave him. I know you hate him, but I promised for better or worse. And, even though I'm not happy, I will uphold my vows." Both women were crying openly now. Mary wanted to explain more but just then, the waiter arrived with their food.

They ate in silence while they were both deep in thought, when the waiter came to clear their table, he bought a bottle of nice red wine.

Ivory looked up to tell him they didn't order it, when the waiter said, "Compliments of the gentleman at the bar."

When they both looked towards the bar, what they saw caused both of them to smile and wave the man over.

He walked with the grace of a born predator. He was a bald, black man, in his mid 30's from the look of him. He was about 6-foot tall, with light-brown skin, stretched tightly over what appeared to be solid muscle. With his dark suit and midnight blue tie, he cut quite a dashing picture. He smiled and both women moaned a little bit.

Ivory was the first to extend her hand to shake. Mary was faithful to her husband, but there was nothing wrong with saying thank you to the sexy gentleman.

"Thank you for the wine, sweetie. Would you like to sit down?"

Shaking both of their hands, he smiled and replied, "You're very welcome, and I'll only sit if I'm not intruding on a private moment between sisters."

The women both laughed, and Mary did the introductions. "Hello, and you are not intruding at all. My name is Mary, and this is my beautiful daughter, Ivory."

"Nice to meet you both. My name is Manny." He took pains to be polite to both of them, but Ivory could tell he only had eyes for her mom. From the blush on her cheeks and neck, Mary could tell also.

After some idle chit-chat, Mary looked up to find Manny staring into her eyes. To her, it felt like he was staring into her soul, and seeing things no one except her husband was supposed to see.

"I'm sorry if I am stepping over boundaries," said Manny, "but I happened to see you crying earlier. I figured the wine would make you feel better. Is there anything else I can do to make you feel better?" Reaching over and taking her hand, he added, "You have such a beautiful smile."

Mary felt like she was floating. To have such a fine, young man blatantly offer her sex, had her mind wandering.

Ivory, wanting to give them a little privacy, said, "Mom, Manny, excuse me for a second while I use the Ladies room. Manny, don't run off without saying bye." With an encouraging nod to her mother, she left them alone.

Manny was holding the eye contact, and it was like he was feeding erotic thoughts into her mind. Certainly, she couldn't be coming up with them on her own. "Manny, I am really flattered, but I am married." She tried to sound kind but also forceful.

"Damn," Manny said, while staring at her mouth. "I knew I couldn't be this lucky, but you know you're not wearing a ring?" She had stopped wearing it about 5 years ago because that was the first time Robert had beat her. Manny was staring into her eyes again and it seemed they were both drowning in each other. They were both so lost, they didn't notice Ivory come back.

"Huh-uh, well how are we getting along?" she asked with a sunny smile.

Mary actually jumped with guilt from the thoughts and images in her head over the last few minutes.

"Ivory, Mary, it was so nice to meet two such lovely women. I will tell you this Mary, if your husband isn't a total dumb ass, he will make sure you never cry again, unless it's from happiness or passion." The last was said with the promise of unimaginable passion for her if she ever gave him a chance. "Ladies, have a wonderful rest of the night." When he stood, he took Mary's hand and kissed it. With a polite wave to Ivory, Manny turned to walk away.

As he walked out, they both watched him go and then turned to look at each other.

"Ivory, not one word," Mary said, with a huge smile.

"Come on, Mom. That man was gorgeous, and he never even looked twice at me. Why, Mom? Why would you let him walk away?"

"Stop it, Ivory. Now, let's get drunk with a little help from 'Manly Manny' and then go home to face 'the beast'."

CHAPTER 5

The killer, A.K.A. 'Manly Manny', was very proud of his performance. The Dennis residence was built like a fortress, and not only was the security top notch, but they had cameras everywhere. He had hacked into their camera network and found a path to the home that would keep him off the cameras. The problem was that anybody who got within 25 feet of the house without a fob on their body, would set the alarm off. No other way around it. If he wanted in, he would have to be walked in by someone with a fob or have one of his own.

He looked up what the fob was, and it really just looked like a key fob for a car. After a little more research, he found that the family had 3 fobs for the house alarm. He had thought about going to Philly and stealing it from the daughter, but needed her in on the action. So, he decided to wait until she visited and steal it then.

After watching Ivory for months in Philadelphia, he found that she never took her purse with her to the restroom. She was also not into witnessing other people's affection towards each other. He also knew the daughter hated her dad and would never go anywhere in public with him willingly. So, he just followed them until they stopped to eat and set his plan in motion.

Seducing women has never been a problem for him. Number one rule, do your research first. Find out what she likes, dislikes, loves and what she hates. Mary likes wine, dislikes hard-looking tough guys. Loves her daughter, and hates her husband. So, he just created a man that she could be interested in.

The killer knew he was handsome and had a body that women loved. After being in prison for so long, he could mold himself into acting or looking like anything he wanted to. Knowing Mary was successful and had money, she wouldn't settle for anything less in a partner at this point in her life. So, who he showed her, had to appear rich and successful. She also wouldn't put up with a wandering eye. So, even though her daughter was very attractive, he only glanced at her to be polite. So, the scene was set, and he played his role to the letter.

Now on the way to the house, the wine was pivotal. He had bought a second bottle to be delivered as soon as he left. He had also written a card that said, "So worth it just to imagine your beautiful smile." He knew after they drank all the wine and talked about him, at least an hour would pass. He needed that time to get to the house, handle the captain, and set up for the next scene.

He hoped the fat bastard was in the bed because it would make this thing so much easier. If not, he would have to sneak him to put him down without too much damage. Which meant he couldn't let the hippo-looking motherfucker fall or he might break something.

The night was cloudy, so the moonlight was nonexistent. He parked his car a quarter mile from the house. He pulled all the way into the woods, so any traffic coming wouldn't be able to see his car.

He changed into his real work uniform consisting of all black clothing and a mask. Then he began to make his way towards the house while staying under the cover of the woods. He had his work bag strapped tightly to his back. He wouldn't need anything until he got to the side door.

When he got to the tree line surrounding the house, he paused. This was the first time he actually felt something about what he was going to do. The women were so beautiful, and not just on the outside, but on the inside as well. But destroying a few lives to help the countless and voiceless in prison, was acceptable and expected in order to achieve his goal. The show must go on.

Because of the fob, he knew Cpt. Dennis wouldn't have any of the added security turned on. Then again, he might just to spite his wife and daughter. The killer just had to take the chance.

When he reached the door, avoiding all the cameras, he took his lock pick set out. Then, just on a lark, tried the door. [Well, what do you know,] the door wasn't even locked.

He put the lock pick set back in the pack and took out 2 needles. These needles were also very important to the success of this job. The dose he had in these two would leave the recipient of the drug paralyzed for at least 30 minutes. He also packed another 10 doses with an hour of effective time each, in case the women didn't come home tonight. The best part is that the drug is flushed out of the system 30 minutes after the effects wore off. It would leave absolutely no trace in the blood. Timing was everything in any operation.

The killer entered into the house through the laundry room. He had studied the blueprints but had never been in the house. It was a sprawling 3-bedroom, 4-bathroom house, where each bedroom had its own bathroom and sitting room. It was situated in its own wing. Each bedroom was also situated in its own wing. Everything was connected with long hallways. It was a very beautiful and expensive home.

The killer crept through the kitchen and into the living room where everything was dark and silent. No alarm had sounded so old, Robert had opted for the other way of things. I guess by cutting off all the lights and going to bed, he was showing his family that he didn't worry about them at all. He didn't have a care in the world.

The master suite was all the way in the back. As he got closer, he really hoped the captain was sleeping. It would make everything smoother and faster.

"This is just unreal how shitty this motherfucker really is," whispered the killer to himself. Cpt. Dennis was on his stomach on the bed in a pair of boxers, dead to the world. The killer walked right in and stuck the needle in his fat ass.

The drug was so strong and fast acting, he was already paralyzed by the time he woke up. "Surprise, you fat piece of shit. I know you wished I would come for you because you thought you had a good plan. Well, your wish has been granted."

The killer had hacked into the NC Correctional Officers forum. He had read the post that Cpt. Dennis had written, talking about his 9mm he had close at hand, even when he took a shit. The killer had factored that into his plan also. The gun was right on the nightstand next to the bed where, in another post, the captain said it would be.

He had thought the captain would be prepared, therefore making this job a little harder than the other ones. It turned out to be so easy it seems he had allotted a little too much time.

Cpt. Dennis couldn't be hurt, or it would fuck up the killer's plan. He also didn't want to talk too much and have the captain start putting things together to reveal his identity. That was because, if the plan went right, fat ass would survive this encounter. The killer was mad at himself for not thinking of getting a voice box. Then, he could at least talk shit to him without fear of discovery.

Another good part of the drug was that the victim still had all of their senses. The killer rolled the fat bastard over and locked eyes with him. He could see the fear and anger on Robert's face, but that wasn't enough. He punched him in the balls. Okay, that's what he wanted to see. Now, you had pain mixed in with everything else. He didn't hit him hard enough to rupture anything, but still, a good solid hit to the balls would hurt even the toughest man. And this fat, pasty, soft pussy was anything but tough.

"Now, we wait for the girls to come home so we can start the party," the killer whispered to the captain.

He looked at his watch and saw he still had 15 minutes on the first dose. He didn't want to leave his DNA on anything, so he didn't go exploring. All of a sudden, he heard 3 short, soft beeps come from the front of the house. He sprinted to the front door and saw the women getting out of an UBER. He ran back to Robert thinking, [Damn, if the captain had been awake, the 3 beeps from the panel to alert the fob had entered range, would have warned him.] He got lucky with that.

He jabbed another needle into Cpt. Dennis, grabbed the captain's gun and then walked out of the room, closing the door behind him. The door had to be closed so the captain couldn't hear what was said or see what the killer wanted to show.

CHAPTER 6

The ladies were wasted. Ivory being younger and more of a drinker, was holding up pretty good. Mary, on the other hand, wouldn't stop laughing and mumbling about Manny.

They stumbled out of the UBER and gave a heartfelt farewell as if their driver was a loving relative. Mary was leaning on Ivory as they mounted the stairs to the front door.

"Damn, I should have let Manny rock my world," said Mary. "I mean, it was like fate. Could you imagine how beautiful our children would be? I'm only 46, I could pop a couple more kids out. Ivory, baby, you want some half siblings?"

"Mom, hush before dad hears you. It's already one o'clock in the morning. And you blew it with Manny. You didn't get his last name or his number, so how would you even find him?"

They were at the door now, and Mary was fumbling with her keys. "Give me those," Ivory said, snatching the keys from her mother. "You're such a lightweight, Mom." Ivory had opened the door by now and ushered her mother inside. With her back to the living room as she locked the door she said, "Mom, you're sleeping in the bed with me. I don't trust that you won't call dad Manny by mistake."

When Ivory turned around, it took her a few seconds to process the scene in front of her. A masked figure was standing in front of her mother, holding a gun to her face. Ivory sobered up fast but stayed quiet so she could better assess the situation.

Mary was terrified. She wanted to scream. She wanted to run. Her body didn't listen to her and that was probably a good thing. Her body understood that, if she did anything before instructed, she would die.

The masked man said, "If you do what I tell you, without hesitation or question, I will not hurt you. The second you do either, then you will die. Ivory, come get Mary and take her to the couch."

Both women's mouths dropped open because even with the alcohol and the terror, they recognized the voice. Hell, they had spent the last hour talking about the owner of the voice. Mary was shaking and seemed frozen at the same time. Ivory was the first to move and she grabbed her mother and walked her to the couch.

It seemed Manny knew the jig was up also, so he took his mask off and just stood staring at the two women. He then said, "I am not here because of either of you. I am here because of the racist fucker in that bedroom. Do what I say and you'll both be fine."

Mary was crying but was trying to stay silent. She knew she was being silly, but she felt like she had just lost a lover. Before her brain could catch up to her mouth, she asked, "Manny, why?" The gun came up, but she was so deflated, she didn't even react to it.

Manny said, "First off, my name isn't Manny. Second, you really don't want me to answer that. And third, I said no questions."

"You made me feel alive again."

Ivory tried to make her mother shut up, but Mary wasn't going to stop. "I have suffered for so long. Years! And in 15 minutes, you brought back joy to my life. I was beating myself up for not saying yes to you. Goddamn it, I was just talking about how beautiful our kids would be." Mary was crying as if her whole world had just come crashing down. She was so hurt and angry that she forgot to be afraid.

Ivory could tell that Manny, or whatever his name was, was affected by Mary's speech. He sat down across from them and looked at his watch. He got up again and said, "Both of you, come with me."

He pointed toward the main suite, so Ivory took her mother's arm and walked ahead of the man. When they got to the door, he said, "Hold up. Robert has been given a drug that paralyzes him for a period of time. He has all his senses, but I have to give him another shot, okay?" Both women nodded and they went in the room.

It was dark, but they could see Robert clearly enough to tell he was on his back on the bed in a pair of boxers. Just like Manny had said, he was breathing but couldn't move. Mary went and stood over him and she could clearly see the fear in his eyes.

Manny stuck him with the needle and then said, "Mary, I want you to scratch his face and upper arms as deep as you can. And before you argue, it's either your nails or a bullet. It really doesn't matter to me." He had whispered all this in her ear, and when she glanced back, she noticed he had his mask on again. "Hurry up, we are on a timetable."

Mary looked down at Robert and lightly scratched him on his face. Manny grabbed her arm and Ivory's arm and pulled them out of the door. He was pissed and she didn't understand what she had done.

He marched them both to the living room and ripped his mask off. He asked Mary, "Do you think this is a game? You caress that fat, abusive asshole as if you still love him. I told you to scratch that motherfucker but let me be clear. I want to destroy him, and you both are going to help me, or you all will die." He paused and looked at both of them to make sure they understood that he was serious. "In about 20 minutes, you will call the police and say your husband is trying to kill you. Ivory, you will be screaming for your dad to put the gun down. The scratches have to look like you were fighting him off of you. Both of you play your roles right, and the captain goes to jail where I want him, and you both are free of him. Now, let's try this one more time."

They all turned to go back to the suite, but Manny stopped them again. "Mary," he said, "I want you to know that you are perfect. You are beautiful, smart, sexy, and everything a man could dream of calling his own. Earlier tonight, I was not faking. You mesmerize me. I was lost in your look and your smell, as well as your heart. I almost couldn't go through with this because I knew we had a connection. I'm truly sorry and I'm hurting because I will never get to hold you and love you like you deserve. I don't want to hurt you, so just do what I say."

Mary looked in his eyes for what seemed like hours, and then turned towards the bedroom.

When they went in this time, Mary attacked without further provocation. She scratched his head and face and upper body to the point where Manny had to pull her back. Her husband was breathing harder but couldn't react in any other way to the pain.

Ivory loved her mother and hated her father, but she didn't know how to respond to such a brutal attack. Manny said, "Alright, that's good enough. Both of you come with me."

They walked back to the living room with Manny holding Mary and telling her how good she did. He ended with, "I know that felt good to get it all out of your system, but we have one more step before I can leave."

He motioned them to sit down on the couch again while he sat in the recliner across from them. He looked at Mary and said, "This is the make-or-break part, and this will decide if I leave you alive or dead." He paused and looked at each of them in turn. "Mary, you have to sound hysterical, and tell the operator that your husband has a gun and is trying to kill you. Ivory, I want you in the background yelling for your dad to put the gun down. You do this right and no matter what he says, he goes to jail."

Mary raised her hand for permission to ask a question. When Manny nodded, she asked, "So, you're just going to trust us not to tell the police about you? I mean, come on, you have terrorized us. Why would we turn on a husband and a father for some guy to get revenge on him?"

Manny leaned back and stared at her. "Mary, Ivory, you both hate him. He treats you both like shit. He looks like shit. Mary, you don't believe in divorce, but you've wanted to

31

leave him forever. Ivory, you want your mom to be happy, to come up to Philly with you. Well, that selfish bastard is the only thing in your way. You do this and you are free. Everyone wins except the one who deserves to lose."

Mary and Ivory were both silent because they knew he was telling the truth. Ivory said, "Mom, he hits you all the time. The verbal abuse was just as bad. He's my father, but you know how I feel about him. Come on Mom, let's do it."

Mary dropped her head in thought. When she looked up, she said, "Okay Manny, how do you want this done?"

Manny explained what he wanted them to say, and Mary took out her phone. She let out a deep exhale and called 911.

The operator answered on the 2nd ring and heard nothing but screams from what sounded like multiple women. "Ma'am, ma'am, what is going on? Hello, ma'am, can you talk to me?"

Mary responded, "Please, help, my husband is trying to kill me, and he has a gun. Ahh, Robert, please stop. I'm sorry."

Ivory just kept screaming, "Dad, put the gun down. What is wrong with you? Stop trying to hurt Mom."

Through all the screaming, Manny just sat in the recliner with a smile on his face, waiting for the finale that only he knew about.

When Mary got to the last line, Manny stood up.

Mary, reciting her line, said, "Robert, no, what are you doing? Noooo!"

Manny had told her at the end of the long 'noooo' to scream and hang up. What happened was something else entirely.

Mary really got into playing her role, the reward of freedom driving her performance. So, when she heard the gunshot, she thought Manny had improvised to make it sound real. But Ivory's scream cut off and she fell back on the couch with a hole in her head. Mary screamed, dropped the phone, and ran towards her daughter. She never made it, and she also never heard the shot that ended her life.

Manny hit the end call button on the phone and rushed off to the bedroom. Being careful not to leave a blood trail from the fresh scratches, he dragged Cpt. Dennis into the living room. Manny put the gun in his hand and fired off a couple of shots into the ceiling. This was done to put gunshot residue on the captain's hands. The captain was just starting to move around a little bit when the sirens were getting close. Looking around to make sure everything else was perfect, he ran back through the house, out the side door and into the tree line.

Ten seconds later, the cops kicked in the front door and started yelling, "Put the gun down. On the floor you piece of shit."

[Job complete,] Manny thought. He hated what he had to do the women, but he knew after the emotions wore off, they would tell the police the truth. He used everything he knew how to do to manipulate them as far as he could. Their deaths had been planned, but it wasn't easy. It was a necessity that he would have to live with for a very long time, hopefully. He saw the police bring Cpt. Dennis out in cuffs, and with that sight, he turned and ran for his car.

CHAPTER 7

"I really don't care what you have to say. This is an open and shut case and you're not coming here and stirring up shit." Det. R.B. Mitchell of the Greenville Police Department was livid. "No one called you to come over here. We don't need your help. Goodbye."

Det. Mitchell had over 20 years on the job, and he had never been a part of an easier case. But these two SBI idiots were determined to come in and fuck it up just enough to give the culprit a way out at trial. All these ifs, ands, and buts were deadly to a case if you had a good lawyer and it just so happened that the asshole suspect had one.

R.B., as his friends called him, was a 6-foot, 205-pound, black man who still had the body he had when he played college football. He worked out and tried to eat healthy because you never know when that edge would come in handy for chasing a suspect or helping a victim. With light brown eyes and a distinguished amount of gray on his temples, the ladies couldn't get enough of him. He could have made lieutenant or captain long ago but wanted to stay on the streets where he felt he could do the most good. The normally even-tempered Det. Mitchell was having his patience tested today.

"All I'm asking is for you to listen to what we have to say, in its entirety before you discount what we're trying to tell you." Sgt. Det. Rogers was trying to be patient with the man, but he was also getting upset. "Robert Dennis is a piece of shit, we all agree on that, but are you comfortable with sending an innocent man to death row?"

"We have a lot of information to add to what you have already." Det. Grace was trying to convince the detective to take the bait. No detective worth his or her salt could turn down genuine information about a case they are leading. "If what we tell you doesn't sound right, then ignore it and keep pushing your investigation where it leads you."

"That's what I'm trying to tell you, my investigation was laid out in front of me from the very start. I have an airport security guard who saw the suspect arguing with the victims. I have camera footage of the outside of the house. The suspect and the victims leaving and coming home and no one else at all coming or going. I have a 911 call where both victims are telling
Mr. Dennis to put the gun down. You can also hear both gun shots on the recording. Police found the suspect standing over the victims with the murder weapon in his hand. GSR test came back positive. Come on, what more do you want?" Det. Mitchell had ticked off each point by counting fingers and then threw his hands up in disgust.

But Det. Rogers was ready with a list of his own. "Victims didn't come home for four hours after the airport incident. When we tracked their movements, we found that a 6-foot-1, bald head, black male was interacting with them in a restaurant called Marco's Place. This man fits the description of our Prison Guard Killer. When we looked at the video, at no time could we get a look at his face. He avoided the cameras like a criminal. He also wore gloves into and out of the restaurant. Ann, tell him about the security."

Det. Ann Grace stepped up and said, "We went deep into the security system and found some interesting information about those security fobs. Each of them, the victims, and the suspect, was given a specific fob with a digital signature on it. Well, it seems that out of nowhere, Ivory's fob entered the house while she was still in the restaurant. It's not on camera, but the company has a digital vault that records these things for some reason. Also, when the women returned, only Mary's fob registered. Eight minutes after the police kicked the door in, Ivory's fob leaves the house again. It was never recovered. It seems that the Dennis' asked for a 25-foot alert zone. So, as soon as anyone enters that perimeter around the house, it records. If it's a person without a fob and they are not with someone who has one, it alerts the security company as well as both Mary and Robert's cell phones. A video of the person is sent and either of them can accept or reject the person. But, if they have a fob, the vault just makes a note of who comes and goes and when. The thing is, if the black guy was a decoy, why did he wait outside for eight minutes after the police got there. The record shows that ten seconds after they brought Robert Dennis out of the house, Ivory's fob left the house's perimeter."

Det. Grace could see the interest on his face but also the determination that he had his man. They had agreed to meet in front of the victims' home to go over what they had. Det. Mitchell didn't want to come, but his boss had made him. Apparently, when the SBI called, you went.

It was a month after the murders and everyone in the department and the D.A.'s office felt Mr. Dennis was guilty despite all the claims he made that some guy had set him up. He claimed he was drugged with something that had left him paralyzed. When the blood test came back negative, Mr. Dennis had deflated in front of the detectives. He said that a masked man had held a gun to Mary and made her scratch him. With the extent of damage done, when he told them it was done on the bed and he was dragged to the living room, they went looking for blood trace on the bed and the floor. The only blood found was in the living room. When Robert was informed of all of this, he put his head in his hands and cried.

Mr. Dennis was in solitary confinement in Pitt County Jail. That is where he will stay until trial because he had already been denied bail. Det. Mitchell had to admit that what the detectives had to say was interesting, but it still didn't negate the evidence that they had. For all they know, Robert hired someone because he couldn't pull the trigger himself. Even that theory doesn't add up because of the 911 call. That recording played in court will hang Robert and everyone knew it. Det. Mitchell's job was done and now it was in the hands of the D.A.'s office. These detectives were talking to the wrong person.

"Okay, I admit, what you have is good stuff. You have to know that everything you are saying will just muddy the waters. What you have is all guess work and what we have is fact, proof. Right now, Mr. Dennis is on his way to death row. You asked me how I feel about an innocent man in prison. Well, how do you feel about a guilty man using what's been going on to create confusion so he could kill his family? Now, you come in with, really nothing, and if the defense hears about this, then he could walk." Det. Mitchell turned away and looked at the house. He finished with, "Take what you have to the D.A., or not, but I'm done. I did my job, and I got my man. Nice meeting you both." He got in his unmarked car and drove away.

. . . .

Ann had never seen Walt so mad. The D.A. had to have gotten a heads up on why they were coming because he wouldn't even meet with them. Everybody felt they had their man and didn't want to hear anything to contradict it. The thing is, Ann felt like they were right. She just didn't know how Walt would take what she had to say."

Spit it out, Ann. You keep cutting your eyes at me like that and they'll get stuck." They were sitting outside the D.A.'s office in their rented Jeep Grand Cherokee.

"I'm not sure you want to hear what I have to say."

"The fact that I'm sitting here, mad as hell, because a bunch of people don't want to hear what we have to say, should tell you to say it anyway."

Ann hesitated, but finally said, "I think he killed them." She waited for him to call her an idiot or a trader, but all he did was look at her and nod for her to continue.

"Every prison guard in the state has been given the general description of our suspect. Mr. Dennis could have hired a black man to steal Ivory's fob and bring it into the house. I think he wanted to kill them himself, but with the fob and the black man, it would cause just enough doubt to set him free. I believe that after he killed them, he froze up and that's why he didn't cover it better. Remember, he has been a guard for 28 years, he is an Army veteran, and he has been under investigation for violent behavior against inmates in the past. Now, the last could help him because of the M.O. of our killer. Except, as far as I can see, the two women were innocent, and our killer has never hurt the family in any way. I think Robert Dennis used his knowledge of what's been done by our killer to murder his family."

They both sat in silence while Walt absorbed everything Ann said. "So, do we let it go or do we keep pushing it?" Walt finally asked.

"I hate to say this, but I think we should let it go. I mean all we could do is find the black guy, but we have nothing to go on. He paid for the wine with cash, and no one can say more about him than we can see for ourselves on the video. And even if we do find him, we have no proof that he committed a crime. So, what could we do to him? Let's head back to the hotel and get some food and rest."

The two detectives would get their food, but the killer wouldn't let them rest.

CHAPTER 8

Sgt. Marshall Oakland had never been in so much pain in his life. The killer could tell because you don't cry like this if you've been through it before. Then again, it wasn't physical pain that had him crying.

The killer had the whole family shackled to a wall in a warehouse. The family consisted of Marshall Oakland, of course, his ugly wife Debbie, and their two equally ugly children, Matthew and Robert. The killer was torturing all of them, but Marshall had yet to be touched.

This time, the killer was holding nothing back. After what he was made to do to Mary and Ivory, nothing was off limits now. That is why the two little boys were dying slowly at his hands.

"No more tough talk, Sarge? I thought you were going to do something to me if I touched your family. How about this?" he asked, as he stabbed Marshall's eight-year-old son, Robert, in his stomach. When he twisted the knife and pulled, blood and guts flew everywhere.

Debbie was screaming, "Why, why, why? Please stop. He's just a little boy." She was fighting her shackles so hard, she was bleeding freely at her wrists.

Sgt. Oakland just said, "My son. My sweet little boy. I don't know you man. What do you want from us?"

The whole family was in good shape and good health. Good for the killer but bad for the family. With good health comes longer life. And with longer life, comes longer torture.

"Well, Mr. Oakland, it seems young Robert has left the building. But we still have plenty to play with. Like your ugly as sin wife, Debbie. I'll let you make the call on this next bit. Haha, get it? Bit." The killer had a drill in his hand with a 10-inch concrete bit in it. "So, this either goes in your knee, your wife's vagina, or your son's head. Which one is it going to be? I bet your wife wants it because nobody with this much dick would ever share it with her ugly ass. You have 5 seconds to decide." The killer started the countdown, "5,4,3."

"Okay, you son of a bitch. Okay." Marshall couldn't see his family suffer anymore, and he hoped he would pass out from this. "My knee. Use the fucking drill on me, and let my family go."

The killer advanced with the drill. "What are you doing? I said me, motherfucker. I said me. Noooo!"

The drill went into his other son's head. It was messy and gory, and the killer laughed out loud as the parents screamed.

"Damn, that boy had a lot on his mind. Hahaha. I think I said something about your wife's ugly ass. Should that be the next stop for my drill?"

"Why, man? Please, just tell me why you're doing this to us. I know who you are. I've never done anything to an inmate."

"Fuck what you've done. What about what you haven't done? You've worked at Pamlico for 8 years. Have you ever lied to help another guard? Have you ever let another guard torment an inmate and turned a blind eye? Fuck you and your innocent act." The killer was furious, and spit was flying with every word shouted.

"I'm using you to send a message to every officer in the world. I want all of them to quit. To fear even going to work. That's why I have that camera right there. None of you will suffer in vain. Your suffering will stop the needless suffering of inmates. When officers see what I will do to them and their families for getting out of line, who will dare to hurt another inmate?"

He walked over to Sgt. Oakland's wife and started the drill. She screamed until blood started streaming out of her mouth. She didn't die until the batteries in the drill died.

The killer locked eyes with Marshall Oakland and said, "I didn't show you my face because I want you to live. But, whether you live or die is up to you. I am going to shoot you in your knees and elbows and then I'm going to set this building on fire. Make it out, and you'll live a pain filled life. Don't make it out and die a painful death. It's up to you."

The killer had drums full of gas and he just kicked them over, causing gas to flow everywhere. Before he did anything else, he took down the bodies and soaked them with gas also. He pulled out his gun and shot Sgt Oakland just as he promised. While Marshall screamed from the pain, the killer removed his shackles and he fell heavily to the floor.

The camera equipment might lead back to him so he soaked the floor around the base so it would fall over and burn up. He had the video feed recording on his phone, so even after he left, he would get all the details going on inside the warehouse. At least, until the camera burned up.

As Sgt. Oakland whimpered on the floor, the killer said, "You motherfuckers act so tough when you're in those uniforms. Be tough for me now so you can be a living testament of my hate for you oppressive sons of bitches."

The killer walked out of the warehouse and threw the match over in the gas. Within seconds, the warehouse looked like a hellscape with fire everywhere. "Fight for your life and live you piece of shit," he whispered to himself as he walked over to the van.

Sgt. Oakland was one of the good ones, but they're all good until they're not. Hopefully, this will be the last warning that the guards need to start treating the inmates with respect. If not, then he had plenty more he could use to drive his point home.

. . . .

The killer had been making calls for the last hour, and he was ready to give up. He was calling reporters in Raleigh and asking them some basic questions to determine if they would be able to help him with his agenda. So far, none of them would do. He was looking on the internet at past reports done to see if he thought they could deliver the message that he needed out there.

The next call would be the last one for tonight. It was already 1:30 in the morning. and the killer picked up his phone and dialed the number provided on the reporter's website. After the 3rd ring, a woman picked up all business-like. "Denice McCarthy, and this better be good."

Denise McCarthy was a beautiful black woman with short dark hair. Her bio listed her as 5-foot 5-inches, 120 pounds, and 40 years old. She graduated from Duke University with a degree in Journalism. She seemed to concentrate on crime and punishment, which is exactly what he needed.

"Hello? Listen, I don't have time for this crap. Either state your business or I'm gone."

"Ms. McCarthy, I'm sorry for bothering you this late but I was wondering if I could ask you a couple of questions." The killer was using his most non-threatening, but also sophisticated voice. He knew from her background that he couldn't intimidate her, and she wouldn't put up with ignorance.

"Make it fast," she said. "I'm on a deadline and I don't have all night to chit-chat."

"Have you heard about this Prison Guard Killer that's been running around killing people?"

"Of course," Denise responded. "Probably every reporter in the world has. But really, you need to get to the point. I have things to do."

"Alright Ms. McCarthy, I'll get to the point. What have you heard about a fire at a warehouse in Pamlico County?"

"Not much, just that some people died in a fire. It's not exactly on my beat. Why? Do you have information on it?"

"Three dead, one survivor. Sgt. Marshall Oakland survived but his wife, Debbie, and his two sons, Matthew and Robert, were killed after being tortured."

When he paused for 5 seconds, Denise said, "Okay, I'm pulling it up, but I don't see…"

The killer talked right over her. "Robert was stabbed to death. He was the eight-year-old son. Matthew, who was the 12-year-old, was killed by having a 10-inch concrete bit drilled into his skull. Debbie was tortured with the same drill until she bled to death from her wounds. Marshall was shot 4 times and left alive to deliver a message to all the other guards."

There was silence on the other end for about 10 seconds. "Okay, I just looked at the media releases and almost none of the information you just gave me is on them. Would you care to tell me how you came upon this information, Sir?"

"Ms. McCarthy, can I call you Denise?"

"Sure. Is there something I can call you?"

The killer decided to ignore that question and get to the point. "I got all the information from a recording that contains the crime from start to finish."

Denise asked, "And, where did this recording come from?"

Again, the killer ignored her question. "I have been calling reporters for the last hour. I have done my research and I think that you would be the perfect person to send this video to."

"Well, I don't know," replied Denise. "It would depend on what you wanted me to do with it."

"You see, that's what I'm talking about. Every other reporter jumped on that line to tell me why they should be the one. But not you. See, I knew you would be perfect."

"Okay, well, you still haven't answered the question," Denise pointed out.

"Well, I want to show the video to the public so they can see that inmates will no longer be just victims. That they have someone who will fight for them, literally. If you watch it and report it with an air of fairness, and a warning to both sides, then there could be more stories to come."

"And how can you possibly promise more stories to come? Didn't you say you found a recording?"

"I said, I have a recording, not found one. Anyway, I have it because I'm the one who made it. I'm the Prison Guard Killer, and if you play this like I know you can, then all my messages will go through you. Now, do you have a secure email I can send this recording to, or do I keep looking for a reporter?"

Denise McCarthy gave him an email address for him to use. After he sent the video, there was about a full minute of silence over the phone.

Then Ms. McCarthy murmured, "Dear God."

The killer only said, "Yeah. Dear God," and then he hung up.

CHAPTER 9

There was someone banging on her hotel room door, yelling at her to get up. She was still half asleep, and she could see it was still dark outside. Ann Grace was not a morning person. When she looked at her phone and saw the time, she let out a deep moan.

"Open the fucking door, Ann. We have an emergency out here."

"Is there a dead body in the hallway?" she yelled back.

"No," Walt replied. "But there will be one in your room if you don't get your ass up and open this door."

"Come on Walt, give me ten minutes to get myself together."

"Ann, because I love you, I'm giving you five, but if you're still in that room after five minutes, I swear I will kick this door down."

She knew that he was dead serious, so she jumped out of the bed and ran for the shower. She took care of all her hygiene needs, used the bathroom, and pulled on jeans and a t-shirt, all in about three minutes, awesome multitasker that she was.

"Ann, get your ass in gear."

"Leave me alone Walt, I still have two minutes."

It would only take a man five minutes to get ready for the day. Most of them didn't wear makeup or worry too much about their hair, or how they smelled in some cases. But a woman was expected to be fast and perfect at the same time. She knew Walt would really kick the door in, so she grabbed her hair care products and her makeup and ran for the door.

When she opened it, her partner was standing with his hands on each side of the door, leaning towards her, looking more tired than she had ever seen. "Okay, now what's the big hurry?"

"Come to my room and I'll show you. The shit has finally hit the fan."

She ran back in and grabbed some white tennis shoes and then followed behind him to his room. "I'm getting nervous," she said. "Tell me what's going on. Is someone else dead?"

Walt didn't answer. All he did was walk over to his laptop and hit a few keys.

On the screen, a petite, very attractive, black woman was reporting on a fire in Pamlico County. The banner on the bottom of the screen said, "Contact With a Killer." Ann focused on what the woman was saying.

"The Prison Guard Killer has claimed 4 more victims in addition to setting last night's fire. The target was the family of Sgt. Marshall Oakland, 38, who has worked at Pamlico Correctional Institution as a guard for the last eight years. Sgt. Oakland survived, but his family was tortured and brutally murdered before being set afire at an abandoned warehouse. Marshall Oakland was also tortured but was given a chance to "fight for his life," as the killer called it. Debbie Oakland, 34, and their two children, Matthew, 12, and Robert, 8, were all murdered in front of Mr. Oakland. Then he himself, was shot 4 times and told if he could crawl out of the burning building, then he could live. In a stunning move, the Prison Guard Killer contacted me and admitted to these horrendous acts of violence. He claims that he is doing these things, and will continue to do them, until prison officials start treating inmates with respect. Our research team has found that over the last few years, more than a dozen assaults and murders on prison guards have been attributed to this killer. Also, some inmates have been targeted for assault or murder. The thing they all have in common is they all abused inmates in some way."

"I would now like to show you a video that the killer sent me. Even though it has been carefully edited, it is still wise for parents to use discretion towards young viewers."

The video started by showing all four family members shackled to a wall in a semi-dark warehouse. Thankfully, it skipped all the tortures and murders, and the next scene was of the masked figure piling the bodies and pouring gas on them. The next scene showed Mr. Oakland out of his shackles but twisting on the floor in pain and the killer walking away. The killer is off screen when fire seems to engulf the whole area. Mr. Oakland is dragging himself off to the side when the camera falls over and cuts off.

"Most of the video was too brutal to show over network television, but I will say that it lasted more than 3 hours long. With the video, the killer also had a message. He says that inmates will no longer be just victims. He adds that now they have someone who will fight for their right to be treated as humans. In the video, the killer can be heard telling Sgt. Oakland that he wanted him to live so he could be a living reminder of what he will do to officers and their families if anymore inmates are abused. The message is clear. Even though I don't condone the methods being used, if this will stop the needless suffering of our prison population, then maybe some good can come out of all of this bad. This is Denise McCarthy reporting for your Channel 3 News. We will have updates on this story all day long."

Walt slammed the lid on the laptop, and they both sat at the table in silence. Finally, he whispered, "What the fuck, Ann?"

"First off, no way what that reporter did is legal. No police department in the state would have okayed her to use that video that fast. We need to be on our way to Raleigh to arrest her."

Walt just looked at her in silence. She finally asked him, "Are you going to say something?"

"You said first off. Normally, when someone says that, it means there is at least a second thing."

"Okay, well secondly, our M.O. for him just went to shit. We thought he wouldn't hurt the families. It makes you second guess if he really did kill Cpt. Dennis's family too."

"We need to watch the whole tape before we start guessing at anything. Bayboro is way closer than Raleigh, so let's head that way. In the meantime, let's call that reporter and see if she can send us the full recording. Maybe I'll do that while you finish getting yourself together."

Ann had forgotten all about her makeup and hair. After she was reminded though, she grabbed her things and headed to the bathroom. Even though she looked at Walt like an older brother, it was ingrained in every female to always look their best in front of an attractive male. In the beginning of their now six-year partnership, she had had a major crush on him. Any female with a brain soon learned that he was so into the job that he had no time for anyone on anything else. So as not to embarrass herself, she fell into the little sister role, and now they are truly like family. But she still wasn't comfortable enough to go with no makeup on and crazy hair.

She was not trying to eavesdrop, but she could hear Walt out there on the phone trying to work his charms on the reporter. From the sounds of it, the reporter was not giving in as easy as he would have liked. When Ann was finished, she returned to the sitting area.

"Listen, I understand you have a career to think about," Walt was saying to the reporter. "All I'm trying to do is stop the deaths. I am a cop. I don't want anyone else to get hurt and what's on that tape could help me stop him from hurting the next family."

He kept his head down while he listened to something being said on the other end. When his head came up, there was a perfect white smile on his face. "Great," he said, "Let me give you the email. Thank you so much for this, Ms. McCarthy. I owe you one." He gave her the address and a few seconds later, Ann heard a beep from his laptop. He looked at something on the screen and thanked the reporter one more time and hung up.

"There is over three hours of uncut footage on this video. What do you want to do? Watch it here and then decide where to go, or go to Bayboro and one of us can watch it on the way?"

"Well, if one of us watches it while the other is driving, the other one will still need 3 hours to watch it later. Let's go to Bayboro and watch it together when we get there," Ann answered.

"Do we really even need to go to Bayboro? I'm running out of clothes and I'm tired of fast food," complained Walt. "I say we hop on a plane back to Raleigh. We spend the time until the flight and on the flight, watching the video, and get to sleep in our own homes tonight."

"Yeah right. Are you sure you're not just trying to go see the sexy reporter chick?"

"Ann, what the hell are you talking about?"

"I heard you flirting with her on the phone." Ann was only teasing him, but it looked to her that he was blushing. "Oh my God, are you blushing?"

With his most severe face, Walt said, "I don't blush. Don't we have work to do?"

"Whatever. Anyway, what if we see something that will make us have to go to Bayboro? Then, knowing you, we will be right back on a plane out to the coast."

"Good point," Walt said. "Okay, well, let's watch the recording here, but we set our flight to Raleigh in five hours. Or as close to that as we can get. Then, if we see something, we drive to Pamlico County. If we don't, then we still have enough time to make the flight."

Ann thought that sounded like a reasonable plan. So, they ordered some breakfast and set everything up to watch the video. Walt called the SBI travel agent and set them up on a mid-day flight.

When the video started, it showed the family shackled to the wall talking shit to their soon to be killer. Ann hit the pause button then asked, "Are we going to discuss it when we see something, or do we watch the whole thing and then talk?"

"How about if you see something, make a note of the time and we'll come back to discuss it. If we stop the video every time we see something, then we might not finish it in the time we have."

With that decided, they sat down and watched the whole video. They were making notes of places they would talk about later. Ann felt sick after the first ten minutes, but she knew this was her job and if she turned away, she might miss something. So, she put her big girl pants on and sucked it up. She didn't understand how someone could brutalize a child like that. He didn't make either of the kid's deaths easy. He used the children's pain to add to the parent's pain. He tortured both of them to the point of unconsciousness before he brutally murdered them. And he did it all with a smile on his face.

If Ann was truthful with herself, she could admit that she hadn't been really upset by some of the people killed by their guy. She had felt he was sending a noble message, just not in the right way. Now, she could see that he was just a maniac who enjoyed other people's pain. Maybe, he had always been like this, but his target of choice made her think prison had turned him into a creature worse than what he was when he went in. When they caught him, she would be sure to ask.

When the recording ended, neither of them said a word. Ann was sure that this had been the most horrific crime either of them had ever seen. She knew Walt had been a cop in the Army, but to see a mother have to watch her two children die, had to be at the top of his list also.

"Walt," said Ann, "Is this the most sadistic crime you have ever seen in your life?"

"In war, people do things that you couldn't even imagine a person could do to another person." Walt paused, and she could tell he was seeing something from his past. "When your commander is trying to get you to go into that dark place in your head in order to get you to walk willingly into suicide, for some it's impossible to leave that dark place. I've seen psychos that are made. They are worse than the born psychos because, the ones who are born, don't know they are doing wrong. It's just life to them. This guy is gone. For him to get so much pleasure out of these acts is scary."

Walt was looking at her with tears in his eyes. "Ann, something made him. Someone made him. This is not about getting officers to change or justice for abused inmates. This is payback against the people who made him into this."

Ann was seeing something in Walt that was almost painful. This video was hitting him hard because of some inner demons. She was worried that she would do the wrong thing. She wanted to hug him but didn't know if he would accept her sympathy. On the other hand, she wanted to put his mind somewhere else to take that look off his face. She chose the latter.

"It's the worst I've ever seen and ever wished to see. But I'm wondering, how in the hell do you kidnap four people and shackle them to a wall without one of them getting away?"

"He had to have used some kind of leverage. Let's call Bayboro P.D. and find out all the details they have."

Ann pulled out her phone to do as Walt instructed. On the second ring, a man picked up. "Bayboro P.D., this is Officer Fields, how can I help you?"

"Hi, Officer Fields. This is Ann Grace with the SBI. I'm calling to find out who I need to talk to talk to about the Oakland family murders?"

"SBI, huh? You fucking reporters will try anything. No comment. Press release sometime this afternoon. Call back if you need any…"

"Officer Fields, I am serious. I am with the SBI, and my partner and I are helping investigate the video…"

"Yeah, yeah, and you need a copy. Listen here," the officer interrupted. "If you keep wasting my time, I will find you and lock your ass up. Watch the fucking press release…"

The phone was snatched out of Ann's hand and Walt lit into the officer.

"Look here you stupid, red neck, hillbilly, piece of shit. If you ever talk to my partner like that again, I promise you, I will drive to Bayboro and kick the fucking shit out of you. My name is Sgt. Det. Walter Rogers, and my partner, Det. Ann Grace, asked you for some information. I am now going to give her this phone back. And if you don't cooperate, or if you speak disrespectfully to her again, I will personally knock all your fucking teeth down your throat. Do I make myself clear?"

Walt must have heard an affirmative because he handed her back the phone. The good thing is he was actually smiling and had a twinkle in his eyes.

"Hello, Officer Fields?"

"Yes ma'am, I am so sorry, Detective Grace. I will have that information for you in a second."

He put her on hold, and she glanced back up to tease Walt. He had that faraway look on his face again, so she held her tongue.

In a minute, Officer Fields was back. "Okay Detective, sorry to keep you waiting. Det. Brian Wytaker is over that investigation. Let me give you his cell number."

After Ann got the number, she thanked him, wished him a good day, and hung up. She said, "Walt, I got this Det. Wytaker's number. If he's anything like his coworker, maybe you should make the call."

The request was for two reasons. First, Ann did feel like he would get better results from the boy's club. Secondly, and just as important in her eyes, was giving him something to do to take that look off his face.

She gave Walt the number and he called the detective. Not surprising, he seemed to get all the information he asked for with no problem. In law enforcement, it could sometimes suck to be a woman.

Walt was on the phone with Det. Wytaker for about 30 minutes and Ann used that time to look at parts of the video again. [God, when he put that drill bit up inside the woman,] it made Ann hurt on the inside. She knew a lot about the law, but she wondered if this constituted rape as well as murder.

She was still watching the video when Walt slammed the lid down and said, "Ann, I cancelled the flight to Raleigh. We have to go to Bayboro."

"Did you find something interesting?"

"Yeah. They have a video of the abduction. It was at a supermarket. It was simple and fast and very brutal. He's sending the video to my email. Ann," Walt said, with concern in his voice, "Det. Wytaker is pretty good. If you want to go ahead to Raleigh for a little downtime, I can handle everything up there."

Ann went through a range of emotions in about five seconds. It started with confusion but ended with anger. "Don't you ever treat me like a fucking girl. This is my case. You go back to Raleigh and have fun with your new girlfriend. I'm going to Bayboro."

"Ann, I just…"

"Fuck what you have to say, Walt. After all this time, now the truth comes out."

"Ann, I'm only…"

"We're partners, Walt. No, we're family. So just this once, I'll act like the last minute never happened. So, we will rewind a bit. Did you find something interesting?"

"Yes, but let's go so we can get to Bayboro at a reasonable time."

"Alright, partner, anything you say," Ann said, with a smile on her face.

CHAPTER 10

Denise McCarthy had never been considered a celebrity or a star. She knew she was attractive, some people even called her beautiful. But at only 5-foot 4-inches, she was too short to be a model. She also had a little bit too much T&A if you know what I mean.

The thing is, she was also smart. She graduated from Northwest Cabarrus High School in Concord, NC with a perfect 4.0 GPA. From there, she went to Duke University on a full academic scholarship. She had always wanted to be a reporter ever since she watched Superman fall in love with Lois Lane, so she majored in Journalism, but also minored in Criminal Justice. It was a little girlish, but it was who she was.

At 40, she had made it as far in her career as she could go. She hated the politics involved in television, but there was nothing like the exhilaration of delivering breaking news in front of millions of people. She didn't get to go on live often, but that was a good thing. Now, when people saw her, they knew it was for something important. And right now, there was nothing more important than this serial killer running around free in her state.

When the third victim popped up and they knew they were dealing with a serial killer, she had gone live to inform the public. With Central Prison being right in downtown Raleigh, where she now called home, she wanted to let the people know that it was possible this guy could be in their area. She also told them to pray for the safety of the officers in Raleigh.

Secretly, Denise had started doing a little digging of her own. She was owed some favors by some of the SBI agents who could get her all the information they had on this killer. What they gave her left her boiling mad.

The information the media had been given was all about Officer Trevor Jones, and Officers Josh O'Neal and Thomas Fields. They were not given the information on the three inmates who also appeared to be targets. Matter of fact, the officers, O'Neal and Fields, were thought to be bystanders and the real target being the inmate they were transferring, Jamar Edmond. The report she got from her source also included two other inmates.

Former inmate, David Prig was a 38-year-old white guy who had done five years for sexual assault. He had raped several other inmates while incarcerated, but nothing was ever done about it. He had been found in Elizabeth City tied to a tree with a branch shoved in his anus. He had been kept alive and assaulted for several days before his internal bleeding caused him to die.

Then there was Bruce Battle, who was still alive. He is a 34-year-old black male, and he is actually housed at Central Prison right now. He is a known Blood gang member and is serving a 10 to 13-year sentence for armed robbery. He is also known to use gang intimidation on his fellow inmates. The SBI believes that is why he was targeted. He was shot in the arm and had to have it amputated at the shoulder.

So, when she was reporting on the third victim, the killer was really on victim number six. That night, she went live to deliver that news to the public. Some noise was made about her sources, but ultimately, the SBI had admitted to it.

She wasn't the only reporter on the story. There were a lot of famous national reporters from some major networks on the chase too. But ever since she had talked to the killer and been given that video, she was at the top of the heap.

Everyone wanted to see the whole recording. All of the talk shows wanted her to come for a segment. The craziest part was that now, all of her bosses were taking an interest in her. After all the promotions she didn't get. All the transfer requests denied, the condescending remarks she put up with every day. Now, the powers were talking about her future with the station.

Personally, she was fine with where she was in life. She made good money but also had some free time to herself. She did not envy the lives of some of the anchors or daily reporters employed by Channel 3. She wouldn't turn down more money, but no way was she giving up her free time She had even thought about finally getting a man.

Speaking of men, Denise had become curious of this Sgt. Det. Walter Rogers. All her sources named him as the head of the investigation. She had looked him up on social media, but he was on none of the platforms. So, she had looked him up on the SBI website to get a look at his bio. She could admit that she had been impressed with his resume. He was a little older than her, but he looked ten years younger than his listed age of 49. He was in good shape and was very handsome. She didn't really have a type, but if she did, he would be it.

She had called an SBI friend and asked her about any rumors floating around on him. What she heard only intrigued her more. It seemed no one there had ever seen him with a woman. He was definitely not gay, but he was super committed to his job. Everyone thought he would fall for his stunning partner, Ann Grace, but he had firmly put her in the little sister role. All the women had given up on him long ago.

The conversation they had had was all about business, but she could hear the charm in his voice. But the thing she could hear the most was his dedication. So, even though she would love nothing more than to get to know him better, she would keep her distance. Nothing would ever come in between Sgt. Det. Rogers and his job.

Now, with her star shining bright, she wanted to make the most of it. Some of the other channels in the Raleigh area were trying to lure her away from Channel 3. She was grateful for the opportunity they gave her, but they did kind of hurt her when they kept passing her by for promotions. Channel 5 offered her $50,000 more a year with a $100,000 signing bonus. They also would give her a car up to the amount of the bonus. And they would let her go on live whenever she wanted, with whatever she wanted. It was a reporter's dream contract. She was very tempted to leave.

When she had shown her boss the offer, instead of him trying to match or at least get close to the offer, he had just bitched about loyalty and how they had kept her on when she wasn't producing stories like she should. That was her last day at Channel 3. The managers tried to talk her back on, but she had made up her mind. So, she packed up and left.

Channel 5 welcomed her with open arms, gave her a soundman and a cameraman. She chose a black Mercedes Benz S550 and, after her first day on the job, when she came home, it was sitting in her driveway. She had to admit, it felt really good to be wanted.

Now, she had to do something to show the station they had made a good investment. She really hated to say it, but she needed something to happen that would prolong her star shining. She did have the recorded phone call of the killer. She had wanted to hold that for if things got desperate for her and she needed a wildcard. What she really needed was another video or another murder. But from her research, she knew that the killer went months sometimes with no activity. She didn't think it would go over very well if she didn't report anything for her first months at a new job.

She could call Det. Rogers or Det. Grace and ask for an interview. Or she could go on some of those talk shows and give her new station some free publicity. Or better yet, she could go try to interview some of the survivors.

There was Cpt. Robert Dennis, who was charged with murdering his family. He claimed that it was the Prison Guard Killer who did it and set him up for it. Everyone knew he was a racist, so with her being a black woman, she could probably rile him up to say something crazy on camera.

Then, there was Marshall Oakland. She didn't know how he would react to her after she showed the video of his family. He probably thought she was a glory seeker and was just trying to feed some more on his family's blood. She would still call and ask, but she didn't have a lot of hope.

Bruce Battle would most likely love to give her an interview. Guys in prison tend to have a lot to say to the public if given a chance. Maybe he had some insight as to who is behind the assaults going on.

One way or the other, she would have something for her new bosses by the next day. She had tried to call the number the killer had called her from, but it was no longer in service. She was still weighing her options when a text came through on her phone. It was short and sweet but powerful, none the less. Four little words that sent her heart into her throat. 'Expect Another Video Soon.'

CHAPTER 11

Lt. Candace Price was at home getting ready for work. She was just stepping out of the shower after a two-hour workout. If you wanted to bring the money in, you had to give the customers something to lust after.

Standing in front of the mirror naked, Candace knew she was a certified dime, a perfect ten. She was 35 but had a better body now than she did when she was 25. All those edges were now lush curves. And what she couldn't tuck or tighten with diet and exercise, well the doctor could certainly fix that.

The tall, light-skinned, black woman with long, jet-black hair, perfect D cup breasts, and forty-two-inch hips flaring out from a thirty-inch waist, stared at her own natural green eyes. Thanks to good genes, she had perfect pink lips that never needed more than a little lip gloss. Light touches of makeup emphasized her high cheek bones and long eye lashes.

She began to rock her hips side to side to a beat that was only in her head. With water dripping off her body, she was what 500 body squats a day could do for a woman. Well, that and the shots she gets, every now and then.

She was reaching for her lotion when the doorbell rang. She lived in an apartment complex about 10 miles from the prison. She made enough money to be able to live in a big house in a gated community, but she couldn't make the move while she still worked at the prison. That would make the administration very suspicious of her. She had already been investigated over 10 times for sexual relationships with inmates, but she was always very careful. Just because she was a whore didn't make her stupid.

She grabbed her robe and made her way to the front door. She lived on the second floor of a three-story building. The stairs led up the middle of the building, and on the second-floor landing, her door was the first on the left. After moving to Tabor City from Wilmington, there was not much crime to speak of. But a single woman living alone, who looked how she looked, had to be careful. Whether home or not, she always kept the deadbolt locked.

Looking through the peephole, she didn't see anyone. She turned to go back to the bathroom connected to her bedroom when the bell rang again. She stopped and glanced back at the door over her shoulder, then turned around and looked out of the peephole again; no one there. She walked over to the window and yanked the curtains aside; no one in sight. Sucking her teeth, she started back to her bedroom.

All of a sudden, she heard a noise in her kitchen area. She stopped and wrapped her robe tighter around her body.

"Hello, is somebody there?" She had no friends in the area and no family that had a key. "I'm calling the police right now," she yelled at the kitchen. She didn't even have her phone on her, but maybe whoever it was would get scared and run. The problem was, the front door was the only way in or out. So, if someone was in there, they would come straight at her.

Her apartment was only two bedrooms, two bathrooms, a kitchen, and a living room. The second bedroom was right across the hall from the master, and it was full of her workout equipment. Two steps from her living room was her kitchen, so she didn't know what to do. Figuring she was being ridiculous, she stepped into the kitchen. It was absolutely empty.

Laughing at herself, she went back into her bedroom to keep getting ready for work. She had about ten clients lined up for tonight, so she wanted to look her absolute best. She could make a thousand dollars tonight if she could make it to everyone safely. This being a Monday night, it was only safe to do hand jobs. Some of the administration would be in the house, and they were fond of just sitting in their offices and watching the cameras. She was too careful and too smart to ever let those idiots catch her.

She had actually been caught three times over her ten-year career at Tabor City Correctional Institution. A well-placed blow job when she was a regular officer got her out of the first one. The sergeant that walked in on her and the inmate had actually watched while she locked eyes with him. When the inmate was done, he left, never having seen the sergeant. Candace had walked to his office and asked if she needed to pack her stuff and leave. He had gotten up and locked the door and just pointed to his hard cock. She did what she was good at and, in only five minutes everything was right with her world again.

The second time was when she was a sergeant. It was a good thing the inmate had wanted to role play. He wanted to hold her down on her desk while he held a hand over her mouth, and she was to act like she was trying to get away. When the Unit Manager came in, she just fought harder and made more noise. The Unit Manager, who was a Marine before coming to work for the prison, took the inmate down with ease. As soon as his hand was off of her mouth, she started yelling rape. With the statement from the Unit Manager, she still had the $1000 from the inmate, and she also sued the state and took a settlement for $280,000. The inmate received an additional twelve years for 'raping' her.

The last time was only last year, and it had been a very close call. She had been riding the inmate, who worked as a janitor in the captain's loop. This is where her office was relocated to after she became a lieutenant. She had been facing away from him and bouncing on his lap, because he said for $1000, he wanted to watch her ass jump. When the captain came in her office and caught them, because he was a lifer, he kept a knife on his person at all times. The captain had become so irate that the inmate had pulled his knife out and attacked him. When it was all said and done, she was able to get away by saying the inmate had held a knife on her and made her do it. The inmate had gotten fifty years added to his life sentence. Not wanting to rock the boat, she decided not to sue this time around.

With her past, she had become a living legend at TCI. The inmates couldn't get enough of her. She was making $50 just to feel her up. She was charging $100 for a hand job. For $300, you could get a lap dance with your dick out. $500 for a blow job, which no one lasted more than five minutes for. And for a full-on fuck, that would run between $1000 and $5000. That price was determined by how, in what position, and if you wanted to wear a condom. Every hole with no condom on would cost you $5000. Hell, she had some guards and administrators paying for that once a month.

So, the little, skinny, hood rat chick from Wilmington was now a rich, beautiful, young lady worth almost $2 million. Shit, if she didn't have to keep paying all her family's bills, she could have had double that by now.

Most people would wonder why she didn't branch out as a call girl or a stripper, but the truth was, she was scared to do what she did without the power she possessed. She could say yes or no, stop or go, and it was just safer for her. Even though she wasn't supposed to, she looked at the medical records of all the inmates first to make sure they were clean. A call girl couldn't do that. And because of some of her friends dying from STD's, she was terrified to do anything with someone she couldn't check out first.

It was crazy how a little tailoring could change the look of a uniform. She stood out from all the other pretty officers by paying to have her uniform fitted perfectly to her body. And when she could go to work in her normal clothes, she made sure she wore something that would have the inmates calling home about those CashApps.

CashApp was the best thing to ever happen to her bank account. All she had to do was give out a phone number to a few throw-away phones and the money was untraceable. She had paid a random dude in Wilmington $200 to buy her

$1000 worth of prepaid phones. He came out of Walmart with 20 of them. She also gave him some head so he would never rat her out if someone came asking. She got his information and now, once a month, she would send him $1000 to keep him on her side.

She had made it back to her bedroom and she put on some sexy panties before sitting down at her vanity. Her breasts were so perfect. She just sat and rubbed lotion and perfume on them for a while. When she was giving a hand job, she would let the inmate feel her ass and titties if it was safe to do so. Sometimes she would let her titties hang out to entice them into spending more money. She knew that God and her surgeon had blessed her with the perfect body for sex.

"What the fuck," Candace yelled when the doorbell rang again. She grabbed her robe off the bed and marched to the front door. Without looking in the peephole this time, she threw the deadbolt and jerked the door open; no one in sight. She walked over to the steps and looked down and up. No way anyone could have disappeared that fast. She walked over to her doorbell and pressed it. It worked just fine. [Maybe there was a wire loose.] She would call the super when she came home from work in the morning.

She walked back inside and slammed the door shut and hit the deadbolt again. She walked into the kitchen and got some apple juice out of the refrigerator. Already forgetting the trouble with the bell, her mind was on her clients for tonight.

There was this Puerto Rican guy named Eli who she knew had some money. He had been checking her out but never said more than a greeting to her. She might have to give him something for free to let him know she was interested. If he had the kind of money she thought he did, she needed to get her hooks into him now because word was, he would be getting out soon. Yeah, he could do for the long run. She knew Puerto Rican and black babies were absolutely beautiful. She could quit her job, move into a big house, and just raise beautiful, rich babies.

With a smile on her face, thinking about Eli, she walked barefoot back to her vanity. She sat down and started looking at her makeup. She would go with the smoky eye thing today, but she didn't see her sponge. She bent down to look on the floor.

"Ouch," she said when something pricked her arm. She sat up and saw a masked man standing behind her with a needle in his hand. Before she could do or say anything else, she fell over onto the carpet unable to move.

CHAPTER 12

The killer was very pleased with himself. Lt. Candace Price was his. He picked her phone up off the bed and put it up to her face. It made a sound to signify it was unlocked. He sent a text from her phone to her shift captain saying she was sick and wouldn't be coming in tonight. Since she had been working a lot of overtime, the only response was a get well soon and to call if she needed anything.

He smiled down at the beautiful, black woman lying on the floor breathing rapidly. He bent and picked her up and walked her over to the bed where he deposited her. He wanted to talk to her and let her show the pain he was going to inflict on her. He tied her down securely to the bed. He removed her panties with a yank and then looked into her eyes. "I have been waiting for this for a long time now. I want to show you something." He walked over to the door.

"Every doorway in your home has a camera with a microphone installed right here in the middle." He was pointing to a little black dot she hadn't noticed, until he pointed it out. "I also put them in your bathrooms and in the ceiling. I've been watching and recording you for over a year now."

Knowing the dosage he gave her would wear off soon, he walked over and gagged her and moved the bed away from the wall so she couldn't bang the headboard against it. They would have their conversation, but he needed her to be able to show her feelings while they had it.

She was tied spread eagle, and just to keep her off balance, he was running his fingers over her body. She really was a perfectly put together woman. It was just too bad that her soul was so corrupted.

He knew when the drug wore off, but she was smart enough to not move at all. He would break her from any form of dishonesty in due time. Quick as a snake, he pinched her nipple as hard as he could. She screamed behind the gag and tried to twist away from him.

He laughed and let her nipple go. "First of all, I want you to understand that I don't want to kill you. You will experience a lot of pain, and you will be forever changed by this experience. But if you are truthful and forthright with me, you will live. Am I being clear?" he asked her. She nodded her head up and down while staring into his eyes.

She kept wiggling her body and hunching up and down, not trying to escape, but trying to entice him with her perfect body. He asked her, "Do you know who I am?" She shook her head no. He shook his head and said, "Okay, that might have been the wrong way to ask that. Do you know what the media has been calling me?" She nodded yes.

"Okay, so this is how you stay alive. I am going to remove the gag. If you make a single sound other than to answer my questions honestly, I will torture you by slowly taking your beauty, piece by piece." The killer stood up and removed the gag before he sat back down on the bed.

He then opened the bag he had set on the floor. He removed a clear jar with clear liquid inside of it. "This is acid. You can survive this encounter with little to no damage to your body and you can live to suck and fuck for money until your heart is content. If you lie to me, or you refuse to tell me what I want to know, then I will drip this all over your beautiful body. So that you know what you will go through, I am going to give you a demonstration."

"No, no, please you don't have to. I'll tell you…"

He put the gag back on and opened the jar. Her eyes were extremely wide and full of fear. He took out a glass dripper and said, "I am going to drip this on your ankle where it will be easy to hide, but I need you to understand that I am serious." He sucked up a few drops and dripped the acid on her leg.

The reaction was instant. She bucked and screamed behind the gag as her eyes rolled back in her head from the pain.

The acid sounded like bacon cooking on the stove. It kind of smelled the same too. The pain was continuous for about ten seconds while it burned through her skin and tissue and muscles. He removed another solution and splashed her ankle with it.

Just as fast as it started, the pain stopped. Candace had tears and snot all over her face. He went to her bathroom and wet a rag and came back and cleaned her face off.

"I'm going to remove the gag, but don't make a sound, okay?" She nodded her understanding. Trying to sound sincere, he said, "I really don't want to hurt you."

Now with the gag removed, he asked her, "Do you know who Timothy Washington is?" She squeezed her eyes shut and more tears came out.

"Yes," she said with resignation. That was the name of the inmate she had yelled rape on.

"Thank you for being honest, if you keep doing that, this will all be over quickly." He was using his softest, most charming voice to encourage her to tell him all. He was also sure she had forgotten about the cameras.

"Did you and Timothy have an arrangement to have sex for money?"

"Yes," she said. She was crying openly now.

"Did Timothy Washington rape you or were you role playing?"

"He didn't rape me. We were role playing a scene that he had paid for."

"How much did he pay you and how did he pay you?"

"Tim paid me $1000 on CashApp."

"What was the CashApp name?" She gave it to him with no problem.

"Okay Candace, you are doing good. Now you have to give me every CashApp account that you own and every password. Also access to all your bank accounts."

"Not all the money came from that." She knew she had messed up by the look on his face. She fixed her mouth to scream, but he was too fast. He put the gag back in place and then stood over her bucking body, shaking his head.

"Damn sweetie, you were doing so good. Now I have to hurt you again." He picked up the acid and the dripper and filled it up halfway this time. She was bucking and pleading with her eyes for him not to do it.

"You are so proud of these perfect breasts. Always rubbing and squeezing on them. After this, you might need another surgery or two." He squeezed out the dripper on her left breast. She was convulsing and shaking. Her eyes rolled back again. This time, he let it burn for twenty seconds before he dashed her with the compound designed to make the acid inert.

The acid had eaten through the flesh of her left breast, taking chunks out of it. She was looking down at the damage, crying like her life was over. "We'll try this one more time. No questions or extra noise. Just give me what I want, and I'll be on my way." He cleaned her face off again and removed the gag.

"Now, give me all your accounts and access to all of them."

"I have so many that I just saved them in the phone. Just bring up accounts and you can access them right there on the screen."

He looked deep into her eyes and said, "Candace, if one cent is not on that phone, tell me now," she started to say something, but he held his hands up for her to be quiet. "Let me be clear, I know exactly how much money you have and if it doesn't add up like it should, the next squeeze is on your face."

She stared at him for a few seconds before squeezing her eyes shut. "A few of the accounts are in my mother's name for her to pay her bills with. Please, don't take that from her. She's had such a hard life, and she can now live a little."

The killer softened a little towards her. She had just risked everything for a chance to keep her mother happy. "Okay, but I'm going to send this money back to your victims' families. I won't leave you broke because I know you've been saving your checks too." He walked off with her unlocked phone and got to work.

After thirty minutes, he came back over to her and sat down. He looked her in her eyes for a full minute. He then glanced at her body and stood up, putting the gag back in place.

"You know, you're not that bad of a person. You give a lot of inmates hope and pleasure and I appreciate that. But what you did to those two inmates cannot be forgiven. And I am only doing this to make sure you can't do to another inmate what you did to them. After I'm done with you, you'll have to pay someone to fuck you."

He left her room so that he could collect all the cameras he had around her apartment. He had already put the extra doorbell, that was just like hers, in his bag. He had been out in the parking lot watching her on his phone until she got in the shower. He had then picked the lock on her backdoor after climbing up to her balcony. He had waited in her workout room until he had crept up behind her with the needle.

After collecting the cameras, he went around with bleach and cleaned everywhere he had been. Just to mess up any other tests they might have, he took out every chemical she owned, from Drano to oven cleaner and just started spraying it around on everything.

This time, he would edit some of the video before he sent it to the beautiful, Denise McCarthy. He had made her a star. It had been close to three weeks since he sent her the last video. He felt she had done an excellent job. It was honest and informative, and it got his point across. This one was straight forward payback, and hopefully, would put pressure on the system to release Timothy Washington. Without the extra time, he would already be at home with his children.

When he returned to Lt. Price, she was crying and bucking on the bed, trying to get free. "I promised you I wouldn't kill you, but I have to tell you that you'll probably wish I had. What I'm going to do is throw this full bottle on you, but I'm going to untie your hands. The counter compound will be right here on your side table. Untie your legs after I'm gone, and you can make it over here and pour the compound over you to stop the effects of the acid. I left you $100,000 to do with as you please. Have a nice life. Oh, and you'll probably go to jail for all you admitted to on camera. As ugly as you'll be, you won't have to worry about the bull dykes."

He ignored her pleas through the gag and dashed her with the remaining acid. [Damn, smoke was coming off the bitch.] Reaching over, he pulled the knot loose to free both her hands. She was screaming, but she had already started on her left leg when he walked out. He left the camera over the bedroom door to record every last detail.

He was all the way to his car, but he could still hear her screaming. He had his phone out, watching as he drove away. She had freed herself and poured the compound over her head. She was off camera now, in the bathroom, but he could picture her standing naked in front of the mirror, looking at herself.

She was still in the bathroom crying and screaming; she never once thought to call the police and try to catch him. He was on the highway now, on his way back to his hotel room to edit the video. If he was fast enough, he could probably make the 10 o'clock news.

CHAPTER 13

Denise McCarthy was on cloud 9. Everything in her life was going right. She was becoming a star in the reporting world. People recognized her in public and asked her for her autograph. And to think, she owed it all to a killer and good luck. Her work was very good but there were a million very good reporters out there. She was just blessed, and she was taking her blessing as far as she could.

It had been more than two weeks since she received the text about another video. When she didn't hear from him the next day, she set a plan in motion. She had contacted the victims and officers to see if anyone would agree to do interviews with her. To her surprise, the only one who turned down her request was Det. Ann Grace of the SBI. She had sounded a little angry that she would have asked her at all. But when she talked to her senior partner, Sgt. Det. Walter Rogers, he had readily agreed. He said he was in Bayboro at the time, and he would call her as soon as he got back to Raleigh. She had butterflies in her stomach all week until his call that Friday. The interview was set up for tonight. He had even asked her to dinner after their seven o'clock interview. She said yes and the date was set.

The interviews she did with all the others had already aired and her bosses couldn't be happier. Her immediate supervisor had shown her that the ratings doubled what they normally were. It was a good thing she had only signed a one-year contract. Secretly, her boss had also told her the executives would beat any contract that anyone else offered her, so next year she could renegotiate for a lot more money and freedom.

The first interview that aired was with Bruce Battle. The one-armed man was bitter as hell and blamed the world for all his troubles.

"Mr. Battle how are you doing this morning?" she had been ushered into a room with glass cutting it in half. On the other side was Mr. Battle sitting on a stool with a phone in his hand. On her side was a stool and phone. She sat down, with her cameraman standing behind her. She had fixed a recorder to the phone to pick up both sides of the conversation.

"I'm doing a lot better now that I get to see your beautiful face. Damn girl, can you stand up one more time for me?"

"Thank you, Mr. Battle," she said, ignoring his request. "The prison has agreed to give me 10 minutes, so I want to get to the point." She paused and stared into his eyes. "Do you belong to a gang, Mr. Battle?"

"Absolutely not. That is a lie the prison system made up so they could keep their foot on a nigga's neck."

"There are plenty of people in prison that have not been labeled. Why would they target you?"

"Because I'm smart and powerful and I'm fine as hell. Don't you think so?"

Denise smiled and asked, "Okay, well how are you adjusting to the use of one arm?"

The change from flirtatious to fury was instantaneous. "What the fuck kind of stupid ass question is that? Let me take your arm, bitch, and see how well you adjust. That coward motherfucker is gonna pay for this shit."

"Do you have any idea who would want to do this to you?"

"Anybody. Everybody. Every motherfucker who ain't me would love to take me down."

"But can you think of anyone in particular who would want you hurt? It's probably the same person killing all these officers," Denise stated.

"Yeah, I got a good idea of who he is. He was a coward when he was in here but, I have to give it to him, he has some major balls now." All of a sudden, the anger was gone, and a smile of respect lit his face.

"So, you mean to tell me you know who it is, but you won't say his name? You can't be loyal to this guy. He shot you."

"That's the thing, I am not loyal to him, I am loyal to his cause. All these guys get out, mad at the system and talking about all they are going to do, but they are so happy to be out that they forget about the rest of us. I've done some pretty foul shit in here, the piece of shit still decided to let me live. He will have to answer for this eventually," he said, pointing at his missing arm. Looking dead at the camera, he said, "But for now, keep doing what you're doing. We're all rooting for you."

"What if they said you could go home today if you told them his name? Would you do it?" Denise asked.

The fury was back. "Fuck you, bitch. You think I'm a rat? Fuck you! If it wasn't for him, you wouldn't be shit. Nobody knew you until he sent you that video. You definitely wouldn't be in here asking questions. I'm not telling you or anybody else shit." Looking at the camera he said, "Bro, kill em' all." He punched the glass and, standing up, yelled, "Kill them all!"

With that, the officers rushed in and took him down. They cuffed his one arm to his belt loop in the back. It restricted his motion, but he was still fighting them pretty good. Eventually, he got tired, and they dragged him out of the room.

She had gotten it all on video and hadn't known if she should air the last bit. If she did and the officers were killed, she would feel horrible. Her producers had wanted her to air it all, so she did. They edited out the curse words and the early flirtation, but the video aired mostly as is. It had been a huge success and added to the brightness of her star.

As good as the Bruce Battle interview was, the Robert Dennis interview shot her into the stratosphere. It had it all; tears, accusations of innocence and corruption, racism, conspiracies. It was so good, the producers thought she might win an award.

Because no one thought Cpt. Robert Dennis was a threat to her, they did the interview in a conference room at the Pitt County Courthouse. There were two guards, but they stood over by the door just watching the show. Denise McCarthy only had her cameraman and her sound guy. After a few instructions, they were ready to go.

"Good afternoon, Mr. Dennis. How are you doing today?"

The jail had granted her one-hour of interview time from one to two in the afternoon. She had been assured that it was okay if they ran over. Her producers wanted to do an hour-long special show on the interview, so she would touch on everything. At least that was the plan.

"Well, I'm living in hell, so how do you think I feel, girly?"

"Mr. Dennis, my name is Ms. McCarthy. I'm actually here to help you. As you can see, not a lot of people are lined up to hear your side of the story. Everyone has already found you guilty and sent you to death row. So, have a little respect for the one person who is giving you a chance to talk to the public."

"I'm sorry, Ms. McCarthy," Robert said, with his eyes now looking downward. "It's just that I'm innocent and no one will even look into my claims."

"Mr. Dennis, every claim that you made was looked into, and no evidence was found to back you up."

"Ms. McCarthy, this guy was a professional. The police have all the evidence in the world that another person was in that house. They just want me so bad that they are using fantasy to connect the person to me."

Denise leaned in and asked, "How are the police using fantasy? Can you explain what you mean?"

"Certainly, Ms. McCarthy. The police have looked at my phone records to find out how I contacted this other person. When they found nothing, they said I had another phone.

75

When they couldn't find a phone or the purchase of a phone, they said I got someone else to buy it and then I got rid of it. How can I defend myself against things that might have been done?"

"But, Mr. Dennis, it sounds like you could have done exactly what they're saying."

"Well, if that's a possibility, why is it not possible that this is the Prison Guard Killer setting me up? It seems to me that only the stuff that makes me look guilty are possible and all the things that make me look innocent are not believable. I mean, I fit his profile to the letter."

"Who's profile, Mr. Dennis?"

"The killer's profile, dammit. You're not listening to me!" Mr. Dennis had slammed his hands down on the table to emphasize his point. The guards had made to move in, so he settled down really fast. If anyone knew what the guards could do to him, it was Robert Dennis.

"Can you explain why you think the killer would target you?"

"Do you want to know the truth?" Mr. Dennis asked. At her nod, he continued. "I've worked in prisons for over 25 years. I'm not the smartest guy in the world, but I made it all the way up to Operations Captain. Whenever I was on duty, that prison belonged to me. I've kicked a lot of nigger ass over the years."

"Mr. Dennis, we don't need…"

He talked right over her. "And it seems one of the sons of bitches got out and set me up to go to prison myself. My career is over, so I'll tell you the truth. If this bastard is going to kill, maim, or set up every dirty prison guard in the state, he'll be a hundred before he's done."

"Why do you say that?" asked Denise.

"Because they're all dirty. They teach us to be dirty. I didn't have a hateful bone in my body when I was in the service. Blacks, whites, it didn't matter. We were all brothers, fighting and dying together. The state sends us to school to learn how to be an officer. My teacher was a racist asshole and he brainwashed me into being one too. They train us to hate all inmates, but my instructor turned me into a nigger hater just because he could."

"Mr. Dennis, I appreciate your honesty, but can we stop using racist slurs please?"

"Well, I wouldn't be honest if I did. You wanted me to be me, and this is who I am. Anyway, chances are, one of the little monkeys whose ass I beat wasn't a dummy and he came back and got his revenge."

Denise asked, "Can you make a list of all the inmates you've assaulted over your career?"

"Haha, we would be here for a month. Anyway, the problem is, what he's doing now isn't going to change a damn thing. The people who direct us to beat them and humiliate them and abuse them are the ones he should be going after. The administrators want the inmates demoralized and treated like animals, so that's what I do. It's what we're paid to do."

"So, you're trying to get the world to believe that not only are you innocent of killing your family, but all of the abuse you've inflicted has been at the direction of the administration of the prison?" The interview was going better than she could have hoped for. If he kept this up, he could bring down the whole system.

"Oh, you think it's just at the prison level. Hahaha! It goes all the way up to the governor's office. Listen, the normal little pissant officers don't know about everything. They're not under control yet, so they're not trusted. But once you get up to Lieutenant or Captain and higher, they give you special training at special meeting."

As Robert Dennis was saying this, one of the officers, who was a Lieutenant, walked out after saying something to the other officer.

Mr. Dennis went on. "You think they are stopping contact visitation and adding private security at the fences because they want to stop contraband in prisons? No, they are trying to stop the competition to their own contraband networks. Officers get caught bringing stuff in. They get caught because they're doing it for themselves and not the network. Officers have multiple charges of assaults. You hear about them only when they want you to. Normally, they just tell us to put them in the hole until they heal up and the proof is gone."

"What about their medical needs? Do you have people to treat them?"

"The whole medical staff at every prison is corrupt. They bring in so much money that they won't hire you unless you are corrupt."

"Okay, Mr. Dennis, we will come back to this later. How do you feel about your family? Do you miss them?"

"I'm not a very easy guy to love. I wasn't always an asshole, but look at me, my wife was way out of my league," The tears started falling now. "And my little Ivory. I was so happy that she took after her mother."

Denise asked the sound guy to give her some tissues. She was a good judge of people, and she could tell that this wasn't fake. She said, "You loved your family."

Nodding his head yes and wiping his face, he said, "Very much. But I was awed they loved me. I was so stupid and abusive. The last time I could have expressed love to them, I left them at the airport and went home to sleep. When the killer told Mary to scratch me and she did it, I thought he was going to kill me and make it look like she did it. I was trying to move but that drug had me in its grip."

Denise jumped in with, "Wait, is this the drug that you told the police about? Because your blood test came back clean."

"I keep telling you people that he is a pro. He knew what he was doing every step of the way." He looked up at Denise like a light bulb had just come on inside his head. "You're not here to help me, you black bitch. Everything you've said only makes me look worse. I saw that shit on the news where he sent you a video. You're working with him, you stupid cunt."

With that, he lunged out of the chair at her.

She was fast and he was 400 pounds of fat. The single guard had jumped in, but he was thrown aside like he was nothing. The guard slid down the wall but was up again in a second. He got on his radio and then guards poured in, piling on Mr. Dennis.

She motioned for her cameraman to keep filming as the officers beat on Robert Dennis long after he stopped resisting. It took eight officers to carry him out, and then it was silent.

Denise asked her camera guy, "Do you think we could stretch that into an hour?"

"After we add in the footage from the night of the murders and commercials, I think we will be alright," he replied.

Alright had been the understatement of the year. Her producers had aired it the next night at seven o'clock. At nine o'clock, they called her and told her they needed her to come back to the station. She had been terrified that she had went too far. When she opened the door to their fifth-floor offices, the whole station yelled, "SURPRISE!" They were throwing her a party. Everyone was happy for her, and the executives were singing her praises. She was officially at the top of her game.

The interview with Marshall Oakland had not really been an interview at all. He had ushered her and her team into the living room. He had still been moving slowly, healing from his wounds. When she went to speak, he held up both of his hands and shook his head. "I will not take any questions. I am going to provide you with a statement and then I will ask you to leave. If this is not agreeable, then I ask that you leave now."

Denise sat down and said, "We are ready when you are. You can look directly at the camera, or you can look at me. I will say, if you are talking directly to the public or to the killer, then it's best to look at the camera."

Mr. Oakland sat and looked at the camera. Not even a month ago he had lost his wife and two kids, so she would give him all the time he needed.

"I want to start by saying thank you to Denise McCarthy for giving me this opportunity. I haven't prepared anything because I want this to come from my heart."

He paused to gather himself again. "I am going to be honest even though some people may not like what I have to say." He looked over at Denise. "You media people are some damn vultures. And you're full of shit. There are no two sides to this crime. You assholes are trying to give him some kind of noble meaning. He is a fucking monster. A monster who killed my children and raped my wife to death with a drill, while laughing the entire time. And you have the audacity to even suggest that he is doing this for a good cause!" He was screaming, spit flew with every word.

"Mr. Oakland, that's not what…"

"Shut the fuck up! You've said enough. You've done enough. You played this asshole's video of him torturing me and my family. I couldn't protect them, and you showed the whole world what a failure I am." Tears were flowing freely down his face now. "So, you are going to sit there and shut up and let me get some of my dignity back."

Denise put both of her hands up to show her surrender before Mr. Oakland decided, the hell with it, and kicked them out of his house. She said, "I'm sorry. No one will interrupt you again."

"Good," he said, regaining some of his control. "Now, I have always been a good and fair officer. I have never abused my authority or lied to cover for another officer. That's part of the reason I'm still a sergeant after working eight years at Pamlico Correctional Institution. Are all officers like me? No. But there are enough of us that are good, for this kind of stuff not to have happened." He was staring at the camera now with a kind of intensity.

"To the killer out there, I don't know what happened to you during your incarceration, and I don't condone what you are doing. If you really want change, start by showing the ones of us who give respect, the respect that we deserve. There are hundreds, no…thousands of officers who would never dream of hurting any ward of the state that we represent. All of the fear that you worked so hard to instill in the bad officers is gone now. In its place is an anger and hate so deep that you are making it worse for the people you are trying to help."

Turning to look at Denis,e he said, "My family is gone. They didn't deserve any of the things that happened to them. I had assured my family that they were safe, and the look my wife gave me in that van, spoke of a betrayal all the way down to her soul. She thought that I had been lying to her about my activities at work. She died thinking that I was one of the bad guys and I brought all this on my family."

Looking back at the camera now, he said, "In closing, I just don't want anyone else to feel this kind of pain. Please, whoever you are, find another way to get your point across. None of us are innocent in this, but try to give us time to make things right. Stop the killing because its only making the situation worse."

He looked over at Denise and said, "I'm done." He then got up and walked slowly to lead them to the door. As soon as they cleared the threshold, he closed the door firmly behind them.

Because there was nothing really complicated about the interview, it had aired that same night. The public had been mixed on its response to Marshall Oakland's words. Some people sympathized with him and agreed with what he said. Other people thought he might have pissed the killer off to the point that he would kill more than he had been just to prove his point.

· ·

All of that was in the past now. She was having a panic attack about what to wear to the interview date. They were to meet at a popular hotel restaurant where she had reserved a back room for the privacy they would need.

Just as she settled on a little black dress, her phone signaled a text. It was from Det. Rogers confirming they were still on. She responded with a quick affirmative and continued to get ready.

She felt like a movie star when she pulled up to the valet in her brand-new Benz. When she got out, people actually knew who she was and hollered greetings to her. On her way through the lobby, she was stopped time after time to sign autographs. Even though she had arrived 30 minutes early, she ended up being 10 minutes late to the restaurant.

When she finally got to the reserved room, she was giddy with excitement. She felt exhilarated by the response the people gave her. She opened the door to find Det. Rogers and her team having a good time. Pretty soon, all eyes were on her, and everything was silent.

"Wow," Sgt. Det. Rogers said. "You look wonderful." He rushed around and pulled her chair out for her. It was nice to see the appreciation on his face. It was weird, but as soon as she saw it, she wasn't nervous anymore.

"Thank you, you look handsome yourself." Denise said, as she sat down at the table.

"Alright children," her cameraman joked. "Let's get the business out of the way before you start that lovey dovey bullshit."

Denise laughed but Walt gave him a look that dried up all the laughter in the room.

"Okay, well, we will start with just a few questions about your background and then move towards what you can tell us about the investigation. I know you can't say much but..."

As she was talking, a text had come in on her phone. She had continued to talk as she read it. It said, "Might as well show lover boy too." Five seconds later a video came through her email.

"Oh no," she said.

"What?" Walt asked with concern in his voice. "What's wrong?"

"He's here. Somehow, he's watching us."

Det. Rogers jumped up and grabbed the phone. He read the text and glanced briefly at the video that was attached. He looked at her and said, "Stay here. Don't leave this room for any reason." He was all cop now, as he dashed out of the room, in search of the killer.

CHAPTER 14

Sgt. Det. Rogers was running out of the restaurant, scanning the crowds of people looking at every face, and talking on his cell phone at the same time. "Yeah, get as many people over here as you can. He's probably gone by now, but he was definitely here five minutes ago."

He was talking to the commander over at the Raleigh Police Department. He could get the troops moving way faster than by calling 911, and he needed people at the hotel as soon as possible.

"Whatever you need. I am sending a Sgt. Gould to lead the ground troops," said the commander.

"Okay, I'm on my way to talk to the head of security to see about the surveillance cameras. We've already sealed the exits, but there's really no way he would have stayed in here. Anyway, I'll keep you informed. And thanks for the help," Walt said before hanging up.

The video the killer had sent Denise was of her signing autographs on her way into the restaurant. He had been within five feet of her at one point. The video was only ten seconds long, but it sent fear running through his heart every time he thought about how close Denise had been to the killer.

The question was, how did the killer know that she was with him? He had been waiting in that room for thirty minutes before she had come in. So, was the killer following him or was he following Denise? He could only wish that the killer would follow him. He would kill the bastard and be done with it. But he knew the killer was following Denise because he would have felt him if he was being followed. So, back to the original question. He would have to talk to Denise about that.

Before he could make his way to the security office, the officers the commander sent over arrived. There had already been five officers at the hotel, and Walt dispatched them to block the exits that by law couldn't be locked. Now, about fifteen more poured into the lobby, looking around for him.

He waved them over and a sergeant stepped up and said, "We're here to help out with the search. We're looking for this Prison Guard Killer, right? We got ten more officers in cars riding around the area with the description that we got from y'all before. Are we searching this hotel?" he asked Walt.

"I'm on my way to security to look at the tapes. If we can see him leave, then there's no need. If we can't find him exiting the building, then he might be in one of the rooms or hiding somewhere."

"Okay, but I'm going with you, and I'll have these guys start the search and ask people if they saw him. Can you send my guys that video? That way, we can start identifying and looking for the other people in it to see if they saw anything," stated the Sergeant.

Pulling his phone out to call Denise and ask her to send the video to him, he saw that she already had. [Smart woman], she knew that he would need it. "Yeah, I got it right here. What's your number? I'll send it to you, and you can send it to your guys." The sergeant gave him his number and he sent him the video.

While they walked to the security room, the Sergeant sent his guys the video. They got to work on finding the people in the video but also clearing people still walking around the lobby.

The first thing Walt did after leaving that backroom was place a call to the hotel to tell them to seal all the exits. Since that time, no one had been allowed to come in or leave. But the people were getting restless, so they needed to start letting people go if they didn't have any helpful information. Walt knew it was too late to catch him on site, but they might get lucky with the surveillance cameras, or someone else's cell phone video. With Denise becoming somewhat of a local celebrity, there was sure to be other videos of her in the lobby.

Walt had been wondering where the manager of the hotel was and when they entered the security office, he got his answer. The manager was dressed in a classic black suit and white shirt and had a tag on his chest that said Michael. He was an older white guy, around 50 or 60, with a bald head. Right now, he was lighting into his security staff.

"What the hell are you getting paid for?" he yelled at one of his guys.

"Sir, this was not our fault. The system was hacked and shut down remotely. We have control back now, but the system was down for about 15 minutes."

Walt jumped in asking, "What's going on? What happened?"

The manager turned on him, "What the hell are you doing in here? This area is restricted. Security personnel only."

"Sir, I am SBI, Detective Rogers," Walt said, taking his badge out. "And this is Sergeant Gould of the Raleigh Police Department. We are here to see the video of your lobby for the past two hours."

"Yeah, well good luck with that. The security system went down about twenty minutes ago, and it just came back online within the last five minutes. We pay this company thousands of dollars a month and all they can say is, 'it's not our fault.' Unbelievable." he said, shaking his head.

"Okay, well sir, can you tell me what happened?" Walt asked the security guy sitting in front of three different computer monitors.

"Sure, our system was hacked by some outside source, and it shut down all the cameras for fifteen minutes. It was freaky. Everything cut off and we were trying everything to get them back up. And then, bam, everything is working again."

"Has this ever happened before?" Sgt. Gould asked him.

"No, never," the security guard replied. "I've been working in Network Security since networks were made and I've never seen anything like this. We have all kinds of failsafe and back-ups built in to block any type of attempt at intrusion. Whatever this was, it took everything down at the same time and it locked us out."

"So, was this a hacker or a device in your opinion?" asked Walt.

"I would guess that it was a device that was programmed to be turned on and turned off at the flip of a switch. You have to understand that most attacks happen in stages. It's when someone ignores one of the warnings that gets you into trouble. But this attack was every stage happening at once. Like ten hackers working simultaneously to bring down a network."

"Okay, I'm lost now," Sgt. Gould said. "So, was it a device or was it ten hackers working together? We're cops, not scientists, try to keep it simple."

"Well, let me explain it to you. One guy could program a device to perform multiple layers of attack, and at the press of a button, all the layers of the program would activate at the same time. Think of our security as a hallway with steel doors coming down from the ceiling. The next door only opens after the one you just went through closes. That would give the system time to understand that an attack is happening. But if you know programming, you could write a code to open them all. And before the system could alert anyone to the attack, you've already taken over. The attack would continue to keep us out. Again, picture the hallway, but now it's us trying to get back in. Anyway, then he would press the button again to return the system to us. By then, your guy is long gone."

"Is every one of the cameras on this system?" Walt asked the manager.

"Yes, unfortunately," he replied.

"How smart would this guy have to be to make this kind of device?" asked Sgt. Gould to the room.

"I didn't even think it was possible," answered the security guy. "This guy is in the wrong business. He could sell this single device for millions. Can you imagine someone walking into a bank with this technology? This goes way beyond ransomware. He pretty much takes over the whole system. Any system! There's no telling what all he could do without seeing the code, but this guy is dangerous. And you think this is that Prison Guard Killer 5from the news? No wonder you haven't caught him. He's the real-life Batman with gadgets like this."

"Thank you," said Walt. Turning to Sgt. Gould, he asked, "So, what do you want to do? This guy could still be in here. You want to search the whole building?"

"Absolutely out of the question," Michael, the manager, jumped in. "My guests have already been put through hell. No way am I letting you disrupt them more than you already have."

Walter loss the battle with his temper. "Let me? Let me?" he asked while advancing on the manager. "Let me explain something to you. You don't let me do anything." By now, Walt was all the way up in the man's face, as the manager cowed against the back wall. Holding his badge up to the managers face, he asked, "Can you read what this says?"

Michael answered, "Yes, it says Sgt. Walter Rogers, SBI. I understand that, but …"

"Shut up. What this badge means is, I don't have to ask anybody for permission to do shit. Let alone some punk ass hotel manager." Backing off the man, he said, "Now either you go with the Sergeant, or you send someone with a master room key card, because every inch of this building is going to be searched, even if we have to kick every door down. Am I making myself clear?"

"Yes, sir."

"Okay." Turning back to the Sergeant, he said, "Sgt. Gould, I'll let you do your thing with the search and just let me know if you find anything."

Smiling, the Sergeant said, "Yes sir."

"Smart ass," Walt whispered, as the manager went out with the Sergeant.

"Sir," the security guy said. "I made a recording of the two hours before the blackout and everything up until two minutes ago." He handed Walt a thumb drive and said, "If you can get to a set up like this, you can watch all the cameras at once. If you can't, then just put that in your computer or laptop, and when it asks if you want to download the viewer, just say yes. It will at least let you watch four of them at a time."

"Is there any chance in hell that you can get the footage from that missing fifteen minutes?" Walt asked him.

"Hell, it's not misplaced, it doesn't exist. He didn't cut the wires, but he took all the power from every camera. Sorry."

"Were the cameras the only thing affected?"

"Nope, the phones, the WIFI, basically anything that used the internet, he cut it off. Our cell phones still worked, but that's about it. The room cards only worked because they are pretty much just a reader with an approval code to unlock the door. He could have written a code to disengage those, but all it would have done was unlocked all the doors."

"Why is that?" he asked the guy. You never know what piece of information would break a case.

"It's simple. All the doors are unlocked and only the power going to the reader keeps them locked. Cut the power and all the doors unlock because now there's no power to keep them locked. You have to do it that way for the fire code. That way, if the power goes out during a fire, the fire department can get into any room at any time."

"Okay, well thank you. You've been a great help."

"You're welcome." Walt heard him say as he left the security room to go back to the restaurant. He really expected to see Denise with her team out in the lobby trying to interview people. But when he got back to the room, she was sitting right where he left her.

"Oh, thank God," they both said, at the same time.

Walt said, "I just knew you would be out in the lobby trying to interview some witness that only you could find."

With a smile on her face, Denise said, "Normally, you would be right, but I want to live. He could have killed me, and I never would have seen him coming." By the end of that statement, the smile was gone, and she just looked worried.

"Hey guys," Walt said, talking to her staff. "Can you excuse us for a minute?" After a second of hesitation, they got up and left.

"Denise, this hasn't been released to the public, but I want you to understand how ruthless this guy really is." He paused and took a deep breath. "You remember I was in Bayboro when you called me about this interview?"

"Yes, you were investigating the Oakland family murders, right?"

"Yeah, but I had to go up there to view the video of the abduction. We couldn't figure out how he could kidnap four people without anyone seeing it or any of the victims getting away. Seems that he grabbed the youngest boy, Robert, who was only eight, and stuck a needle in his neck. He had parked a van next to their car at a supermarket. When they returned, he jumped out and grabbed Robert, and it looks like he forced the rest of the family in the van by threatening to hurt the little boy if they didn't get in."

"Dear God," said Denise. "What the hell is wrong with him?"

"I don't know, but his methods are getting worse. It's almost as if he doesn't care if he gets caught, but he's good enough to take risks as safely as possible, if that makes sense."

"It does, I mean, look at tonight. If I had seen him, he could have just acted like a fan. Since he knows I didn't, he felt safe enough to send the video."

"Alright, Denise, I need you to think. How in the hell did this guy know you were here with me? He followed you here. I would have known if he followed me. So, he could see you were here, but how did he know you were right next to me?"

She had no doubt he was right.

"I didn't tell anyone but my team, and I called them one hour before I got here. They are on call 24 hours a day so I only call them if I know for sure, I will need them."

"Do you trust them?" he asked her.

"They haven't given me a reason not to, but I haven't been working with them long. Do you think one of them is helping the killer?"

Walt said, "I wouldn't say helping, but a little info here and there for some cash, who knows?"

"I couldn't swear to it, but I would say neither of them is helping him. I could be wrong, but I just don't get that feeling off of them."

"Alright," Walt said, "But I'm going to have them checked out anyway. I'll be very discreet, so don't worry about it.

Dammit Denise," Walt said, pulling her into a hug. Holding onto her, he said, "I was so scared. I don't want anything to happen to you."

Pulling back after a full minute, Denise said, "I don't think I'm in danger. If he wanted to hurt me, he could have."

"We have no idea what his M.O. is anymore. Maybe he likes to play around before he kills. I need you to be careful, okay?" he pleaded with her.

"I didn't know you cared, but I'll be as careful as I can."

Her phone rang at that moment, and she looked at the number. It was not a number she recognized, but for some reason, her pulse picked up.

She answered. "Hello?"

"That was so sweet. I almost shed a tear. Put me on speaker," the killer demanded.

Setting the phone down on the table she said, "Okay, you're on speaker."

"Hello, you two love birds. Seems I've been really good for you, Denise. Rising career, finally got a man. And you, Sgt. Det. Rogers, I knew with a little help, you would come out of your shell."

Walter had pulled his phone out and was calling the crime lab. He would know exactly where this fucker was in thirty seconds. He put his phone down and responded to the killer. "Seems you know everyone on this side, but we don't know what to call you. You want to enlighten me?"

"Hey Detective, are you trying to trace this call? HaHaHa! Remember, I'm the Batman. You can't trace Batman."

"How in the hell?" Walt looked up and saw the camera in the corner. "Son of a bitch, that's how you knew I was here. You're still using the cameras."

"Bingo, genius. And you're the one who is supposed to catch me? In your dreams."

Walter picked up his phone and the tech said, "It bounces every few seconds. I'm sorry sir, but we can't get a lock."

"Alright, thanks for trying," Walt said to the tech. Looking up at the camera, he said, "Why go after Ms. McCarthy? She has done exactly what you wanted."

"I'm not going to hurt her. She's my star. I respect her and I like the way she works. As long as she doesn't turn on me, we're good."

Denise said, "Why send me a threat if we're good? That was a clear message that you could get to me if you wanted to."

"Denise, Denise, Denise. I can get to anyone at any time. For instance, Sarge here likes to keep his fruit on the shelf, and he puts his drinks in the fruit drawer. Doesn't make sense to me, but hey, a man likes what he likes."

Walter exploded, "You coward motherfucker! That's the only way you'll come at me is behind my back. Come at me man to man and let's see who walks away."

"Whoa, whoa, whoa man, chill out. I like your spunk. But seriously, I don't want to hurt anybody that doesn't deserve it. You get too close, and I might have to take you up on that offer. But remember Superman, Batman lost the first battle, but he ended up beating the shit out of you. Every day you live is because I let you. Don't get it twisted, I will destroy you if you cross me."

Walt, still boiling, said, "Tell me how I can cross you and I'll do it just to meet you. Give me a hint. I want to cross you so bad. See, the problem is you've been running up against these soft ass prison guards and you're getting cocky. Make sure when you step up to the big leagues, you're ready."

Denise decided to jump in, "Please guys, stop this. I don't want to call you The Prison Guard Killer, so what can I refer to you as?"

The killer said, "Since we are working together, you can call me…Carl."

"As in Carlton Porter?" Walter asked the killer. "Bullshit, tell us your real name."

"Denise, take me off speaker so we can talk." She took him off speaker and picked up the phone. "Okay, I'm here," she said.

"Listen, I don't want to hurt either one of you. I know he is just doing his job. To tell you the truth, I like him. Other than him wanting to kill me, he seems like my kind of guy."

"Carl, you called me for a reason. I'm tired and my day has gone to hell because of you. Did you need something?"

"Sorry about that. I want you to only have good days, but I do need you to do something for me."

"If I can, I will. Ask away."

"Yesterday, I tortured a woman named Candace Price. She is a Lieutenant at Tabor City Correctional Institution. She's fucked up, but for some reason, she's sitting in her house and hasn't reported it yet."

"Is she alive?"

"She was an hour ago. I need you to give her info to your boyfriend and get the ball rolling on this thing."

"I hate to ask this, but if you tortured her, why are you now trying to help her?"

"I promised her I wouldn't kill her, but if she isn't treated, then she will die. I need her to stand for the wrongs she did."

Denise gave Walt the information and he got to work on his phone. "Okay, I told him."

"After she comes out with her public statement, I'll have a surprise for you."

"What do you mean, public statement?"

"She's waited because she's trying to come up with the best way to spin it. After she tells her lies, then I'll force her to tell the truth."

"Okay, but why the rush? Eventually, she would have gotten help and told her story."

"Well Denise, I'm on a timetable. Today is Tuesday. I need this done and over with by Sunday."

"Please Carl, just tell me, why?"

"Because, if Timothy Washington doesn't make it home for his daughter's birthday party on Monday, I'm going to kill a guard every day until I am in jail or dead. I promise you that. And to show you how serious I am, I'll kill one tonight to seal the deal."

"Wait, no Carl...Carl?" But Denise was talking to dead air. Carl was gone.

CHAPTER 15

The killer was in a bad mood, and someone was about to feel even worse that he did. He had followed Denise, but he hadn't planned to hurt her or anything like that. He had planned to catch her somewhere by herself and approach her with his mask on and ask his favor. Watching her on the cameras he had put in her house, he could tell that she was going out on a date. He hadn't had a clue who it was with, so he followed her to find out.

He figured, when she went to the hotel, that she was going to the restaurant. He knew she was single, and she didn't come across as a woman who would go up to some guy's hotel room on a first date. He was just going to follow her in and make sure the restaurant was her destination, then go back to her house and wait for her. He turned on his device and followed her into the hotel.

Programming had started out as a hobby, but pretty soon it became a fascination. Everything these days ran off the internet or some other network. So, to stay ahead, he had written a very complex code with thousands of commands to be performed in such a way to crash any network that he chose. He had then embedded the commands into a device that looks like a cell phone. It wasn't strong enough to take out a cell phone network, but a building's security was a piece of cake. And once the system went down, he had another program on his laptop to piggyback his way into the system with the people who booted it back up. It had taken him a year of writing code every day, but it was worth it. All his skills would mean nothing if he couldn't get people to carry out their parts of his plan.

Lt. Candace Price was really starting to piss him off. He had thought about going back and fucking her up a little more to force her hand. The problem with that was, he had only left the one camera so they could have set up a trap for him and he wouldn't know. [Stupid, it was only a few hundred dollars.] He should have left all the cameras so he would know if it was safe to go back. In his defense, as vain as she is, he had thought the second he was gone, she would have been on the phone calling for help. Now, it was out of her hands and maybe his plan could still work. At least that punk ass cop was good for something.

The killer had put cameras in Det. Rogers house, as well as his partner's, Det. Ann Grace. They had been a hundred steps behind him from the beginning. He still wanted to keep tabs on them, just in case he made a mistake and they got too close. He would have loved to bug their offices and their cell phones, but he couldn't figure a way to do either safely. Their homes had been simple. He cut his device on and walked right in. Sadly, at least for them, they both had smart locks, which unlocked as soon as the device turned on. They had both been out of town looking for him, so he took his time and did it right. Every move they made or word they said, he had a recording of it. [Yeah, cops were totally smarter than criminals.]

Anyway, the killer was mad at himself because he spoke out of anger and promised to kill a guard tonight. It definitely had not been part of his plan. Not even ten minutes after he made that promise, Ms. Denise McCarthy was live, giving a warning to all the correctional officers in the state. She had even told them he was in the Raleigh area. Now, they were probably loaded up and waiting for him. He wasn't scared of the challenge, but he hated going in not knowing what to expect. One thing for certain, he was going to keep his promise.

. . . .

He had been sitting down the road from Officer Greg Black's house for an hour now. The killer hated owing people, and he felt he owed Bruce Battle. The punk ass gang banger knew who he was, and he kept his mouth closed. He had to give him some respect for that.

Back in the killer's first year of incarceration, Bruce had gone into his cell and stolen all of his stuff. With him being in a gang, it wasn't much that could be done to him without serious repercussions. The killer had beat the shit out of him and took all his stuff back, and some of Bruce's stuff for his troubles. The Bloods came back and jumped, him but didn't take any of his stuff. That was the highest respect the gang could pay him. Once they knew he wasn't scared, they left him alone and showed him all the respect in the world. The killer had vowed to pay Bruce back for his ass whipping. The shot that took his arm was all the payback he needed.

Now, the killer was sitting outside the house of one of the men who had beat on Bruce in that interview he gave Denise. This officer was on his list anyway, so this seemed like the perfect time to end him.

He didn't know everything about Officer Black, but he knew enough to know that he needed to die. Officer Black lived in Dunn, NC, right outside of Raleigh. He was 42 years old and had worked at Central Prison for 20 years. He lived with his husband Nick and their two adopted daughters, Emily and Gabby. The killer had no interest in hurting his family, so he was out in his car doing some research.

Officer Black's husband, Nick, who was also 42, worked nights at Wake Minimum Custody Prison and was on duty right now. The older girl, Emily, is 20 years old and was on campus at North Carolina State University. The problem was, he didn't know if the 10-year-old, Gabby, was in the house. The car that was registered to the officer was in the driveway, so the killer decided to take a chance. If he had to, he would drug the little girl to keep her out of the way.

Slipping out of the car, he made his way to the house. It was a small, one-story home that was surrounded by a lot of open land on three sides. On the portion of the property that bordered the back of the house was a dense wooded area. He could see a swing set in the small backyard, as well as toys all over the front lawn. The blueprint he found on the place showed three bedrooms and two bathrooms that were all on the small side. Seems everyone had their own space but not a lot of space.

The killer could see that the master bedroom was on the opposite side of the house from the two slightly smaller rooms. With that in mind, he made his way to where the little girl would be if she was home. Better to take care of her now than to have her walk in on him killing her dad.

When he made it to the side of the house where the two rooms looked out onto the yard, he took a needle out his pack and cut the device on to disable any alarms. He peeked into the smaller of the two rooms and found that it had been turned into a small workout area. He turned to the other window and peeked in. There, sleeping on her side with her back to the window, was little Gabby.

This was the dangerous part. He had never been in the house, so he didn't know if the doors squeaked, or the floorboards creaked. He knew he could get in with little effort, but he didn't want to get shot in the face for his troubles.

Figuring the front door would be better maintained, he went around to the front. Walking carefully up the steps and over the porch, he reached the door. [The moment of truth,] he picked the lock in five seconds and turned the knob.

He opened the door super slowly. The door didn't make a sound. He stepped into the house and stopped to let his eyes adjust to the darkness. When he could see, he almost shit himself. Sitting on the couch, with a gun in his hand, was Officer Greg Black. The good news was that he was sound asleep.

The killer almost laughed out loud with relief. He eased over to the man and saw that his finger was not on the trigger. He stuck the needle in his neck and held the officer's hand down with his free hand. All Greg Black had time to do was tense his body before the drug forced him to relax. If his finger had been on the trigger, he could have gotten a shot off. Just like football, killing was a game of inches.

Since he had every intention of torturing the officer and then killing him, he still needed to secure the little girl. First, he would make sure the rest of the house was empty. He walked to the master bedroom side of the house and found no one else there. With that done, he made his way to the little girl's room.

He stood in her doorway looking in on her. He wished there was some way to do this without hurting her. There was nothing he could do about the pain of losing a parent, but he would do everything he could to keep her away from the violence. He stuck her in the leg with the needle. Her eyes opened and her breathing picked up, but other than that, she stayed still.

The killer kept her on her side and walked around the bed to where her phone sat on the dresser. It was unlocked, so he plugged in the headphones that sat beside the charger and turned the music on. Before he put the ear buds in her ears, he leaned down and said, "I'm so sorry." He made sure she was comfortable and them went to see her dad.

Officer Greg Black was right where he left him. The killer had to admit, without the drug, he would be dead or in jail by now. You couldn't buy it in the United States, but it was plentiful in Russia. It had cost him $100,000, but it was worth every penny. Plus, money wasn't a factor. For a hacker with his level of talent, money was just a few clicks away.

He stopped in front of the officer and punched him in the face twice. "For your crimes against helpless inmates, you have been sentenced to death. You will suffer, but you will suffer in silence. I don't want your little girl hearing your screams." He stuck him in the neck again with the needle.

The killer picked Officer Black up and carried him to the bedroom. There was no need to tie him up, so he went to work. He punched the officer again and again, in the body and face, until he was tired. Then he pulled out his knives.

With the officer laid out on the bed the way he was, he was completely at the killer's mercy. Unfortunately for the officer, the killer had none for him. He stabbed the bottom of both feet as hard as he could and laughed at the man's rapid breathing. He pulled the knives out and stabbed down into the officer's hands. He twisted the knives until most of the center of his hands were missing.

Pulling back, but leaving the knives in the officer's hands, he said, "I'm going to check on your daughter. Don't go anywhere because, when I come back, the real punishment will begin."

The killer walked back to the little girl's room to find her sitting up on the bed facing towards the door. "Is he dead yet?" she asked him.

The killer didn't know what to say. He had given her a small dose because she was so little. Obviously, it hadn't been enough.

"Is he dead yet?" she asked him again.

"No," said the killer. "Did you call anyone to help?" he asked the little girl. When she shook her head no, he asked, "Why not?"

"He doesn't only like boys, he likes girls too," she stated calmly. "He told me that you might come and to stay in my room. I've been praying that you would show up and save me."

The killer had tears in his eyes when he said, "I can promise you that he will never hurt you again. I have to stick you with another needle to protect both of us."

She rocked his world when she said, "Leave the headphones off. If it's okay with you, I'd like to hear him hurting."

The killer pulled his mask off and smiled at the little girl. "It would be my honor to carry out that request. Now, get comfortable."

When she laid on her back and smiled up at him, his heart broke for the pain she had been through. He delicately pushed the needle into her calf and smoothed the hair out of her face.

The killer whispered, "Sorry I didn't come sooner." Then, with a smile, he said, "Enjoy the rest of the show," and went back to work.

He knew he should have covered her ears anyway, but he couldn't bring himself to deny the child anything. He was hurting because he should have killed Officer Black years ago.

Officer Black had been accused of raping several inmates while working at Central Prison. It had been common knowledge that he was a rapist.

He liked to shackle inmates to the beds in solitary confinement and force himself on them. Anytime someone reported it, the administration went through the motions, but would ultimately say, there was no proof. Well, now it was time to pay the piper.

When he walked into the bedroom, he took out the ropes from the bag that he carried with him everywhere. He tied the officer securely to the bed and sat down to wait for the drugs to wear off.

As soon as they did, the officer started talking. "Don't kill me man. I'm fucked up enough. Just leave man. Please, just leave."

Seeing as the killer didn't have a mask on, he thought it was a foregone conclusion that the officer would die. "You were dead the second I stepped into this house. You're a rapist and a child molester." The killer punched him hard in his balls. "How could you hurt that little girl?"

He could barely be heard over the officer's screams and cries for help. The killer used his knife to cut the rapist's pants and underwear off. Then said, "You will suffer for all you've done. Then you will die. Do you know what your little girl said to me?"

"Fuck you man, and fuck her too."

"Yeah, that's what she told me. You like to fuck little kids. Well, you won't be fucking anything anymore. Not even when you get to hell."

The killer cut his privates off and the officer howled until he passed out. Movement at the door caused the killer to reach for his gun. "No, sweetie. Go back to your room."

"I wanted to make sure he was dead." It was only then he noticed the kitchen knife gripped tightly in her hand.

"I am going to chop him up into little pieces, but you don't need to see this, okay sweetheart? Please. I promise he will be dead, but I need you to trust me and go back to your room. When you hear the front door slam, call the police, but remember, you never saw me. I had my mask on the whole time. Okay?"

At her nod, she turned around and walked off in the direction of her room. The killer went to the door and watched her put the knife back. She then walked over to her room with a look of peace on her face.

He walked back to the bed and continued to beat on the rapist until he regained consciousness. "Wake up, you dickless motherfucker."

"Ung, unh," was all the officer could muster.

The killer again stabbed him where his penis used to be.

"Ahhh, ahhh!" the officer screamed over and over from the pain.

Finally, the blood loss was too much, and the killer couldn't revive him. He stabbed the officer in the neck until his head separated from his body. "See you in hell, you worthless piece of shit," were the killer's parting words.

He walked to the front door and put his mask back on. He had blood all over him but better safe than sorry. He slammed the door hard to alert Gabby to call the police. He had taken two steps to cross the porch when he saw a car turning into the driveway. It was good that he had put his mask back on and was in shape to run. The car belonged to Sgt. Det. Rogers.

CHAPTER 16

As soon as the killer made his declaration about killing an officer, Sgt. Det. Rogers said, "I'll be back," to Denise and he took off. Knowing the killer could use the cameras to spy on him, he exited the building and made his way out to the street to make some calls.

The first call was to Denise. "Listen, am I on speaker?"

"No, and why did you leave?" she asked him.

"I wanted to talk to you, but I didn't want him to hear my side of the conversation."

"Okay. What's up?" asked Denise.

"You need to go on live right now and warn every officer that the killer is coming after one of them tonight. I will alert the Wardens to lock down their facilities and also to start some kind of call chain to make sure the officers at home are safe."

"Alright, as soon as I hang up, I'll get started on that," said Denise, being careful of what she said. The killer could still be listening to every word.

"I also need you to find an officer and give him your keys. I am going to have the crime lab agents go over to your house and find those cameras."

"He never said anything about mine, just yours," stated Denise.

"Denise, trust me, he doesn't leave anything to chance. There probably isn't an inch of any of our houses that he can't see. Our cars also. The security guy said he probably has some sort of device that can kill a building's security, so it wouldn't be a problem for him to get into our homes or our cars. Anyway, just to be on the safe side, do that now and I'll get it checked out."

"Okay, what else do you have planned?"

"I'm going to get Det. Grace and we're going to catch this motherfucker tonight. His pride won't let him back out of a promise. If everyone does what I say, we will have him tonight."

"Well, I'm going to find a cop right now and then I'll go live. Be careful out there tonight. You still owe me a first date."

"I will," Walt assured her. "Go do your thing," he said, and hung up.

The next call was to the crime lab. When his communications guy came on, he told him about the possibilities that the three houses and three cars could be bugged, and his men dispatched field agents to the four locations.

He went back in and found the officer who had Denise's keys sending him to unlock her car and then to take the keys over to her residence to meet the agents.

He watched Denise set up and then deliver her dire warnings to all officers, but specifically the ones in the Raleigh area who were at home tonight. She also pointed out that the killer seemed to target officers with a reputation of abuse on inmates. She closed with, "Not all the officers affected have been dirty, but if you know that you have stepped over that line, then be on the lookout because the killer might just target you tonight. This has been a channel 5 breaking news report by Denise McCarthy. Now back to your regularly scheduled program."

When she started breaking down her set up, he left to continue making calls. Detective Ann Grace answered on the third ring. She had been asleep, as it was close to midnight, but her voice sounded wide awake.

"What's going on, Walter? If you're calling me, I guess your date didn't go good?"

"Not good at all. The killer dropped in on us at the hotel, but he got away before we even knew he was here."

"What the fuck? Was he following one of you or was it just a coincidence?"

He could hear her jumping out of bed.

"We think he was following Denise, but the bastard just happens to be some kind of coding genius, and he made some device that can shut down and take over any security system. He used the device to shut down the building security and took a video of Denise while she was signing autographs. He was about 5 feet from her at one point. We are tracking down everyone we can to see if they have any cell phone footage of him. So far, nothing."

Ann was in the shower now, but she had him on speaker.

"Okay, I'm like 20 minutes away, so I'll be there in 10."

"Ann, the killer made some statements while we talked to him that leads me to believe that he has cameras in all of our homes and vehicles. So don't leave, I am coming to get you. I already sent the lab guys to search mine and Denise's homes, and they're on their way to you also."

Ann, who was never slow to catch on said, "Cameras, here? Oh my God. Wait, you said you talked to him. You talk to him?"

"Yeah, he used the cameras here to see Denise and me setting up to do the interview, and he called to have a chat. I have a recording of the conversation. I will send you a copy. He also promised to go after a guard tonight, so Denise went live to warn everyone. Anyway, as soon as they go over my car, I'm on my way to you."

Ann was out of the shower and getting dressed. "So, what are we doing about the guard?" Walter heard her doorbell rang.

He wanted to warn her to make sure it was the crime lab agents before she opened the door but knew she wouldn't take too kindly to his warning. Also, he heard her chamber a round in her gun, so he stayed quiet until he heard her talking to the agents.

At the same time, the other agents showed up to search his car, so he said, "Ann, listen, I'll explain when I get there. Let those guys do their thing and I'll be there as soon as I can."

They both hung up and he greeted the lab guys letting them into his car. They were done ten minutes later and what they found astonished them.

Not only were there cameras and microphones to cover every angle, but there was also a tracking device so sophisticated, the lab guys thought it was military grade. It didn't come up on any scanners, they only stumbled upon it by mistake. It was leather and perfectly matched the seat, but one of the ends was curling off. It was solar powered so it didn't need a conventional battery to work. It was just another clue that they were dealing with someone who wasn't just your run-of-the-mill killer.

After they assured him that he was clean, he took off to Det. Grace's house. He didn't want to waste time, so he called the Warden at Central Prison. He would have a better idea on how to get the word to each Warden in the state.

"Warden Thomas speaking, how may I help you?" It was almost one o'clock in the morning, but Walt guessed Wardens had to be on alert just like cops.

"Yeah, sorry to bother you Warden, but we have a situation that might mean trouble for your guards."

"Okay, who am I speaking to, if you don't mind me asking?"

"Oh, sorry. This is Sgt. Det. Walter Rogers of the NC SBI."

"Alright, I just wanted to be sure. My nephew is Sgt. Gould of the Raleigh Police Department. He called me about fifteen minutes ago and told me what was going on. He told me I might get a call from you. I turned on the news and caught the warning and have already set some things in motion."

The SBI could pull rank and Walt could tell the Warden to stop whatever he set in motion and to do Walt's own plan, but maybe Warden Thomas' plan was better.

"So that we don't step on each other's toes, can you tell me what you set in motion?"

"Sure. All the facilities in the state have gone on lockdown to minimize targeting of officers and inmates. And in the Raleigh area, we have set up a thirty-minute call chain where every officer has to call into the prison they work at. If they don't call, and we can't get ahold of them, a cop will be dispatched to their residence to check on them. Some of them are probably dead tired but we stressed how important this is."

Walt had to admit it was a good plan. It was almost exactly what he hoped for. "That's a very good plan. Let's hope the killer was just blowing smoke and everyone stays safe tonight."

"Alright Detective, I'm still coordinating everything, so let me get back to it. I'll keep you informed with any new developments, and if you will, please do the same."

"Most definitely, Warden Thomas. Just use the same number if you need to contact me. All our resources are yours if you need them."

At the Warden's affirmation, they both hung up. Walt felt better after speaking with the Warden about their chances of keeping everyone alive tonight. He would still proceed with part of his plan and needed to talk to his partner about it. He knew she would be a little off her game thinking about the videos the killer could have made. But her instincts would make the plan so much easier.

When he pulled up to her house, the crime lab agents were standing around her car looking at something on the hood. He walked over and saw about seventy black dots that looked like sprinkles for ice cream. He also saw five cameras and a patch just like the one taken out of his car. Obviously, the agents who found his, had given this team a heads up.

"What's going on guys? What are the black dots?" Walt asked the agents.

One of them replied, "You would never guess, but they are all the cameras we could find in the house and on the property."

Walt was speechless. "Cameras? Those little black dots are cameras?"

"Yeah," the same agent answered. "Not just cameras, but a microphone and a power source too. I've seen one at a Law Enforcement convention. That power source can last up to twenty years. No scanner can detect it, so without tearing the house down, there is really no way to make sure we got them all."

"How did you find these in the first place if you can't detect them?" asked Walt.

"The officers in Tabor City went to check on that Lieutenant up there. They finally got her to open the door, and she's fucked up bad man. Infection all over her torso from some kind of acid scars. Another day without help and she would be dead."

Walt hated to sound callous, but he didn't really care about Lt. Price. "Okay, and what about the cameras?"

"Well, she told them what happened and how the guy recorded everything and left one of the cameras in her bedroom. The cop actually broke it trying to get a look inside. When they went through her apartment, they found these small drill holes in all the thresholds. They called their boss, who called our boss, and he told us what to look for. The cameras that actually look like cameras, and the tracker we found in the car."

"Do you think those black dot cameras are in the car too?"

"I don't think so. It would be too easy to spot a hole in plastic, so I think he only used them in the wood frames."

"Alright, where's Det. Grace?" Walt asked, looking around.

"Last I saw, she was sitting in the living room waiting for you to come get her so y'all can track the bastard down. Her words, not mine."

Walter started towards the house but then turned back and asked, "Why don't we have cameras like that?"

"For one, we would lose too many of them because they're so small. Secondly, they run about $2,000 for one."

Walt stared at him like he was crazy. "So, this guy put over $100,000 worth of camera equipment in Det. Grace's house, just in case she said something?"

The guy answered, "More like $200,000 when you add what was in the car. We're getting reports that it's the same for you and Ms. McCarthy. Add in the cameras from Lt. Price's apartment, and you're looking at close to a million dollars."

"Something isn't right here," said Walt. "How can a deranged serial killer stay ten steps ahead of us for this long, while making millions of dollars to throw away on cameras?"

"I know you're the Detective and I'm just a lab worker but, honestly, he moves like a cop. This guy might have done some time. If I was looking, I would be looking for an ex-Military Intelligence guy or some kind of Law Enforcement. The skill level to do some of the coding we've seen, companies would pay this guy millions. That could be where the money is coming from. He could even be CIA. I mean, who knows?"

"But what would the CIA or Military Intelligence be doing killing a bunch of correction officers?"

"Okay, I don't want to speak out of turn here, but I think you are looking at this from the wrong angle. The SBI puts people into prisons undercover all the time. So does the FBI. The skillset this guy has is world class. He doesn't just get caught and go to prison unless it's something in prison he needs to accomplish. Then, something might have happened to him while he was inside. I don't know but it's almost like he's too good, too precise. I would call up some of these agencies and find out if they have a rogue agent."

Thinking about that, Walt thanked the agent and walked off to get his partner. He found her sitting on her couch in deep thought. "Get your laptop and let's go," he said to her before turning and walking out of the house.

Hurrying to catch up to him, Ann said, "What the hell, Walt? What the hell is going on?"

Walt stopped halfway to his car and said, "Get in and don't talk." They both walked on and got in, and Walt drove away. It was after one o'clock in the morning, but there was a Wendy's still open about a mile from her house.

They pulled in and got out. Ann asked, "Are you hungry or something? Seems we got better things to do than sitting around eating bacon cheeseburgers."

Walt didn't respond until they were in the restaurant. "Sit down and stop with the smart-ass routine. This guy is a piece of shit, but he only goes after who he thinks is bad. I know you are angry and scared, but let's use that to catch him. Okay? I need you."

Ann had tears in her eyes when she said, "But you don't understand. You're not a woman. If he puts those videos of me online, my career…"

"Will not be affected," Walt finished for her. "And you're right, I'm not a woman. And, I can't understand, but I need Detective Ann Grace to help me catch him. It's done. It's out of our control. All we can do now is catch him before he has time to do anything with the footage."

"Alright Walt, what do you need me to do?"

"Thank you," he said with feeling. He knew it was hard, but he also knew she was a very strong woman. "I need you to pull up a map of the Raleigh area." When she had it up, he asked, "Is there a way to pull up every officer's house on the map?"

"Sure, if we had a week and two more people. What are you trying to see?"

"I'm trying to find a house that is isolated but still in the Raleigh area. It would have to be an officer who was already under investigation for something. I don't think he would want to go in completely blind. He would go after an officer that's already on his list."

Ann was typing furiously on her laptop and mumbling the whole time. After what seemed like an hour, but was really more like five minutes, she said, "Okay, we got five possibilities." She turned the laptop around and showed Walt the map with the five addresses highlighted.

"Anyone of these could be a target. Or none of them," Walt said. "What do you think?" he asked Ann.

"I don't know but…. wait, wait. Why does this name sound familiar?" Ann asked, tapping a name on the screen.

Walt said, "Greg Black? Doesn't ring a bell for me. Why was he under investigation?"

Ann pulled up another screen and said, "Says right here, he might have raped a few male inmates at Central Prison where he works. Hold on, that's it. He's one of the guards who beat up Bruce Battle during that interview with Denise McCarthy."

"Okay, let me make a call." Walter called Warden Thomas.

"Sorry to bother you sir, but has a guard named Greg Black reported in yet?"

The Warden said, "Oh shit, not Greg. Hold on, let me check." About twenty seconds later he said, "Okay, he called in the first time, but he missed the last call in. We've had a total of twenty-two officers miss the last call in. We were in the process of calling them all before we send in the calvary."

Walt said, "Okay sir. Well, we are about fifteen minutes from his listed residence, so me and my partner are going to check on him. If you get in touch with him before the fifteen minutes, please call me and let me know."

"Will do, and be careful, he lives far away from any back up." With that last warning, they both disconnected.

Walt stopped Ann at the exit of the Wendy's. "We can't talk in the car. He still might have bugs we can't find."

"Okay, so what are we doing?"

"Going to Dunn and seeing if this officer is still alive. We might get lucky and catch him there."

"Yeah right, because we are so lucky," said Ann. "How long is the drive with you driving?"

"With me, maybe eight minutes. Remember don't talk, he could still be listening."

They both exited the restaurant and made their way to the car. They stayed quiet and Walt was hoping the Warden would call and say the officer checked in. Ten minutes later, they were pulling into Officer Greg Black's driveway.

Everything happened at the speed of light. Ann said, "What the hell is that?" Walt glanced at her and saw her pointing towards the house.

Walt looked closer and yelled, "Motherfucker! Got his ass!" Both of the agents slammed out of the car as the masked man jumped off the far side of the porch and disappeared around the side of the house.

CHAPTER 17

Detective Ann Grace was hyped. Her heart was beating so hard in her chest that she thought she was close to stroking out. She was heading towards the porch when she heard Walt yell, "No Ann, I'll follow him around the far side. You go the other way and we'll cut him off." Ann shot down the closer side of the house. Walt was super-fast, so she had no doubt he could run the killer down.

When she turned at the back of the house, Walt was halfway to the wood line. She went to follow, so he would have some backup, but he yelled, "Clear the house, Ann. Someone might need help."

The killer only had about a ten second head start on Walt, and she was reluctant to leave him in the woods alone with the killer, but she did what Walt told her to do.

She approached the backdoor slowly and tried the knob. The door was locked. Instead of kicking the door in and causing unnecessary damage to the house, she ran back around to the front and found that door unlocked. Even though she figured there wouldn't be any threats in the house, she still entered with her weapon drawn.

The house had an open floor plan, but all of the doors leading off the main living area were closed. She scanned the open area and didn't see anything out of the ordinary. She went towards where she thought the master bedroom would be and pushed the door open.

It took her mind a little bit of time to catch up to her eyes. When it did, only her training kept her from running out of the house, screaming like a mad woman. The man was tied down to the bed, spread eagle, and his private parts had been cut off. He had also been decapitated, his head sitting on his stomach. It looked like something was hanging from his mouth. When she leaned in closer to see what it was, she ran out of the room, out of the house, and threw up on the side of the porch.

The man's private parts had been stuffed into his own mouth. Ann knew she was being very unprofessional, but she had never seen that one before. They needed to get the lab agents out here as soon as possible. She still needed to clear the rest of the house, but she put her gun up and pulled out her phone to call for back up, and to get the lab guys started in their direction.

She saw movement out of the corner of her eye, but she was too slow. She felt a small prick on her back, and before she could do anything else, she collapsed to the floor, unable to move. All she could see, was the killer's black shoes as he laughed and said, "My lucky day. This will sure get some attention."

They had been in so much of a rush to chase after him, they left the car running. The killer picked her up and walked over to the car. He was strong, as he carried her with one arm, and opened the back door with the other. He dumped her in the backseat and then reached in and took her gun. She had dropped her phone when she went crashing to the porch floor. He patted her down very professionally, and took everything he found, including her back-up gun.

The killer didn't seem in any rush when he closed the door and walked off for a full minute. Ann didn't know what he was doing because she was laid out on her back and could only see the roof of the car. When he came back, he got into the driver's seat, turned the car around and drove off.

Ann knew she was in trouble. She was fighting with all of her might to move just one finger and it wasn't happening. The crazy thought that entered her mind was that Cpt. Robert Dennis was innocent. There had been no mention of this drug until he said it, and everyone thought he made it up to get away with the murders. He had been telling the truth. He had not killed Mary and Ivory Dennis. If she made it out of this alive, she would tell the truth about this drug.

The killer said, "You cops are so predictable. I knew the super cop would want to keep his little partner away from harm. I mean, who would let a pretty lady like you follow a deranged serial killer into the woods. By the way, I never went into the woods, if you haven't figured that out. I picked the back door lock in about two seconds and then watched your dumbass boss go tearing away into safety while he sent you into danger. After watching you for years now, I figured it was time to meet the beautiful Det. Ann Grace."

Ann's mind was racing. [Years? This motherfucker has been watching her for years?] All those private moments, captured on video by this lunatic. She really had no idea what this guy was capable of, but she had a bad feeling that she was about to find out.

The killer pulled over and cut the car off. She heard him get out and shut the door and then another car door opened. He came back and opened the door at her feet then stuck her with the needle again. It was crazy to be able to feel everything but not be able to move at all.

He reached in and started to undress her. In her mind, she was screaming for him to get his filthy hands off of her. Of course, she didn't have the ability to talk, so she stayed silent. Her breathing was picking up and her heart was beating out of her chest. When he had her down to her bra and panties, he picked her up and carried her over to another car.

"I know better than anyone that anything can be a tracker. I will have leave all of your clothing behind, and I do mean all of them. Hey, it's not like I haven't seen it all anyway, right?" he said, leaning over, smiling in her face.

He put her in the back seat and then removed the rest of her clothing. His reminder only sharpened the fear coursing through her. She was losing her mind not being able to at least try and talk her way out of the situation. She was completely alone and at the mercy of someone who she was pretty sure didn't have a lot of mercy as a rule.

He ran his hands over inches of her skin that hadn't been touched by another person in years. He also went through her hair in search of any trackers. He removed all her jewelry and walked off. She guessed, to throw all of her things into Walter's car. When he came back, he pulled a black cloth from a bag and blindfolded her. The killer wouldn't have to kill her if her heart beat any harder.

She heard him say, "Now, for the last step." There was about ten seconds of silence and then he said, "Oh, sorry, Ann isn't available right now. Let me put you on speaker."

Ann heard Walt say, "I swear to you, if you touch a hair on her head, you will die."

The killer laughed and said, "Yeah, yeah. How about this? Come out of your mouth wrong to me again, and what I do to her, she'll wish you were dead. Anyway, your dumbass isn't still in the woods, are you?"

"No, I was on my way back to the house when you pulled off. Why didn't you stick around and wait for me to come back?"

The killer said, "Well, me and your partner decided on a last-minute date. But enough with the bullshit. I gave you and your girlfriend a job. Maybe with just the lives of a few guards in the mix, you wouldn't try as hard. So, in addition to more guards dying, the beautiful, and at this time, very nude, Det. Ann Grace will also die. As she is a very good woman, and not my usual target, I would hate to kill her. Timothy Washington goes free and so does she. It is now Wednesday; you have five days counting today. Use them wisely."

"Wait," Walt screamed. "How do I know she's not already dead?"

"You don't and you won't. You're an investigator, investigate. Free that innocent man and you get your partner back. Fail, and you will never see her again. So you can concentrate on what is important, I won't kill anyone else. Well, until Monday if you fail. Don't waste time looking for

117

us. Trust me, we will have fun with our time. At least I know I will."

"Listen man, I understand you taking a stand with the prison system. But I'm begging you, please don't hurt her. No matter how you feel about me or the system, don't take it out on that girl."

"Walter, I'm not a monster. I promise you, just do your part and she will be good. If she doesn't try to escape or kill me, then she will be released the same way I found her. I have to go. Before I hang up, Officer Black has a daughter named Gabby who is probably still in her room. The guard was molesting her. When your team talks to her, take it easy. She's a sweet kid."

With that, Ann heard him break the phone and start up the car.

The killer pulled away and nothing else was heard except the tires on the road for a long time. Occasionally, the killer would stick her in the arm or leg with the needle. Eventually, she fell asleep and dreamed of being chased by a masked man while running in a field naked. He kept saying, "Come back, I'm not a monster." He also had a big needle in his hand. No matter how hard she ran, or how many turns she took, the masked man kept gaining on her. Right when he was about to stick the needle in her, she was jerked awake by the killer.

"Wakey, wakey, sleeping beauty," the killer taunted her. All she could do was open her eyes, but her breathing and heart rate were still up from the dream. "We have reached our final destination. It's a good thing for you that I only like the best. I figured that I would need one, so I built the best prison in the state. You'll have your own room and television. The food isn't great, but it's not all that bad. Hopefully, you won't be here long enough to get used to any of it."

Ann had no idea how long she had slept. Although she could hear everything he was saying, it really didn't make any sense to her. It didn't help that she was still blindfolded and couldn't see anything.

She heard the killer get out and after about 15 minutes, her fingers started to tingle. She was able to make small mumbling sounds and twitch a little, but that was all. The door opened and the killer said, "Don't remove the blindfold and when you can, wrap this around your body." She felt something clothlike land on her body.

After another five minutes, she was able to move as if the drug had never been in her system. She grabbed what felt like a robe and wrapped it around her body, tying the belt tightly. The door at her feet was open and she scooted that way until her bare feet hit the rocks.

"Okay, that's far enough for now," said the killer. "Only a few rules. Don't try to run. Don't try to attack me. Don't take the blindfold off until I tell you to. Are we clear on all those?"

"Yes," Ann said. "Will I get yard time and a phone call?"

"Sorry, but no. I do have some puzzles and some novels for you to read."

"Alright, can I stand up now?"

"Sure you can," the killer said with cheer. "When you stand up, take ten steps forward and then stop." She stood and walked ten steps as he instructed. She heard a key go into a lock and then a door opened.

"Your castle awaits, my lady. Go ahead and walk forward." She took about four steps and then she entered some kind of a structure. After two more steps, he told her to stop. She heard the door close and lock and then he said, "Okay, you can take the blindfold off now."

Based off of what he said about her going to a prison, she expected to see something like an old jail. What she saw was the inside of a dark, run down cabin that was one strong breeze from falling down. She turned and looked at the masked man with confusion.

He smiled and said, "I thought ladies liked mysteries. You haven't figured out that things with me are never what they seem?" He walked to the only door other than the door leading outside. He opened it to reveal an elevator. "Well, get in. Your 5-star accommodations await."

She stepped into the elevator, and he told her to face the backwall. The elevator looked like any other elevator, but only half the size. The killer got on, the door closed, and they started to descend. After about twenty seconds, which seemed like a long time to be going down into the earth, the elevator stopped, and the door opened. She heard him doing something with his keys behind her back.

"Alright Ms. Grace, walk backwards off of the elevator." She took four steps and stopped facing a concrete wall with the elevator door in the center of it. "You're doing good. Now turn to the right and keep walking until I say stop."

When she turned, her mouth fell open in astonishment. Opposite the elevator was an all-glass control booth in the shape of a circle. The hallway she was walking down went around the control booth and came back out into the elevator room, making a complete circle. All along the hallway, on the opposite side from the glass booth, were prison cells. All of the cell doors at this time were closed, but the prison was huge. [There had to be fifty cells all together. He had to have spent millions on this thing.]

When they reached the midway point, he said, "Stop." He did something on his phone and the closest cell door opened. The cell doors were all tinted glass, so she hadn't been able to see inside any of them. The glass slid to the side to reveal a modern-day jail cell with a T.V. on the wall opposite the entrance. There was a cot and a sink-toilet combination and that was it.

"I guess all the suites were book," quipped Ann.

The killer did something with his phone, and all the doors along the hallway opened up. "Come take a look." The killer led her back to the beginning of the hallway. The cells closest to the start of the circle looked like suites at a mediocre hotel. They had queen sized beds and shelves containing books and DVDs. The floors had carpet, and the bathroom was behind a partition. It was three times bigger than the cell he had taken her to. It also had a big screen T.V. with a PlayStation hooked up to it.

"Now, come to the other end," the killer demanded. The cells got smaller and more spartan the closer they got to the other end. The cell he had showed her first was like a basic cell. The cell at the end of the circle was like a punishment cell. It contained nothing except a bucket and was about the size of a closet.

"You will go into the receiving cell for today. You give me problems; you will end up down here. You do what I say, when I say it, and you go to the suite. It doesn't matter to me at all where you stay. There is no escape. There is no help coming for you. All you can do is hope that your partner and Ms. McCarthy can achieve their goal. Now, let's go."

He led her back to her original cell, and she stepped inside. "Out of respect for you, I will leave your glass tinted, and I will announce myself before I come in. You will be fed, and I promise I will not harm you unless you make me, or your friends fail."

"Are you staying down here with me?" Ann asked.

"I will be around from time to time. There is a button in your cell if you need me for anything."

"Well, what happens to me if you die? I mean, you do have thousands of cops looking for you. And after this, the FBI will probably join the hunt."

The killer laughed. "The FBI? Do you think they haven't already been in the hunt? News flash, I'm a serial killer. The FBI has been here since the beginning. Anyway, I'm not worried about the FBI."

"Still," said Ann. "If you die, am I just going to starve to death down here?"

"No Ann, you won't starve to death. Let me show you something." The killer pulled out his phone again. "Every cell is assigned a color." He was showing her a diagram with the layout of the cells. "You are in cell 24. I will assign it with the color green. Green means go. Red means stay. If I don't check in with the security app on my phone every 24 hours, then all the cells labeled green will open, and the elevator will take them up to the surface. The cells labeled red will unleash a gas that will kill whoever is inside. Trust me Ann, you are going to be fine if your people come through. If they don't, then I'm sorry, but you will never leave this place."

He did his thing with the phone and her door closed. "Well, you can be thankful that you don't have one of the officer's I've killed down here instead of me."

She watched him walk away. She could see almost all the way down both sides of the hallway. She just stood staring out of the cell for a long time. Then she laid on the cot and burst into tears.

CHAPTER 18

Denise was super excited, but also scared as hell. She was 30 minutes away from the most important live interview of her life. It was Friday, and the interview was set to begin at 7:00pm. They were down to counting hours until the deadline the killer had given them. She was scared to death that she would fail, and more people would die.

Denise was also feeling bad for Det. Rogers. He had called her Wednesday morning and filled her in on everything that had happened. Det. Grace really was like a sister to him, and he was blaming himself for her kidnapping. Denise knew that he would never forgive her if she messed this interview up, and Grace was killed as a result. The pressure to perform was making her sick to her stomach.

Carl, the killer, had changed his mind and went ahead and sent her the video of Lt. Price's confession. He had also emailed her copies of screenshots taken from Lt. Price's phones of all the transactions that were believed to be payouts from inmates for sexual favors. Candace Price had been smart to buy all those phones and use the numbers to receive payments. But she had messed up by keeping herself logged into all the accounts on her own phone. With the killer's skill set, he traced each payment back to each inmate that paid it. Bottom line, Candace Price was going to jail.

The SBI wanted to go ahead and arrest her, but Walt put a stop to that. Knowing Ann's life was in the balance, Walt wasn't going to deviate from what the killer wanted done. If he wanted a live interview with Lt. Price being humiliated, then that was what the killer would get.

Carl had also hacked into the prison's network, where they stored all their old videos. He had sent hundreds of short video clips of Lt Price disappearing with each inmate at the prison that had paid her over the past nine years. The amount of work the killer was able to do in two days showed her how important this was to him. He had gift wrapped Candace Price for the authorities, and immediately following the interview, she would be handcuffed, charged, and processed, and the arrest would be done live on camera. They didn't need her confession; they had all the evidence they needed.

The only problem now was the timeframe. With it being Friday, the courts wouldn't open until Monday. Even then, it could take months of legal proceedings to overturn the inmate's convictions. Going through the courts would eventually bring Timothy Washington home. Unfortunately, they only had hours, not months.

Understanding that the courts were a dead end for a fast fix, yesterday Denise and Det. Rogers had gone to see the governor. He had made them wait outside of his office for three hours to see him, and things only got worse from there.

They had gone to the Governor's mansion in Raleigh after their boss had explained to the governor what was going on. He agreed to the meeting and was made aware of how time sensitive this his whole thing was.

When they were finally ushered into his office, the governor stood and shook both of their hands. "Nice to meet you both. I'm sure my assistant has already taken care of your refreshments?" He was a distinguished looking white man, who had the smile and the airs of a born politician.

"Yes, sir," Walt answered, shaking the governor's hand. Walt wasn't looking too bad either in her opinion. He was dressed in a dark gray suit with a burgundy shirt and black shoes. The rumors were that Walter hated to dress up, but when he did, he only wore the best.

"Well, have a seat and let me know what I can do for you today."

Walter laid out everything that they had on Lt. Candace Price and ended with a plea for help. "Sir, we know this inmate is innocent. In fact, he was the victim of a crime. Right now, a lot of lives are in danger, including SBI agent, Ann Grace. If we don't meet this guy's deadline, then she will die, and more officers will also die. If we can get you to give Timothy Washington, even a provisional pardon, then we can save some lives."

The governor looked back and forth between them, and then laughed. "You can't be serious. I'm not giving a rapist a pardon. If you want this guy free, then you need to start filing some paperwork with the courts. As far as a deadline, if I gave into this, then every criminal in the state would start kidnapping people and demanding pardons for their buddies. I'm sorry, but I can't help you." The governor rose, and said, "Now, if you'll excuse me..."

"Sit down," Walt said, in the most ominous voice Denise had ever heard.

"Now you listen here. I don't know who you think..."

"I said, sit your ass down, right now." Walt never raised his voice, or even moved, but suddenly the room was filled with deadly intentions. "So, you are going to stand there and look me in my eyes and tell me that my partner is going to die? I don't think so. Sit down right now or I will make sure you never stand up again."

The governor sat down. "You understand that you are throwing away your career right now? I could press a button and have 20 armed men in here in five seconds." The governor was red in the face and short of breath. He was afraid but trying to cover it up with anger.

"Governor, all we are asking is that you help us preserve life. If you look at the evidence we have on Lt. Candace Price, and her own confession that she lied on the inmate, no one would be calling Timothy Washington a rapist. He was found guilty of armed robbery, but he finished that sentence years ago. Maybe, we can get him to sign some kind of waiver so he can't sue the state if you grant him a pardon. Either way, we have to get this guy home by Sunday night."

The governor sat back in his chair and regarded them warily. "I looked you up Detective, and I know you were in the service. They teach us that if you are captured, the rest of us still have a war to fight. Det. Rogers, we are at war. I can't lose a battle trying to save one soldier. I'm making moves as a General now, and I have to think about the bigger picture. I'm sorry, you can threaten me, even hurt me, but my position will not change. Now, do I press the button, or do you leave with your career intact?"

Denise, who had remained quiet up until now said, "Governor, I'm Denise McCarthy with Channel 5 right here in Raleigh."

Impatiently, the governor said, "Yeah, yeah, I know who you are."

"Well, I want to say that you can't ruin my career so everything you said today will be told to the public. I will make it my lifelong goal to ensure that you never hold public office again. And, if Ann Grace dies because of you, I will use every resource I have to see you locked up."

The governor said, "Good luck and have a nice day." He got up and walked to the door. When he opened it, there were five men in black suits waiting to escort them off the grounds. They had left quietly because they didn't have a choice. They really couldn't help Ann from jail.

They had gone to a few judges with the evidence early Friday morning, but none of them could do anything without the correct proceedings in court. All of them had agreed that he would be freed, but they were looking at a few months before they could get his case on the docket.

The two of them had been sitting in her new Benz outside of the courthouse, feeling dejected. Finally, Walt said he couldn't sit around doing nothing, so he went out looking for Ann. He didn't say how he thought to find her, and she didn't want him to snap at her, so she wished him luck and watched him walk away.

Now, their last hope was the court of public opinion. The interview and arrest were only part of the program tonight. They were going to play up the fact that his daughter was turning ten years old, and the state was keeping her dad from her. He should have been home four years ago, but that extra twelve years was going to keep him away until his little girl turned 18.

They were going to tell the public what the governor said and see if they could get the Director of Prisons to release him. Basically, they were going to make a last-ditch effort to come up with a miracle. Then again, maybe Walt will find Ann and take some of the pressure off.

It was now fifteen minutes until show time. Denise was making her way to the studio. They were set up to do the interview in a small cozy room off of the main studio. They wanted to make Candace Price feel as comfortable as possible while she told all of her lies, not knowing they were going to play the video of her confession as soon as she finished. After the video went off, or whenever the Lieutenant started going crazy, the police would come in and do their thing. If Lt. Price wasn't such a stone-cold bitch, you could almost feel sorry for her.

Lt. Candace Price looked like exactly what she was. A former, very beautiful woman who had been attacked with acid. Denise had read the statement she gave police and had seen the photos taken. Lt. Price had agreed that Denise could show the photos, but the Lieutenant still fixed herself up as best as she could.

It had only been five days since the attack, but none of the injuries were life threatening. They were life changing for a beauty like Lt. Price, but it was all cosmetic. Whatever the acid and counter agent had been, within 24 hours, all of the wounds had scabbed over. The chunks of flesh wouldn't grow back, but with antibiotics, her health was as good as ever. She was supposed to see a plastic surgeon about repairs, but Denise didn't know if the prison would let her keep that appointment. Then again, she had money for bail. Or at least someone to bail her out. It was funny how women like her never had a shortage of male helpers.

Denise was wearing a royal blue, knee-length dress with just a bit of cleavage showing. She had her hair in the classic 'Ms. Berry' look that was very good for television. She wore diamond stud earrings and a thin, gold chain. Three-inch heels completed her outfit.

Lt. Candace Price was wearing a form-fitting black dress that showcased her perfect butt and long, toned legs. She did have a bandage wrap on her left breast, and the rest of her upper body had pock marks and craters all over it. Lt. Price was wearing a wig that was just like her natural hair because the acid had made most of her hair fall out. Her whole face had been eaten up with acid, so she wore huge sunglasses to cover most of it. The gag had saved most of her mouth. She was using the collar of the leather jacket to hide the damaged part.

They had both taken their seats. The producer was counting them down from one minute. Denise was smiling and trying to keep the woman at ease to keep the shock value of the surprise. No one knew how Lt. Price would act, so a plain clothes cop was standing about ten feet behind her.

The producer came over and made sure they were both ready and then started the countdown. When she hit one, Denise was ready to go.

"Hello everyone! This is Denise McCarthy reporting live from the Channel 5 studio. We are pleased to have been granted this stunning exclusive with the brave woman who was brutally attacked by the Prison Guard Killer five days ago. I am talking about Lt. Candace Price. Lieutenant, do you mind if I call you Candace?"

"Not at all, Ms. McCarthy," answered the Lieutenant.

"Sweetie, we are family here. Call me Denise."

"Well, Denise, thank you so much for giving me this opportunity to tell my story."

"Candace, it is definitely my privilege and honor. Before we get into that horrendous attack, why don't you tell the world a little about yourself."

"My full name is Candace Shada Price. I am thirty-five years old. I was born and raised in Wilmington, North Carolina. I graduated high school and joined the Army when I was eighteen. I did my four years and was honorably discharged. Then, I fell into a little bit of a depression, and I went home to live with my mom for the next few years. Ten years ago, I saw an ad in the paper about the desperate need for prison guards. I went to the prison in Tabor City and was hired almost immediately. With my Army background, I met all the qualifications. Well, after ten years of working my tail off, I am the first black woman to make Lieutenant at Tabor City Correctional Institution."

"First off, let me say thank you for your service."

"You're welcome," replied Candace. "It was just something I felt compelled to do for my country."

"Alright, so you live in Tabor City now, right?" asked Denise.

"Yes ma'am, I do. It is a little slower in Tabor City than in Wilmington, but sometimes what we need is slower."

"That is the absolute truth. By the way, I wanted to say to the viewers that, because of the importance of telling this story, we will be commercial free for the first hour."

"Denise, I just want to say that it is hard being a black woman in today's world. The success we both have should be an inspiration to the little black girls all over the world."

"Thank you for that." Denise decided to try to shake the Lieutenant up a little bit. "Now, just in the state of fairness, I do have to ask this. What's going on with all these investigations for sexual misconduct with the inmates?"

"I am going to be totally honest with you. Sometimes, as a woman, we have to use what we have to get what we want." Lt. Price took a deep breath and then continued. "These inmates look at me and they lust after my body. Some of them would do anything for a chance with me. So, I flirt a little and give them hope. In return, they tell me everything that's going on in the prison. They will tell me things, to try and impress me, that that they would never tell a male guard. The reason I was able to move up like I did was because of all the busts I made in the prison."

"I have seen your write up history and it is impressive, but if all you did was flirt, how does it turn into sexual misconduct?"

Denise could tell that Candace wasn't liking the direction of the questions, but Candace thought she was smart enough to give credible answers on the fly.

"Well, the answer to that question has two parts," explained Candace. "First off, sometimes the inmate will be mad that he was set up and they lie on the officer to get them into trouble. Sometimes it works and the prison will drop the inmate's charge in order for their accusation to go away. Secondly, and more bizarre, other officers lust after me and when I shoot them down, they lie and say they saw things that never happened."

"Well, there has to be some truth to that, seeing as how all the investigations have been cleared," said Denise. "It is shameful that all those men would lie on such a strong, independent woman like you."

"You know, not all men are bad, but it happens so much to women. It's funny how they call us the weaker sex, but they are so intimidated by us," said Candace.

Denise cleared her throat and said, "I want to ask you about a couple of times when the inmates took your flirting too seriously. Tell us about the time when you were a Sergeant."

They had spoken on the topic a couple hours ago, so Denise was sure Candace knew where she was leading her.

"There was this inmate, named Timothy Washington, who I reprimanded about the things he would say to me. He would always compliment me on how I looked and smelled. It got to the point that I would go the other way when I saw him. Well, this day, I had just gotten my hair done and he commented that he would love to pull my ponytail and ride that horse. I told him to watch his mouth and told him to report to my office after last meal." By now, her voice was rising and falling, and tears were leaking out from behind her shades. She was an Oscar worthy actress.

Denise said, "I know this is painful for you. Continue whenever you are ready." Denise handed her a few tissues to wipe her cheeks.

Candace continued. "Normally, there are two or three officers hanging around in the Sergeant's office. That day, we were grossly understaffed, but I really didn't think he would hurt me. Other than a few lewd comments, he seemed like a nice guy." She paused again and took a deep breath.

"When he came in, I was on the visitor's side of the desk straightening some papers. Before I could do anything, he grabbed me from behind and used his weight and strength to force me down on the desk. He said, 'I told you I was gonna ride this horse.' He punched me one time in the stomach, so all the air left my body. He had his hand over my mouth so it was all I could do to breathe. I could feel him pressing into my back with his penis. Then he reached up under me and started to unbuckle my belt. Oh God. Give me a minute. I'm so sorry."

Candace was full on, snot bubble, crying now. She was rocking back and forth as if she was reliving one of the worst moments of her life. Denise was dry eyed only because she knew the woman was lying. But the woman was extremely convincing. If they didn't have all the evidence they did, there would be no way to convict Lt. Price.

After a minute, Candace went on. "I started to fight him, and he punched me in the stomach again. I couldn't draw a breath and I thought if I kept fighting, he would kill me. When he got my pants down past my behind, he forced his way inside me. It hurt so bad that I started to fight him again. It only seemed to excite him more because, the harder I fought, the harder he pushed. Then he was yanked away from me. The Unit Manager had come in so I could sign some paperwork. He saved my life that day, and I will always be grateful to him. Mr. Washington did three years in Restrictive Housing and received an additional 12 years for his crime."

"Thank God you were strong enough to fight for your life. And thank God for Steve Corban, the Unit Manager who saved you that eventful day." Denise thought it was strange that Candace mentioned the inmate by name but didn't say the Unit Manager's name.

"Alright Candace, if you're feeling up to it, can you walk us through the second attack?"

"It is hard for me to relive these horrible events, but I do think it's important for the story to be told." Lt. Price wiped her face with the tissue and acted like she was preparing herself for war. It took everything Denise had to keep a look of disgust off of her face.

"Larry Milton was the inmate's name and he forced me to have sex with him at knife point. It started out as just another day. Mr. Milton was the janitor assigned to clean the area where my office is located." She started sniffling and she said, "I'm sorry, this all happened last year, so it's still kind of fresh for me."

"Take your time, and just tell us what you can," said Denise, in her most sincere voice.

"I had come into the office that morning and there was a horrible smell coming from something in the trash can. I went and got him and asked him to take the trash out and freshen up the office a little bit. He went off like he was getting the supplies. I sat down at my desk to start my paperwork when I heard him come in. I didn't think anything of it, but then the door closed. When I looked up, he was standing in front of the desk with a knife. I said, 'what do you want?' He replied, 'Bitch, you know what I want, and if you scream, I'll slit your throat!' I begged him to think about what he was doing, and he said it was because of my looks and the way I smelled that made him want to do it. He told me he wanted me to ride him, then he placed the knife to my neck. I was scared, but I wanted to live, so I did what he wanted. The captain came in and started yelling and the inmate pushed me off of him, got up, and attacked him, allowing me to call for help. It was terrifying because he had life without parole and had nothing to lose. I thought he would kill us both. They gave him fifty more years, but it won't really affect him."

"Any woman in your place would have been terrified. I don't think I could have gone back to work with all that has happened to you. But you are so strong that you wouldn't be defeated. Thank you so much for protecting your community from these monsters."

Denise was enjoying herself, and despite the theatrics, Candace seemed to be as well. Denise was certain that Candace's enjoyment was about to come to an end.

"With so much stuff coming at you back-to-back, this latest episode with the Prison Guard Killer has to have you thinking about calling it quits," stated Denise.

"Not at all," said Candace. "I will be out for a while to have all the surgeries required to repair my body, but I do plan on going back to work."

"Good for you, Lieutenant. Now, in your own words, tell us what this psycho did to you."

"Well, it was brutal, but it was simple and fast. I was sitting at my vanity getting ready for work, when a masked man stuck me with a needle. It had some kind of drug in it that paralyzed me. The guy put me on the bed and tied me up naked. I thought he would force himself on me, but he just tortured me with acid. He said he didn't want to kill me, just steal all of my beauty. So, after dashing me with the acid, he untied my hands, and ran out of the apartment. There was a compound that he had left behind to make the acid inert, so as soon as I was free, I poured it all over myself."

Denise jumped in. "Can you explain why the attack happened on Monday and the authorities had to get a tip to check on you over 24 hours later?"

Candace still looked confident when she said, "I was embarrassed about my looks. It might sound unreasonable, but I didn't want anyone to see me like that."

"But you do understand that you allowed the killer to get away by not calling it in, don't you?"

"I really didn't care about him at that point," said Candace, showing a little of her selfishness. "All I could see was my ruined face and body in the mirror."

"So Candace, did the killer leave any kind of message with you or give you a reason why he picked you?"

"No, nothing. He just tortured me and left. He had me gagged, so I couldn't even try to talk to him."

"Can you tell us why he took all of your money?" asked Denise.

This was a very dangerous question. Candace had told no one, not even the police, about any money being taken. Denise could tell Candace was trying to think of how she knew about the money.

Candace, deciding on ignorance, said, "I didn't have any money in the house. He never said anything about money."

"So, Lieutenant, I am going to be honest with you. What you have told us tonight has been heartfelt and intriguing, but also full of lies."

"Ms. McCarthy, I don't know why you would say that to me." Candace was getting angry now but was still trying to control the situation. "I have been honest with you, and even while I am in pain, I agreed to do this stupid ass interview. Now, if you want to start accusing me of doing something wrong, then I'm out of here."

Candace went to stand up, but she froze when Denise said, "So, the video the killer sent me is a lie? You see, the killer sent me the recording of the whole incident, and since you have done nothing wrong, I guess you won't mind if I play it for the world."

CHAPTER 19

Sgt. Det. Walter Rogers was having a hell of a week. It had started out looking so promising. He was going to do an interview with Denise and then have a wonderful evening with a wonderful woman. But then, the killer always seemed to have other plans for him.

They had come so close to catching the bastard. If they had taken backup with them, the killer would be dead or in custody right now. Instead, he had gotten his partner kidnapped, and now, if this last-ditch effort didn't work, his partner was going to lose her life.

Walt had no clue where the killer was or even who he was. He was about to talk to the only person who had admitted to knowing the killer's identity. This was a highly sensitive case, and he was about to take extreme measures to save his partner's life.

Det. Rogers was sitting in a room in the basement of Central Prison waiting for the inmate to be brought in. Bruce Battle had admitted to knowing the killer, and Walt had no reason to doubt him. In fact, the killer had turned around and admitted it by killing one of the guards who had roughed him up during his interview with Denise.

Right as Walt was getting impatient, the door opened, and Bruce Battle walked in. This was their first meeting, but Walt had his badge hanging from his neck, so it didn't take a master criminal to figure out he was a cop.

"Man, hell no," Bruce said, trying to turn back out of the room. At one time, he was a big, strong, muscular guy. Since his incident with the killer, he had lost most of his weight.

"Get your skinny ass in there," the guard said, pushing him in. "Detective, if he gives you any problems let us know and we'll handle him. Do whatever you have to do to get him to talk." Walt had filled the officers in on what he was doing, and since it could ultimately save their lives, they were willing to go the extra mile to help him.

After the officer left, Walt said, "Please have a seat, Mr. Battle."

"I don't have anything to say to you. I want a lawyer present for any questions."

"You are not under arrest for anything, so you don't have the right to a lawyer," Walt explained patiently. "All I want to do is ask you a few questions, and then I will be on my way."

"You think I don't know why you're here? Cops have been coming asking me questions ever since I got shot. I'll tell you just like I told them, I'm not a rat and I'm not telling you anything. I showed him my loyalty and he did the same in return. Stop wasting your time and leave now."

Walt stood up and faced the man head on. "I want you to understand something. I know who and what you are. I know that you are a tough guy. But I want you to know I am on a timetable and neither one of us are leaving this room until I get this guy's name."

"Man, you swelling all up like you gonna do something. Fuck you man. You think I'm scared of you? I ain't telling you shit."

Walt let the young man run his mouth, and then when he stopped, Walt hit Bruce in the stomach with everything he had. Bruce sank to the floor, throwing up and trying to draw a breath at the same time. When he uncurled himself, and was finally able to breathe, Walt drew back and kicked him in his stomach, causing him to convulse on the floor.

It seemed five minutes had passed by the time Bruce was able to draw an even breath. He still couldn't sit up straight, and the next few minutes would say whether that was next week or next month.

"Bruce, I am going to take you apart," Walt said, in his most calm voice. "You see, your friend has my partner, and I will do anything to anybody in order to get her back. Now,

136

I am going to give you one more chance to tell me who this guy is before I really hurt you."

Bruce was on his hands and knees now. He waved his hand to tell Walt to back up. Walter moved to the other side of the table. Bruce used the table and chair to pull himself up, so he was sitting down. Walt sat down also, to hear what the man had to say.

Walt could tell Bruce was really hurting, but he still had that look of defiance on his face. Bruce looked up with a smile on his face and said, "You said her. Your partner is a bitch? She got a fat ass? You know my man probably got her tied up, naked somewhere laying that wood to her, right? If it was me, I'd fill up every hole and then bury the bitch where nobody would ever find her."

Walt stood up again, shaking his head, and walking around the table. When he stood right next to Bruce, he said, "It's been a long time since I got to do this. I want you to know, even when you are ready to talk, I won't stop until I'm done."

"Fuck you cop. You'll kill me before I talk."

"Okay," Walt said. Then he started to work on Bruce Battle again.

Twenty minutes later, Walt knocked on the door and the same officer opened it up. He saw Bruce laid out on the floor and said, "Oh shit, man. Please tell me he is still alive."

"Yeah, but I would get him some medical attention really fast," answered Walt.

"Well, did you at least get what you were looking for?"

Walt looked the guard in his eyes and said, "If I didn't, he would be dead."

The officer shivered and turned out of the room to talk to the other guards. Three of them came in with gloves on and carried the inmate out of the room. They gave Walter wary looks but didn't say anything as they went about their task.

Walt asked the guard, who seemed to be the leader, if he could have access to one of their computers.

Without a word, the officer turned and lead Walt out of the room and down the hallway. 30 yards later, they turned into an office that didn't look like it had been used for a while. It did have a computer, and that was all Walt cared about.

The officer said, "Let me log you in under my name. I do need to know what program to bring up."

"I have a name, and I need all the information you can get me."

"Alright," said the officer. "I'll bring up the OPUS system. It has everything from what his initial crime was, to write ups, to work reports." The officer typed for about 10 seconds, and then gestured for Walt to take over.

"Okay. Here we go. Last name, ADAMS. First name, MANUEL." Information started scrolling down the screen.

"That's strange," said the officer, standing behind Walt.

"There isn't a photo of the guy." The officer was pointing at a box on the top, left side of the screen. The words, NO IMAGE, were printed inside the box. "I have never seen a file on OPUS that didn't have an image of the inmate."

"How long have you been working here, Officer Woods?"

"I've been here for over 14 years now. You see, they do have a description. Damn, his date of birth is missing also. Hold up a second. Let me have the seat."

Walt stood up, but stayed leaning so he could still see the screen. Officer Woods logged in and out of several different programs, and all of them were missing the photo and the date of birth. Walt just felt more frustration at how many steps this bastard was in front of them. He left just enough information to tease them but nothing that would help them find him.

"Well, his initial crime was done in Rowan County, and if we trace everything back, then you can definitely get a mug shot of him there," said the officer.

"Don't you guys keep hardcopies of these files?" asked Walt.

"Sure. Actually, they are further down this hallway. But hold on, let me try something real quick."

The officer went back to the OPUS program and pulled up a screen on previous bed assignments. It showed that nine years ago, Manuel Adams had been at Central Prison. He had been housed on the WRB unit for one year. The officer wrote down some room numbers and some dates and exited out of OPUS.

"What I'm going to do now is log into the video archives and pull up some videos that we might can use to identify this guy," Officer Woods explained. "We started using HD cameras about ten years ago, so we should get some good shots of the inmate."

Walt watched as the officer logged in and began putting in the information to bring up the right camera. "The day he got here, the log shows that we had a bus arrive at 2:00pm. I'm pulling up the receiving area video now," explained Officer Woods.

Walt was praying that this would work. As far as being witnesses, the average person sucked. You put pictures of a suspected serial killer on the news, and they would most likely have him in 24 hours. Everyone wanted their 15 minutes of fame for catching a killer.

"And here we go," Officer Woods said. Inmates were seen getting off the transfer bus, one at a time as a guard stood at the back door reading from a list. They were fully shackled and moving very slowly. There were three cameras with views of the bus from different angles. After the sixth guy got off the bus, the three cameras that could see the bus went black.

"What the hell is wrong? Why did it go black?" asked Walt.

"I don't know what the fuck happened," replied the officer. "The video is still playing, hold on. It's clear now." As he was saying it, the camera that would have had the next view of the inmate went black.

"You have got to be fucking kidding me!" exclaimed Walt. The officer might not know what was going on, but Walt sure as hell did. "The son of a bitch went back and erased his image."

"That would have taken forever. Says he was locked up for ten years. Some of the places he was housed would have had him on camera 24 hours a day."

"Can you get to the archives of one of the other prisons?" asked Walt.

"Yeah, give me a minute."

Walt already knew what he was going to find. It was like the killer just enjoyed fucking with them. He could have just deleted his name from the system as well as all his records. Or he could have just killed Bruce Battle. It was like he was leaving just enough out there to keep everyone running around in circles. Manuel Adams was definitely not this guy's real name.

"Alright, this was Maury, six months before his release," Officer Woods said, pointing at the screen. When the bus pulled into the receiving bay, the same sequence of events from Central Prison happened all over again. As soon as the third man started to get off the bus, the camera blacked out. They fast forwarded through a week, following where the inmate was going to be. Every time he would have been picked up on a camera, the screen would go black. Walt didn't think that this was a program. He felt that the killer had put in a lot of time and effort to completely erase any image of him they were likely to find.

"Is there any way that the images can be recovered?" asked Walt. "Maybe a backup drive somewhere?"

"This archive is the collection of what is loaded from each camp every thirty days. After it is stored here, the camps delete their history and start fresh. In other words, this is the backup. There is nowhere else that these videos are stored other than this archive."

"Hold on. This is Maury, right?" asked Walt.

"Yeah," the officer replied.

"I remember seeing that the inmate was released from Maury Correctional Institution," said Walt. "Go to the last month of his incarceration."

After three minutes, the officer said, "Alright, here we go. What are we looking for?"

"Anything that looks like an altercation or anything out of the ordinary."

They went through Manual Adams's day to day routine of yard calls, chow calls, and lock downs without being able to see any of it, but piecing it together by the times and the area where the cameras blacked out. Then, one week before he was to be released, he was sent to receiving for something. Right before the camera blacked out, Walt yelled, "Hold it!" Officer Woods hit the button to pause the video.

Standing in a group of officers, who seemed to be facing off with a group of inmates, was Captain Robert Dennis. "Okay, let it play out," said Walter.

The screen stayed blank for about ten minutes. Then a group of medical personnel entered from a side door and the next screen to go blank was the hospital wing. The Medical area stayed black for almost four hours before the receiving camera went back out. A car pulled up in the sally port and then that camera went out. When the officer looked up the log, it showed one car going to Pitt Memorial Hospital. The inmate never came back to the prison, he was released from the hospital. For the inmate to stay in the hospital for the whole week, his injuries had to have been serious.

"It was him all along. That fucking Cpt Dennis." Walt was mad as hell. He was going to have to drive or fly over to Greenville. But either way, that fucking Cpt. Dennis was going to talk to him tonight.

"Thank you for your help, Officer Woods. You can keep looking for some kind of way to identify this guy, but to tell you the truth, you would be wasting your time. Can you print

141

out the information you have on Manuel Adams, and I'll leave you alone."

"No problem," said the officer. After he printed it out, he handed it over to Walt and then led the way to the exit.

"Did you want to check the hard copies before you left?" the officer asked.

"Waste of time," said Walt. "This guy is way too far ahead of us for that. Lead me out of here."

CHAPTER 20

Lt. Candace Price was in deep shit. She prided herself on being a fast thinker as well as a fast talker. When she heard Denise say the killer had sent in the video, she knew it was over for her. She could claim that what she said was spoken out of duress. But Denise had already mentioned the money. If the killer had made copies of the money transfers, then losing her job was the least of her worries.

Lt. Price was kicking herself for doing this stupid interview in the first place. Wednesday, after the police showed up at her apartment, she had been scared to death that the killer had turned the evidence over to the cops. Hour after hour, more officers and detectives asked her questions and all of them seemed to take her story at face value. She had let her guard down and actually started believing her own lies.

She was released from the hospital the next day and twenty of her coworkers were waiting in the parking lot. They cheered and clapped like she was a hero returning from a war. The Warden told her to take all the time she needed, and all her surgeries would be paid for by the state. She almost passed out from relief, knowing the $100,000 wouldn't go far with the level of surgeries she would need.

They had all piled into their cars and drove over to her apartment. The killer had destroyed pretty much everything by dumping chemicals over all her stuff. In the one day she had been gone, the crew had gotten her all new furniture and cleaned the place to look like new. They had also stocked her refrigerator and all her cabinets with food. They ushered her into her bedroom and fussed over her until she begged all of them to please let her rest. They didn't want to, but reluctantly, they left.

About two hours later, her phone had rung. She ignored it because it was not a number that she knew, and she didn't know anyone in Raleigh. Over the next two hours, the phone wouldn't stop ringing. Finally, she picked up, if only to tell them to leave her alone.

"Who the hell is this and why do you keep calling me?" asked Candace.

"Hi, Ms. Price. This is Denise McCarthy with Channel 5 news in Raleigh. I was wondering…"

"Let me stop you right there. I don't have anything to say to the press."

"I was just wondering if you would like to…"

"No comment. Damn, I just got out the hospital. Leave me alone." Candace was about to hang up the phone when she heard something that couldn't have been what she heard.

"What did you say?" asked Candace, bringing the phone back up to her face.

"I said, we will pay you $100,000."

"What do I have to do, get naked on T.V.?"

"No, nothing like that. We just want to have the exclusive interview about your life story. We will pay for all your travel and right after you do the live interview, you will be paid in full."

There had been something in Candace's gut telling her to say no, but the promise of all that money lured her in. Still, she decided to push it a little bit. "$150,000 and you have a deal. But I want the $50,000 paid up front."

"Okay, no problem. But the interview has to be tomorrow night. We will have a driver there to collect you in the morning and when you get here, we will have a contract for you to sign. After you sign, $50,000 will be deposited in your account. After the interview, you will receive the balance. Does that work for you?" Denise asked her.

After Candace had agreed, they talked about travel and lodging, and they hung up with Candace feeling a whole lot better about her future. She had fallen asleep with a smile on her face.

The next morning was hectic. The interview was scheduled for 7:00pm, but Denise wanted her there by 1:00pm. The limo arrived to pick her up at 8:00am and took her to breakfast at IHOP. They arrived in Raleigh at 12:00pm and the driver took her to a really nice hotel, where she was given a suite for 3 days. By 12:45pm, she was on her way to the studio in downtown Raleigh.

Denise herself greeted her when she arrived at exactly 1:00pm. She escorted her to a conference room where three people waited for her. It was the producer of the show, a lawyer, and a PR lady. They presented her with the contract and went over what they were going for, as far as content for the show.

Everything sounded good to Candace. The contract was only three pages, so she read everything, agreed, and signed the contract. Five minutes later, she got a notification of the $50,000 deposit on her phone.

They did stipulate that she would be assigned two guards because, when they started advertising the interview, the killer might come after her to shut her up. Candace thought it had more to do with making sure she didn't run off with their money, but she wasn't going anywhere without that $100,000.

She was driven back to the hotel to do whatever she wanted until 5:00pm, when she was expected back at the studio for a briefing. Pretty much just a meeting with Denise to go over the questions so the transitions would go smoothly.

Because of Candace being shy about how she looked now, she spent all the time in her room resting and thinking. The doctor she had talked to said they had a synthetic skin that they would use to fix her up as good as new. He even said that if she wanted a few minor changes here and there, he would do it for free. He said the procedures would be painless and the downtime would be days instead of months. With the State paying for everything, she would get as many upgrades as possible.

At 4:00pm, she started getting ready. She took a long, hot shower and then stood in front of the mirror naked, just like she would have done at home. She turned around and looked at the back of her body. It was still perfect. All smooth, toned skin and flesh. She turned back around and looked at her upper body and she immediately started crying. She was hideous, and doing this interview would expose her to ridicule from all over the world. She started having second thoughts about whether the money was worth it.

She turned away from the mirror and walked back into the sleeping area. She would do this, even if it killed her. $150,000 was the equivalent of 150 nasty ass inmates pumping away at her body. If she could endure that, then she could definitely endure one night of embarrassment.

She went over to the closet where she hung the sexy dress that she would wear that night. Not wanting to risk further embarrassment, she wore a thong instead of nothing, like she would normally have worn. All she needed was flashing the camera during a live interview. They would blur it, but she didn't need the ridicule. She went ahead and put the dress on.

She walked over to the full-length mirror and loved what she saw from the back but almost started crying again when she saw her face and chest. She had fingernail sized chunks of flesh missing, and the spaces were a bright pink. She remembered seeing a coat and jacket store in the lobby and decided to just wear the dress, but cover the top with a jacket.

The vanity already contained all her make up, so she sat down to do what she could with her face. Denise had told her they had excellent make up people, but Candace didn't trust to be made up by someone who really didn't care how she looked. Ten minutes, and a big pair of sunglasses later, she was ready to go.

The phone rang, and when she picked up, the front desk informed her that her driver was outside. She did have butterflies in her stomach, but she walked back to the mirror for one final look, grabbed her purse, and was out the door. The two guards were waiting for her in the hallway. She

146

didn't acknowledge them at all, just kept walking to the elevator with the absolute sureness that both men had their eyes glued to her ass.

In the lobby, she went into the clothing store to buy a jacket. It was summertime, so even at night, it was close to eighty degrees. Denise had told her it would be chilly in the studio, so she went to the leather jacket section.

"Ah, Ms. Price," said one of the guards. "Your driver has the car at the door. We need to get going."

She acted as if he didn't exist, took her time trying to find the perfect jacket, and was on her way across the lobby after a brief stop to pay.

The car ride was uneventful, as well as the briefing between her and Denise. They went over about a hundred possible questions that might be asked on air. The only thing Candace had demanded was absolutely no questions about her family. She wanted to keep all this as far away from them as possible.

7:00pm had come fast and she was nervous as hell when Denise started the questions. But Denise was very good and lulled her into feeling secure and protected. She was asking all the questions that Candace had ready-made lies for and Denise was giving all the correct responses. Then she asked her about the delay in her alerting the authorities. It was an innocent enough question, but for some reason, the butterflies had returned to Candace's stomach.

When Denise had accused her of letting the killer get away, she had to admit that she had lost a little bit of her control. She knew as she was talking, that she sounded selfish and uncaring. That was exactly how she really felt, but she couldn't let the world see it. She needed the world to see a hero that has survived some serious adversity.

Then she mentioned the money. Candace had actually watched the previous interviews Denise had done with the other survivors of the Prison Guard Killer. She had also seen the video of the Oakland family massacre. She had not put it all together until that very second; Denise was working for, or with the killer.

Candace needed to get out of the studio as fast as possible. She decided that she would act offended at one of the questions and storm off. She needed to still keep her image intact, so she acted as if she knew nothing about any money.

The comment about her being a liar was her cue to leave. She pulled out her best indignant act and started to walk off. Now, she sat frozen, looking at Denise like she was a monster. Denise was a very pretty woman, with her short hair and classy act, but she was a straight barracuda.

"Lt. Price, are you in shock or are you just speechless with surprise?" asked Denise. "A lot of people have been hurt because of you and tonight the truth will be told." Denise stood up and moved a curtain to the side to reveal a big screen T.V.

"Don't do this," said Candace. "I said whatever I had to say to survive a madman. Now, you and your friend, who happens to be a serial killer, are going to try to make me look guilty for trying to stay alive."

Denise sat back down with a look of disgust on her face. "You see, this would have been the time to start with a little truth. You are still under the delusion that you are the smartest person in the room. Candace, I hate to tell you this, but you're not."

Candace looked around the room and noticed that a lot of the people who were in the room at the beginning of the interview were gone. In their places were a lot of serious looking men who could have been cops. One of them had moved to stand about four feet behind her.

Denise made a motion to someone Candace couldn't see, and the video started to play. Candace didn't know what to do. She wanted to jump up and try to knock the huge T.V. off of the wall. She had a feeling that if she tried, she would find out why all the big, angry men were brought into the room.

The video started when the killer had asked her if she knew who he was. She was noticeably naked, but her private areas were blurred out. She sat and watched the video with tears running down her face, knowing it was really over. Everyone in the world would see this video and know the things she admitted to, she had really done.

Candace saw the officers come in the door that was off to the side behind the cameras. Her heart dropped down to her stomach because the worst nightmare of any law enforcement officer was about to happen to her; she was going to jail. They had to have more than the video and she knew the killer had given it to them. For him to be a criminal, he sure did work with the cops a lot. He may have sent her to jail, but he had also turned over evidence on himself. Just this tape alone would get him 20 years. But I guess, after you show the world a tape of you killing two kids and their mom, it really didn't matter what else you did.

The video ended after the killer told her that he would send the money back to the victims, but he would not leave her broke. Everyone was quiet for about ten seconds. Then Denise asked, "Do you want to say something in your defense?"

Candace was silent for a while, just staring at Denise. Finally, she steeled herself and said, "Yes, I believe I do have something to say." This was when she normally would have lied and begged and did whatever she had to do to get away. Knowing that it was over came with its own kind of relief. It gave her the strength to say what she really needed to say.

"You know, good people do make bad decisions," said Candace. "Good people are also put into bad situations. I went overseas for my country. Put on a uniform that is despised all around the world, for my country. And when I came home, I had to go live with my mother because I was broke and broken." This was probably the first time she was being totally honest in the last ten years.

"My mother is an angel. She did everything she could possibly do to help me, but she was just as broke as I was. When I got the job at the prison, I thought that I could enter into something with structure, something I could use to pick myself up with. I don't know, maybe put the pieces back together. But what I found is the most corrupt system on earth. And I'm sorry to say, I let it corrupt me."

Candace was hurting. The killer might have showed a little mercy, but the world would not. The police would confiscate every dime she had, as well as what her mother had. She would be the one going to prison, but she wouldn't be the only one to suffer.

"Look. It doesn't matter what I say. No problems I had will be taken into account. But my family had nothing to do with this. It was my greed and my determination to be something that led me to do these things. Just place your hate where it belongs and leave the innocent alone."

Denise was looking at her with a newfound respect. "So, what about this inmate, Timothy Washington?"

Candace said, "I am not going to go into details and incriminate myself. We'll let the lawyers handle all of that." Candace glanced at the officers and held her hands out in the classic sign of 'come and cuff me.'

"Wait," Denise said. "You sat here and gave the world a heartfelt speech about all your bad decisions and how you want to do right by your family. Well, there is an innocent man who is in prison right now because of your lies. Do right by him. He is labeled as a rapist right now. How do you think his little girl feels about that?" asked Denise.

Candace laughed and said, "It's funny that you and the killer only have questions about Timothy Washington. Now I know why you paid me all that money. And I swear that I will sue you for everything you have if you don't honor that contract."

Candace stood up and held her hands out again. "All she wanted to do was humiliate me and have me locked up live on her program. Officers, please come and get me or I'm walking out."

Two officers came over and cuffed her hands behind her back as they read her her rights. As they were leading her out of the door, Candace heard Denise say, "We'll be right back after these messages."

[Stupid, cold-hearted bitch. If she thought this shit was over,] Denise McCarthy had another thing coming.

CHAPTER 21

"I don't know," said Robert Dennis. "He was colored, or African, or black, or whatever y'all are calling yourselves these days. Hell, it could have been you. Y'all all look the same to me."

Sgt. Det. Walter Rogers kept the smile on his face. Mr. Dennis was about a second away from having all of his teeth knocked out. If Walt didn't need what was in his head, it would already be split open.

"Alright Mr. Dennis. We already know he was black, but do you understand that I am trying to help you here? A double murder charge as high profiled as yours, you could be sitting in county for years. You've already been denied bail. Help me, and all that can go away right now."

Walter was sitting in a cell with Robert Dennis at the Pitt County Jail. After leaving Central Prison, he headed in the direction of Greenville. He did call them with his estimated arrival time so they would be ready for him when he got to the jail.

The captain on duty had demanded to know what Walt wanted with his inmate. Walt didn't have time to tell him anything, but he couldn't afford any delays. He told the Officer in Charge everything. He threw in the fact that the killer could start going after county detention officers next, so it was imperative that he have access to Mr. Dennis as soon as possible. The captain agreed and told Walt to follow him.

Robert Dennis had attacked Denise the last time he had a visitor, so this time he was fully restrained and shackled to the table separating them. He was not being very cooperative right now. Walt also made a call to the Pitt County District Attorney on his way to the jail.

In light of some new evidence that had come from the Lt. Candace Price investigation, they now knew that the killer did have the drug that Mr. Dennis told them about. Denise had edited down the video, but the killer had sent them the whole thing. They even saw him hiding in the workout room laughing his ass off as Candace kept going to the door after the killer pressed the button on the fake bell.

The most important part was when he stuck Ms. Price with the needle, and it paralyzed her. That piece of evidence was going to free Cpt. Robert Dennis because, when they tested her blood, it came back negative just like his blood had. They could still sit back and wait for his trial, but the DA had agreed, if Robert helped him, he would drop the charges and he would go free. The DA knew he couldn't win at trial anyway, not with the new evidence.

"So, you mean to tell me, if I help you with the identity of this spook, I get to go free?" asked Robert.

"You won't go free right this second, but your lawyers will be provided with a key piece of evidence that will free you." explained Walt.

"So, you motherfuckers know I'm innocent, but you're still going to hold me?"

"Absolutely. The main reason is just that everyone hates you. The thing is, we still have the 9-1-1 recording and we could convict you with just that. Now, the new evidence does place you in a better position, but you could still be guilty." Walt had a smile on his face that was designed to really piss Robert off.

"Man, all you niggers are the same. You still think that you are smarter than the white man. It doesn't matter how much money you have or what position you hold. You are still nothing but monkeys that talk."

Walt made a decision that could go one of two ways. He was either going to be a hero or he was going to lose his job. He laughed and said, "Have you looked around this room? There are no cameras or two-way mirrors. No one can see you or hear you. So, Mr. White Power, do you think it's smart to say all these things while you are shackled to a table?"

Walt saw the laughter and joy melt away as it dawned on Robert that he might be in a little bit of trouble. "Listen man, I'm just talking shit. I really can't remember what the guy looked like."

Walt stood up and walked around to stand behind Robert. "You see, this is where your mouth has put you in a fucked-up position. I remember every person I have ever beat up. I might not remember their names, but I definitely remember their faces. With you being so much smarter than us monkeys, I figure you know exactly who he is. And if you don't, maybe this will jog your memory."

The punch was a direct hit to Robert's right kidney. With him being so fat, Walt had to put everything into the punch to make sure Robert understood what was about to happen.

Robert was moaning and gasping for breath. Before he could feel even a sliver of relief, Walt hit him just as hard, in the same place.

Robert was screaming for help and trying to get away from Walter. Robert was a big man, but since it was mostly fat, the restraints held him in place. Walt had a frank conversation with the officers about what he was about to do. They told him not to hit Mr. Dennis in his face or break anything. Other than that, he was free to do anything he wanted.

"It's just you and me buddy. No one's coming to help you," Walt taunted the fat man.

"Please man," Robert begged between breaths. "Stop, I swear I don't remember what he looks like. Don't hurt me man. I'm sorry."

Walt was really angry, but even more angry at the fact that he believed the pitiful excuse for a man. Inmates meant so little to him that even one he put in the hospital was not memorable. If Walt continued to beat on the man now, it would just be out of anger and frustration. The man couldn't tell him something he didn't know.

As Robert continued to beg, Walt walked back around the table and sat down. "Alright. Alright. Shut the fuck up!" Walt yelled to silence the man's begging. "I believe you. But you have to remember something man. You and five guards beat this guy and put him in the hospital. It happened in Receiving at Maury." Walt told him the exact date in an effort to jog his memory.

"To tell you the truth, that's where 90% of all our ass whippings are given out. I really can't remember one incident," said Mr. Dennis.

"Well, does the name Manuel Adams mean anything to you?" asked Walt.

"Right before I was set up by this prick, me and my boys had to put it on three motherfuckers in Restrictive Housing. I can't even remember their names. I couldn't even pick them out of a line up. I'm sorry man, but I can't help you." Robert had a pained look on his face like he really did wish he could help. Since the fat bastard wasn't smart enough to be a good actor, Walt had to take his word for it.

Walt stood up and said, "Well, this has been a total waste of time. I'll see you at the trial."

"Hold on man. I was willing to help, doesn't that count for something? I'm innocent, and you know it. Get me out of here."

As Walt walked through the door he said, "We're still investigating. When I'm finished with every possible avenue, I'll turn everything over to your lawyers. You know, us monkeys can talk, but we still think really slow. It could end up being a year from now." Walt waved and walked out the door with a smile on his face. He could hear Mr. Dennis cussing him out all the way down the hall.

He exited the jail and went straight to his car. Denise should have wrapped up the interview hours ago. Instead of waiting to watch it, he decided to call her and get the scoop firsthand.

"Hi, Walt. I was wondering when you would call." Denise sounded like her normal self, so Walt didn't get any clues from her greeting.

"What's going on, Denise? How did the interview go?" Walt decided it was too late at night for chit chat, so he got right down to business.

"Well, it went good, but not great," answered Denise. "We did everything like the killer wanted. I didn't like it, but we let her tell all her lies, then exposed her with the video."

"That's great Denise. Now the killer can't say that we didn't do everything in our power for Timothy Washington," said Walt.

"Well, that's the thing. She wouldn't confirm anything about Timothy. When I asked her to explain the situation, she said that she wouldn't incriminate herself. After they locked her up, I reported about the governor, the Director of Prisons, and the Judges. But, without me telling everyone about Ann, I really couldn't make a strong enough case for his immediate release." They had decided not to go public with Ann's abduction or the deadline. It would make people think he is going free to save a cop, and not because of his own innocence.

Denise sounded totally distressed, and Walt had to reassure her, even though he was hurting pretty badly himself. "Denise, it's okay. I know you did everything in your power to help her. Don't worry. We will come up with some way to find her or either identify him."

"I really just hate the fact that I couldn't do more. I took a few live calls from lawyers and politicians, and they all agreed that Timothy Washington should be free. But they all said that it would take a few months before the paperwork could make it through the courts. Walt, I don't know how we can make this deadline."

"The more I think about it, I don't think we were meant to meet the deadline." Walt had started to come to this realization on his drive to see Robert Dennis. The killer didn't just stumble on this information within the last week. Timothy Washington was supposed to be released years ago, so if he was so keen on getting the man free, why did he wait until less than a week before the birthday to send them on this mission. Walt wasn't often confused, but this whole case just didn't add up.

"So, if we were not meant to meet the deadline, then what does that say about Ann?" asked Denise.

That was the same question floating around in Walt's head. The killer only seemed to kill people he deemed guilty of something. Or, in some cases, just being in the wrong place at the wrong time. So what would be the purpose of killing Ann?

"Honestly, Denise, I just don't know. And I am starting to run on fumes. I had to run over to Greenville to follow a lead. I'm going to get a room for the night and start fresh tomorrow. I can't do much for Ann if I pass out from exhaustion."

"Well, I hope the lead turned out to be productive," said Denise.

"Another dead end. But it did give me some more insight into our killer. A lot of what he is doing is payback for wrongs done to him while he was on the inside. But he's playing some kind of game that only he knows the rules to. We are all pieces on the board, but he's the only one who can see the whole board. Anyway, all of this is leading up to something and our killer is the only one who knows what that is. I need to get going. I'll call you tomorrow after we've both had some rest."

"Okay. And Walt, please be careful," said Denise.

"I will, and good night." Walt hung up and started the car up. He needed to find a place to lay his head before he crashed. He looked on the car's navigation for the closest hotel. Finally, he was at the Microtel, and he pulled into the parking lot.

He went in and got a second-floor room and made his way up the stairs. As soon as he was inside the room, he fell face first on the bed and was fast asleep.

Four o'clock in the morning, he was jerked awake by his cell phone ringing. Walt was still dead tired, and the sudden jolt after so little sleep, made him feel worse. This was not a time when he could afford to ignore a call, so he reached into his pocket to retrieve his phone. He had fallen asleep before he could take it out and charge it. He still had his eyes closed when he said, "Hello."

In an imitation, upper class, white voice, the killer said, "Hello, Det. Rogers. I hope that I'm not disturbing you. I feel that you need an audience with me to discuss an urgent matter."

Walter jumped up off the bed and began looking wildly around the room as if he expected the killer to be standing in the shadows.

"Come on, Walter," said the killer in his normal voice. "That lumpy Microtel bed couldn't have been that comfortable. Wake up!" yelled the killer.

"How do you know where I am?" asked Walt.

"You think those needle dick assholes in your lab are better than me? They found the trackers and cameras that I wanted them to find. But I don't think that's what you want to talk about, is it? You seem to feel like I am being unfair."

"Listen. We have done everything in our power to free Timothy Washington. You saw the interview with Candace Price. And I'm pretty sure you heard what everyone had to say. The timetable you gave us is not doable. If you can just give us a more reasonable timeframe, I promise you, he will go free." Walt was trying to keep all anger out of his voice so as not to set the killer off.

"It is 4:03am right now. You have a little under forty-four hours until your partner dies. You've had since Tuesday night. I gave you plenty of time. It's not my fault that you have wasted most of your time trying to find me. By the way,

158

what kind of shape did you leave Mr. Battle and Mr. Dennis in?"

"They will both live. But you knew I was eventually going to need to talk to both of them. You also knew that Bruce would cave, but nothing he said would hurt you."

"I really didn't think he would cave. He's a piece of shit but he's pretty strong minded. How far did you get with Manuel Adams?" the killer asked with a little laugh.

"As far as you wanted me to get. Which is exactly what I think you did with this Timothy Washington thing. You're too smart and too well planned to think that we could have gotten him out in under a week."

"No. Don't try to put this on me. There was a way, but that way is gone now. I mean, where are you right now? You're so focused on catching me, which you will never do, that you are the reason why your partner is going to die." There was so much anger in the killer's voice and Walt didn't understand why.

"How can you tell me not to put this on you? The whole thing is because of you. If you wanted this guy free, you could have brought this to our attention years ago. You decided to wait until now. So, Mr. Genius, please tell me how I could have freed this guy in five days? Tell me how I could have made a judge ignore proper procedure and let Timothy Washington go? Come on, you fucking bastard. Tell me!" Walt was screaming by the end of his speech. He was so mad he was shaking. [How could this son of a bitch try to place the blame on him?]

"You still don't get it. Your job is not to investigate murders. That's what local law enforcement is for. You have a big position so that you can see the big picture." The killer was back to being calm and was now talking like a teacher to a student. "You're right. I didn't think you could free Timothy in five days. I don't know or care about him anyway. All I wanted to see was you dedicate your time to getting him out when you know that he is innocent. I didn't expect you to dedicate one day to freeing him and the rest of the time looking for me. You just proved the main problem with the system. All you top dogs care about is putting people in prison. Not one of you care about getting people out."

"What was I supposed to do?" asked Walt. "How was that even possible after you took my partner?"

"I wouldn't have had your partner if you wouldn't have used your time trying to catch me instead of trying to free Timothy Washington. You knew that you couldn't stop me from killing whichever guard I picked, but you still delayed helping the inmate to try to help the guard."

"I'm a cop. Timothy Washington wasn't going to die that night. You really expected me to sit back and just let another person die?" Walt asked the killer.

The line was silent for a few seconds. "Well, I guess not. But your choices led to me having your partner. It wasn't in my plan, but soon you will understand that I am always ready for anything. I did give you a mission, and it is too late to back out of it now. You still have today and tomorrow to pull something out of your hat. Do whatever you have to do. You won't hear from me again until Monday morning. It will either be to tell you where to pick your partner up or to tell your partner goodbye. Spend your time wisely or your partner will be very disappointed in you." The killer hung up and Walt fell back on the bed, wondering if it would be possible to break Timothy Washington out of prison

CHAPTER 22

Det. Grace was going to die.

It was 11:00pm, Sunday night and the killer was sitting outside of her cell doing something on his phone, with a gun on his lap.

Ann would have liked to say that she had been a model prisoner, but she would be telling a lie. So, any sympathy the killer might have had for her was long gone.

Tuesday night, or really Wednesday morning, when the killer had brought her here, she had spent all night crying and sleeping. When she finally got up, she had no idea of the time or even if it was night or day. All she had to wear was the robe the killer had given her. She was hungry and she had to use the bathroom really bad. But she was alive, and sometime during the night, she had gotten her resolve back. She had had her one night of crying and feeling sorry for herself. Now it was time to fight.

First things first, she had to piss like a racehorse. She never understood where that saying came from. [Did regular horses not have to piss just as much as a racehorse? Maybe racehorses had to drink a lot more water because they sweated so much.] Anyway, wherever the saying came from, she still had to piss like one.

There were cameras in two opposite corners of her cell, so she had absolutely no privacy. The toilet did look clean and there was a whole roll of double-ply toilet paper. The seat was stainless steel, but there was no cushion on it at all. She arranged her robe around her so as she squatted down, the skin exposed to the camera was minimal.

When her urine stream came out, it was embarrassingly loud in the otherwise silent room. The killer could be listening through the intercom on the wall. She attempted to slow the stream down in order to sound more lady-like and less like a construction worker.

161

That out of the way, she washed her hands and looked at the T.V. There was no remote and when she looked up at the bottom and on the sides, she started putting her fingers on different parts of the screen. Nothing.

She walked over to the intercom and pressed the button. Then she went and sat down on the cot and waited for the killer to answer her call.

Instead of the intercom coming to life, she saw movement coming from down the hall. The killer stopped at the door and knocked. She wanted to see what he would do, so she stayed silent. He shrugged his shoulders and turned to walk off.

She jumped up and yelled for him to come back. She didn't know if he could hear her, so she pressed the intercom button again. He stopped and looked at his phone and this time his voice came out of the speaker.

"Det. Grace, I don't have time to play games. Do you need something or not?" He had stopped about forty feet from her cell and was looking towards her door.

"Yes," Ann answered. "I need you to come back down her and explain some things to me."

"Say please and I'll come back," said the killer, in a teasing voice.

"I thought you didn't have time for games," Ann retorted.

"You're right. That was kind of childish." The killer walked back towards her and opened her door with his phone. "Do you want me to step in or do you want to step out?"

"You can come in. I just have a few questions."

"Okay," said the killer, stepping into the cell. "What do you want to know?"

"First off, how in the hell do I work this T.V.?" Ann asked.

"Oh, it's a smart T.V. Just say T.V. and then give it a command."

Ann said, "T.V. on." The T.V. turned on to an old 'Fresh Prince of Bel Air' episode on B.E.T.

"If you want the guide or to turn the channel, just tell it what to do. Speak to it like it's a child. Just remember, always say T.V. first."

Ann went through a few commands to test what the killer said, and it worked like a charm. She flipped through a few channels and then said, "Okay, how do I get something to eat?"

"That's easy. Press the button and tell me that you are hungry. There is a fully stocked kitchen right next to the elevator. As long as you are good, you have full access to the kitchen area. I will open your door, and the kitchen door and you can fix whatever you want. If you end up in the punishment cell, you will get whatever I decide to give you, when I decide to give it you."

"Okay, understood. What about a shower and some clothes?"

"Every cell except the last ten on this side has its own shower. Just tell the shower to open and it will open for you." The killer seemed to be relaxed and having a fun time playing prison cell guide.

Ann looked around the room and couldn't see another door. "Shower open," Ann said. A panel on the right side of the T.V. opened up a crack. She walked over to it and slid the partition into a recessed nook inside the wall. It contained a single shower head as well as a rack with clean towels and rags, soap, shampoo, and other hygiene products like lotion and deodorant.

"If you act right, you will get to see the showers in the suites. They have a hot tub and a waterfall for a showerhead."

Ann didn't know if he was joking or not, but she was probably never going to find out anyway. "Shower close," Ann said.

The panel slid back out and locked itself into the opposite side of the recess. Even knowing it was there, the fit was so exact that she couldn't tell exactly where the opening was. "And what about the clothes?" asked Ann.

"You don't need them. No one is here but me, and I've already seen it all," he said with a big smile on his face. "Anyway, clothes give people a false sense of confidence. You might think that with clothes on you could try to escape."

"You ever think that a woman just doesn't want to worry about flashing her ass and breasts with every move she makes?"

"I've had cameras in your house for years now. I've seen so much of your ass and breasts that it's not that big of a deal anymore. Just try to relax and enjoy yourself."

The killer went to leave the room and as soon as he turned his back, Ann struck.

She threw a two-legged kick at the back of his right knee, knowing that with her training, if she took out one of his legs, she could overcome his weight, strength, and reach.

It felt like she was moving in slow motion as her feet flew towards its target. Then, just like that, the target was gone. The killer had to have eyes in the back of his head. Ann didn't scream or make a war cry to alert her adversary like they do in the movies. She could honestly say that she didn't make a sound. But the next thing she knew, the killer was spinning to his left, at a speed that defied logic, and even managed to kick her in the stomach as she flew past.

All the air left her body, and for the moment, took all her fight with it. The killer was standing over her shaking his head but nodded to show he respected the attempt.

"I knew that you were going to be a fighter. If you hadn't tried something, I would have been very disappointed in you." The killer walked out of the cell and said, "When you get up, I am going to take you to your new cell. Even though I respect your attempt, I can't let it go unpunished."

Ann laid there, faking like she was still incapacitated from the kick. She was in it now and even though she was still hurting, she wasn't going to give up that easily.

When she stood up, she didn't even pretend that she was going to go along with his plan. She squared up and said, "You want me to move, come in and get me."

The killer smiled and said, "Ann, I really don't want to hurt you. I'll tell you what. If you just come willingly, I will get you a set of clothes."

"How about after I kill you, I go home and put my own clothes on?" Ann taunted back at the killer.

"Ann. Stop. Please don't do this," the killer begged.

Ann backed further into the cell and waited on the killer. He put his hands on his hips and smiled at her again. "Are you sure you want to do this?" the killer asked her. She didn't respond, just stayed in her stance.

The smile left the killer's face and he advanced towards her like she was a wayward child. She aimed a jab at his throat, but he swatted it away like it was gnat. He grabbed her right shoulder and pulled it out of the socket. Before the pain could even register, he grabbed her left shoulder and dislocated that one too.

When the pain hit, it dropped her to her knees. Every breath she took sent iron pokers through both her shoulders. She fell on her back on the floor and tried to use the cold concrete to ease the pain.

"I will pop them back in when you are ready to go." said the killer. Through it all, his mask never even moved on his face. He wasn't even breathing hard or showing any emotion in his eyes.

Ann hated to do it, but she said, "Please help me. I'll go."

"You can't win against me. Even if you knock me out, you don't know any of the codes to work my phone. You will die of starvation down here. I admire your fight, but I will warn you, the next time I will really hurt you, or kill you, and be done with it. Do you understand?"

Ann nodded her head and said, "Yes. Now, please help me. It really hurts."

The killer grabbed her legs and started dragging her out of the door.

"Ow. Owwww. Wait. Stop," Ann wailed.

"It won't kill you. It's just a little pain. But maybe, you will learn your lesson."

The killer continued dragging her down the hallway towards the punishment cells. She moaned the whole way and screamed every time one of her shoulders bumped the floor. She was close to passing out when the killer stopped in front of her new cell.

"I'm going to fix your shoulders and then I want you to stay on the floor and crawl into the cell. If you try to standup, I will break something that will make you stay down."

He walked over and stopped at her head, leaned down, and propped her up with his knee. He grabbed her right shoulder, and without a word, popped it back into place. She gasped from the pain. He then grabbed the left shoulder and popped that one back in too.

He moved from behind her, and she fell back to the floor. The pain left as if she had imagined the whole thing. She decided to fight another day and crawled into the cell.

"The robe," said the killer, reaching his hand into the cell. "And make a decision fast, because if you don't give it up, I'm coming in to get it."

She looked around the small cell. It didn't have a bed or sink or T.V. All it had was a bucket. It looked to be about five by five, so she would have to be diagonal just to lay down. And worst of all, it had no lights, and it was cold. She didn't even think about fighting. She was no match for him. She snatched the robe off and threw it at him.

Without a word or a backwards glance, he walked away. The door closed and she was left in darkness. This glass was not see-through at all. She was still hungry, and she needed a shower. She was butt naked, but she was alive and no longer in pain. Unless she could come up with a weapon, she wouldn't try to attack him again.

She had no idea how long she stayed in there as she slept on and off. She never got any food or water, and her stomach hurt so badly, she was going to throw up from the pain. It was part hunger, but she also had a huge bruise from the killer's kick to her stomach.

Ann sat in darkness, holding in her urine because she didn't want to pee in the bucket again. All of a sudden, the door opened. She crawled out to show the killer that she wasn't a threat, but as she looked around, the killer was nowhere in sight.

A voice that was now familiar to her came out of thin air. "Go back to your old cell. Eat, clean up, and get dressed. I will see you in a little while." The killer didn't sound mad or happy. He sounded like he was explaining something not very important to a stranger.

She ran back to the receiving cell and saw a pizza on the bed along with a pair of jeans, underwear, and a sweater. There was a gallon jug of water and a two-liter Pepsi. A pair of shoes was on the floor with a pair of socks draped over them. It never crossed her mind that the clothes weren't her size. Like the killer said, he had been watching her for years.

Seeing the water made her focus on more pressing matters. She sat down on the toilet, and this time, didn't even think about how long or loud the stream was. [If the killer got his jollies off on listening to women use the bathroom, then so be it.]

After washing her hands, Ann grabbed the pizza box and ripped it open. Meat lovers, her favorite. [Damn, the man did know her.] In between bites, she commanded the T.V. to turn on. When it was on a news channel, she stopped eating and stared at the screen.

It was 5:00pm on Friday. When the killer had taught her how to control the T.V., she had gone to a news station and saw the time and the date. It had been 11:22am on

167

Wednesday. She had been in that hole for over two days. And the fucker never gave her food or water.

The passage of time was just shocking. She knew she had slept on and off, but she had thought of the missing time in hours, not days.

She consumed half the pizza before she remembered that she was standing there, butt naked. She knew not to guzzle the water, so she took several long sips before heading off to the shower with clothes in hand.

After taking the most luxurious shower of her life, she came out of the shower area, fully dressed, to find the killer sitting on the bed.

Whether the confidence was false or true, the killer was right; having on clothes did make her feel better.

Before she could rail away at him for leaving her in that closet for two days, he began to speak. "It is now 6:00pm. Denise McCarthy will be making a last-ditch effort to free Timothy Washington in one hour. This attempt will fail. Ann, I am going to be totally honest with you."

The killer got up and walked over to the muted T.V. that, until he looked at it, Ann had forgotten it was even on. "I feel bad because I gave your partner a task that was impossible for him to do. Without breaking the law, there is no way to get Mr. Washington out in the time I provided him. All I wanted you and your partner to do was dedicate every second of the available time to getting him out. Then, I would have finished my mission, and disappeared into the night."

"Mission?" Ann asked. "What, are you on some secret government mission, or is it just one of revenge?"

Shaking his head, the killer said, "It would take me a year to explain everything to you and you still wouldn't understand. Anyway, I never intended to put you in the middle of all of this. You and Walt stand for everything good in this corrupt system."

"Well then, let me go. I've never hurt anyone who didn't try to hurt me first. Drug me, cover my head, and you can drop me off anywhere in the world."

"I'm sorry Ann, but I made a promise. Your people would never trust anything I say if I don't follow through on my promise. I have the T.V. locked on the channel where Denise will give her last shot. You never know, it might work."

He turned around and walked to the door. He stopped and looked over his shoulder. "Either way, on Sunday night, you will say goodbye to Walt, or you will go free. Believe it or not, I'm rooting for you to go free. Cell one, the suite, is yours after the program goes off. Press the button if you want food. I'll see you Sunday night."

As he walked away, the door shut, and Ann sat down to watch the show.

Ann sat in silence, stunned by the cruelty of the interview. She was appalled because she knew Walt had signed off on embarrassing Ms. Price that way in an effort to get Ann back. No matter what a person has done, or what the reward is, you don't have the right to degrade them like that.

As she sat seething, the door behind her opened. She grabbed up her water and Pepsi, and leftover pizza, and walked up the hall to her new room.

The carpet was white and thick, and it looked like something a queen would have in her room. Ann removed her shoes and carried everything over to the bedside table.

She walked over to the sectioned-off area and saw a real toilet, with a real toilet seat. She didn't see another door, so she commanded the shower to open.

The panel was right across from the toilet, and it slid soundlessly into the wall. She looked in and gasped at the splendor of the room. It did indeed have a hot tub and a shower made to look just like a waterfall. Everything gleamed white and smelled like bleach. This was probably the best jail cell in the world.

Since none of the outcomes could be influenced by her, Ann spent the next two days living the life. Eating meals that she had never tried before. Lounging for hours at a time in the hot tub. Laying back and watching movies that she had never had the time to see when she was free.

But reality soon came crashing back down when the killer showed up 10:30pm, Sunday night, pulled up a chair, and had been sitting outside her cell ever since.

Ann had tried to talk to him. She had pressed the button down for ten minutes straight. She had no idea what he was doing on that phone, but he wouldn't acknowledge her at all.

Ann's heart was pounding, and she had a heavy nervous sweat that she had never had a day in her life. She was totally afraid because there had been no mention of Timothy Washington, or Lt. Candace Price on the news. Denise hadn't been on the air again. Most troubling was that her abduction hadn't been talked about at all.

Ann had been taught to always go public with any crime you couldn't solve. Most people saw things that they didn't even know they saw. All it would take was one person saying they saw a car where it didn't belong, and it could break the whole case. Ann couldn't for the life of her, figure out why Walt wouldn't have gone public.

At 11:50pm, she started to cry. She was begging the killer to talk to her, to look at her, anything but ignore her until it was time for her to die.

When the clock in the corner of the T.V. said 12:00am, the killer stood up and her door opened. She was defeated and deflated, and she sat on the bed and waited for the killer to shoot her.

The killer said, "Showtime." He dialed a number on his phone and said to her, "You have two minutes. I don't care what you say, but if I were you, I would make every word count." He hit send and put the phone up to his face. "Well, I promised you could say goodbye. You have two minutes."

He handed her the phone, took three steps back, and stopped with the gun pointed at her head.

CHAPTER 23

"Ann is about to die, and it's all my fault," said Walter.

It was 11:50pm, Sunday night. Walter and Denise were sitting in Walt's office in downtown Raleigh. They figured it was the only place that they were relatively positive the killer hadn't bugged.

"Walt, it is not your fault. You've done everything in your power to both find the killer and to free Timothy Washington. If Ann does die tonight, then place the blame where it belongs...on the killer."

"I understand what you are saying but the killer was right. I used ninety percent of my time trying to find him instead of trying to help a man that I knew was innocent. I've been chasing this guy for years without getting close. All I had to do was follow instructions for five days and Ann would still be safe, and I could have saved some lives. Now, everything is fucked up."

Walt and Denise had spent all weekend trying to free Timothy Washington. They had gone back and talked to the governor. That had been a waste of time. They had talked to some judges and lawyers, a bigger waste of time. They had talked to the Warden at Bertie Correctional Institution where Mr. Washington was being held. She said she couldn't help them at all, but if they wanted to talk to the inmate, it was okay with her. That trip had been the biggest waste of time to date.

Timothy Washington was an overweight, medium height, bald, black man who was 52 years old. He had dentures and walked like he had bad knees. Just looking at him, Walt would have questioned his ability to force himself on Lt. Price.

They sat down with him at the prison in the regular population visitation room with one guard standing at the door. Because he had been found guilty of sexual assault on a staff member, Timothy would be doing all of his time in a maximum-security prison like Bertie Correctional.

As soon as he saw them, Timothy said, "I have no idea who he is, and I have no idea why he has chosen to help me. Unless you are here to set me free, then I can't talk to you without my lawyer." He came and sat with them anyway with his eyes going up and down Denise the whole time.

"Ms. McCarthy, I do want to thank you for exposing that lying, worthless bitch Candace Price. If she had an ounce of your class, I wouldn't be in this mess anyway," said Timothy.

"You're welcome, Mr. Washington. If it is okay with you, Detective Rogers here would like to ask you a few questions."

Walt could tell that Denise was uncomfortable with the scrutiny she was receiving, and Walt was going to put an end to it.

"Well, Ms. McCarthy," Timothy said, staring right at her breasts. "I would pretty much do anything you asked me to do."

"Mr. Washington," Walt said in a voice that demanded Timothy to focus on him. "How about you show a little bit of class and respect towards the woman who is responsible for your early release. What does it say about your control when you can't be in a room with a woman without you eye-fucking her?"

Denise's eyes flew up to look at Walt's face. She started to say something, but Walt grabbed her leg under the table.

"You're right. You are right." Timothy Washington looked at Denise in the eyes for the first time and said, "I'm sorry for disrespecting you. I know that you have been lobbying to get me out of here and I really appreciate your help." He looked back at Walter and said, "You can ask your questions, but I'm telling you now, I really can't help you."

Walt went on to ask a series of question about friends he had in prison. If anyone had said anything to him about Lt.

Candace Price before the incident? If he had told anyone that he had paid the Lieutenant before the encounter? Anything at all that might help them identify the Prison Guard Killer.

Every answer was a variant of no or I don't know. Walt asked if the name, Manuel Adams, meant anything to him? Timothy had thought for a minute and then said that the name didn't ring any bells.

Timothy's eyes still strayed to Denise every now and then, but Walt couldn't blame the man for wanting to look at an attractive woman. Hell, his own eyes strayed to her a few times. But there was a way to look at a woman without being a pervert about it.

Walt was thankful that Timothy was trying to be respectful. After a couple of thank you's and goodbyes, Walt and Denise took their leave.

Timothy Washington hadn't been helpful at all. they wasted hours in travel time, but whoever wasn't driving, was always on the phone trying to garner some help from somebody. None of it helped in the least.

Now, they were sitting in Walt's office, five minutes from midnight, with nothing to show for the last two days. The killer was not going to be happy. Walt had a feeling Ann wouldn't be overjoyed with the situation either.

"Do you think Ann could get the best of this guy and free herself?" asked Denise.

"I think, if this guy has you, you will be completely at his mercy until he decides what to do with you," answered Walt.

"You trained her pretty well. If anyone can beat this guy, it's one of you two."

"You know Denise, at the beginning of all of this, when I thought he was just some inmate out for revenge, I would have agreed with you. But to be totally honest with you, I don't think any of us can beat this guy. I've helped Homeland Security and the CIA catch terrorists in countries where we didn't have a clue what we were doing. We're in our own backyard now and we can't even figure out this guy's name or what he looks like."

"I get that Walt, but people still believe in you. I believe in you. And more than anything, we need you. Without you and Ann dogging his every step all this time, he wouldn't have had to be so careful. There's no telling how many more people he would have killed."

Before Walt could respond, his cell phone began to ring. It was 12:00am on the head. The killer never said exactly when he was going to call, but some sixth sense told Walt that the person on the other end of this call, was the killer.

When he answered, Walt heard the killer say, "Well, I promised you could say goodbye. You have two minutes."

Walt started trying to talk to the killer. Tried to beg him for more time. The next voice silenced anything else from coming out of his mouth.

"Walt? Walt, is this you?" Ann asked him.

"Yes, Ann it's me. Listen…" Walt started.

"No Walt, stop and listen to me. We don't have time for anything else."

He heard Ann take a deep breath and then she began to speak. "I have no idea where I am, in terms of location. But I am in an underground prison that you will never find. The entrance is inside of a run-down cabin or barn or shed. It was the middle of the night when I got here so I have no idea what else could be around. I couldn't see anything because I was blindfolded, but I didn't hear any vehicles at all."

She took another deep breath and continued. "The killer is 6'1". About 200 pounds. Black. Very educated. He knows several different styles of Martial Arts. I would have put his age around 40, but he moves like he's in his 20's. He also has some kind of law enforcement or military training. I'd say both."

"Ann, thank you so much for the information. I want you to know that we did everything that we could to free

Timothy, and he will go free, just not in time. I'm so sorry I failed you…"

"No, Walt. You did not fail me. I let this bastard get his hands on me and he kept me down with that drug he's been using on everyone. It's over for me, Walt. Just try to catch this asshole, but make sure to tell everyone to be very careful. If you can, kill him. Don't try to bring him in alive. He will have some tricks up his sleeve to get out again."

Walt was crying now because his partner was being so strong in the face of death. "Ann, I love you, and I will never stop looking for him while I have breath in my body."

"I know Walt, and I love you too…"

The next sound Walt heard was the loud bang of a gun going off in close quarters. He sat with the phone clutched tightly in his hand, waiting to hear another sound.

Walt heard the phone moving around and then a voice. "I really didn't want to have to do that, but you left me no choice." The killer did sound remorseful, but Walt had had enough.

He hung up the phone without saying a word. He laid the phone on his desk and cried, while Denise just put her arms around him and stayed silent.

Walt had never felt this much pain in his life. Everyone had thought he was only committed to the job. The truth was, Ann was his commitment. He loved her like a little sister, and his main goal in life had been to keep her safe. He had failed her, the job, and himself.

All he had wanted to do was prepare her for this harsh world of law enforcement. But in the end, his decision to send her out of harm's way, had led to her being killed. One thing was for certain, he was going to keep his promise to her. The son of a bitch would either kill him or he was going to die trying.

Walt gave himself a few minutes to get all the tears out of his system and then he stood up.

He was prepared to tell Denise to go home, but before he could talk, his phone rang again. This time he put it on speaker and waited to hear what kind of bullshit the killer had to say now.

"Det. Rogers. I know you are upset…"

"Oh, you think I'm upset? Fuck upset. I'm pissed off now."

"Okay," said the killer. "So, you're pissed off. Well, I'm pissed off too. You think you're the only person to ever suffer a loss?"

"Fuck your loss," yelled Walt. "I'm going to fucking kill you. Just like I said from the start. You go after weak ass guards and women. You think you're so good? Tell me where to meet you. Right. Fucking. Now. No back up. No tricks. Just me and you. Then let's see how tough you are, motherfucker."

"All in due time, Detective. But first, I want you to know, the other part of this will happen. I promised that I would kill a guard everyday…"

"Yeah. Yeah. Yeah. I know," said Walt, cutting the killer off. "You're going to kill a guard every day. Typical you. Why don't you start with me? I know why. You're a pussy. A fucking coward. A scared ass little boy who won't step up to someone who can give him a challenge."

"Hahahaha," laughed the killer. "You think you're a challenge? That's funny. Anyway, this is just a courtesy call to tell you what's happening next. You'll find Ann's body when I want you to find her body. I will send videos of my kills to Denise, and she will air them every night until I stop sending them."

For the first time, Denise spoke up. "You know, I don't think I want to be a part of your little game anymore. Find someone else to send you snuff films to."

"Hi, Denise. I was wondering if you were just going to sit there or speak up for yourself. I didn't think it would take so long."

"Well, when you start barking orders directed at me, then I will speak up for myself. And like I said, you can find someone else to do your dirty work. Hell, you're the computer guru. Put them out on the internet. Or hack into the network and play them yourself."

"You like your new job, Denise?" asked the killer. "You like that new car? The bigger salary? How about the fact that little girls and grown ass men are running up to you, asking for your autograph? That is all because of me. I turned you into a star and you're going to keep doing what I need you to do. Or are you telling me you are a worthless loose end now? Because that can be handled," said the killer in a menacing voice.

Walt said, just as menacing, "Don't you fucking threaten her, you piece of shit."

"Or what?" yelled the killer. "You going to stop me from doing whatever the fuck I want, like you did with Ann? When I make a threat, it is a promise. So, you want to make it official? Okay, Denise, I will be sending you videos of the kills. Show them every time you receive one, or you will become a featured actress in one of your own. Now, I'm done with all this bullshit. A lot of people still have to die. When Timothy Washington is home, some of the killing will stop. Not all, but you will have saved some lies. Walt, you want to save someone? Talk your girlfriend into following orders. Or the next time you're sitting in your office crying, it will be because of her death."

The killer disconnected the call before either one of them could say a word.

"Denise, what do you want to do?" asked Walt as he retook his seat. He had the fleeting thought that if the killer knew he had been crying, maybe his office was bugged after all.

"Excuse my language but fuck him. I'm not showing any more videos. I will report what's going on, so the public is aware, but I'm done being his bitch." Denise had a look on her face that told Walt he'd better not attempt to change her mind. So, he didn't.

"He's going to come after you. Do you have somewhere to stay that's safer than your house?" asked Walt.

Standing up, Denise said, "I'm not leaving my home and you're not going to make me a prisoner. I can handle myself. Now, we've both been on the go all week. I am going home and getting some rest." She leaned over and gave him a quick kiss on the lips. "I'm so sorry about Ann, but the best thing we can do for her now is to be 100 percent so we can catch this guy. Go home and get some sleep." With that, she walked out of his office and went home.

Walt sat there for another 15 minutes before he got up and prepared to do exactly what Denise said, go home and get some sleep.

He had recorded the phone call and would have to give a full report later today to the brass on what was going on.

It had been their call not to go public with Ann's kidnapping. There had been pros and cons for either side of the argument, but ultimately, he had been ordered to keep it quiet.

The officers from Dunn who responded to the scene at Greg Black's house, had been threatened with jail time or death if they talked. Walt didn't know which threat had done the trick, but they stayed quiet.

Walt pulled up in front of his house and just sat there, thinking about Ann. He wasn't even sure he wanted to continue doing the job without her by his side. He would stay until he got this guy off the streets, and then he would retire. He was getting too old for this shit anyway.

He got out of the car and made his way to his front door. He opened things up, closed the door, turned to go into his living room, and froze for maybe half a second before his gun was pointed straight out in front of him.

"What the hell are you doing in my house?" asked Walt. "Make it good and make it fast because my patience is gone."

CHAPTER 24

"Fuck him," said the killer. "Thinks he's the only person to ever feel the pain of loss."

The killer was mad as hell at both Denise and Walt. The conversation had gone just how he predicted it to go, but he was still disappointed. He had wanted to soothe the detective and maybe have the detective show some kind of understanding for the position the killer had been in.

"Motherfucker acts like I went looking for Ann. He's the one who sent her in that house. Probably knew I was in there and was too afraid to face me. All that big boy talk. Punk ass cop."

The killer was cruising the neighborhood of his chosen victim for the night. Since he had made his promise before he took Ann, he figured that he still owed the world the death of a corrupt guard.

He really needed to tighten up though. The guard he picked for tonight wouldn't be a problem on his worst day, but if he was distracted, he could make stupid mistakes. Dangerous mistakes. And one thing you always had to remember was that every guard was armed.

He pushed Ann, Walter, and Denise out of his head and switched to work mode.

The killer parked a quarter mile from the trailer park that Sgt. Camilla Rodriguez of Albemarle Correctional lived in. She had worked as a guard at the medium-security prison for the last twelve years. She was 35 years old, single, and lived alone.

Sgt. Rodriguez was a big girl. At only 5'2", she was 340 pounds. Because no one wanted her out in the real world, she considered the prison her own hunting grounds. And from his own experience, he knew she did a lot of hunting.

At one point in time, he would have left her alone. His opinion back then had been that a female really couldn't rape a man in prison because no prisoner in his right mind would turn the female down. Over time, he concluded that those rapists were the worst because they made you an active and willing participant in your own rape. The worst part was that the victim didn't even see their attacker as a rapist, they saw them a savior.

Being in prison for even a short period of time can fuck your mind up big time. And those specialized predators that understand and use those fucked up people deserve to die and go to hell. The killer couldn't guarantee the hell part, that was on God. But the dead part, well, he was the specialist in that field.

The killer got out the car with his work clothes on, all black, and jogged in the direction of the trailer park. He had memorized the layout of the whole area, so he made quick work in locating the specific trailer he needed.

The trailer was actually the best one out of the lot of 18 trailers, but that was like being the best-looking piece of shit in the toilet bowl. All of them were pretty messed up.

Sgt. Rodriguez's trailer was painted a bright white with a sky-blue trim around the door and the windows. She even had a small porch that was also painted sky-blue, with two sparkling white rocking chairs, set about four feet apart.

The trailer did show some wear and tear but nothing like that of her neighbors. Scratches and dings but no gaping holes. Altogether, not that bad. But definitely not good.

The killer hated the fact that there was only one door. Sgt. Rodriguez could be asleep on the couch just like Officer Black had been. He certainly couldn't depend on the door to the trailer being as quiet as the door to Officer Black's house.

He decided to walk around the trailer and take a peek in a few of the windows. The problem is how close the trailers were to each other. The Sarge could be asleep, but a noise could have a neighbor calling the cops. [Fuck it,] he thought. He was going to have to take the risk.

The big window on the front of the trailer was covered with blinds from top to bottom and was dark, so that was no help. It was too much out in the open anyway. He decided to walk down the back side.

The first window he came to was too high for him to see in. Because of how small it was, he figured it was for the bathroom. The window was dark anyway, so he moved on.

He was having to move with extra caution because of how close the next trailer was. Also, just like most trailer parks all over the globe, there was trash all over the ground.

The next window was to a bedroom and was actually wide open. The bed was about three feet from the window and Sgt. Camilla Rodriguez was sprawled across it, fast asleep. There were also clothes and other debris on the floor and on the bed around the Sarge.

Deciding that it was fate helping him out, the killer took out a needle and climbed in the window as fast and as quietly as he could.

He still had to make sure no one else was in the house, so he quickly stuck the woman in the leg and kept moving.

After a quick search, it was confirmed that the killer and the Sarge were alone in the house.

The killer walked back to the bathroom and turned the water on in the tub. He made sure to use all cold water for the shock factor. He also pulled out a bag that held ten, quarter-sized cameras, and began sticking them on the walls to cover every angle of the bathroom.

He exited the bathroom after the tub was half full and he had shut the water off. As big as Camilla was, it was probably still going to overflow when he tossed her fat ass in. Not like she would care; she wouldn't be around to clean it up anyway.

When he re-entered the bedroom, he was amazed to find the Sergeant still sleeping. The needle and the noise he had been making hadn't even interrupted her sleep.

He stared down at her disgusting body, and a shiver went through him. She was laying on her back with her legs slightly parted. All she had on was a pair of panties that looked big enough to cover a car. Her big, long breasts hung off either side of her chest like pieces of rotting fruit. He wondered if she slept this way, with the window open, hoping for a late-night visitor. Well, she was about to get all she could handle.

His mind went to the reason she was on his list in the first place. He had been a victim of one of her predatorial attacks, but his own situation had not been as bad as some.

Sgt. Rodriguez used to work nights at the medium-custody prison. The shift she worked on was considered the good shift because all the officers were lazy, and after the 9:30pm count, all of them went to sleep and left the inmates to fend for themselves.

At this time, the prison had no cameras on any of the housing units, so corruption ran rampant throughout the whole prison. Inmates being assaulted by other inmates. Cell phones and drugs all over the place. Sex and gambling were part of everyday life. And the gangs controlled who got to do what.

About 11:00pm on a Saturday night, the killer had just come out of the shower with only boxers and a towel wrapped around his waist.

The Sergeant was in the middle of doing one of her rounds when her eyes locked on him.

"Hey," she had yelled. "Where do you sleep?" After he told her, she said, "When you finish getting dressed, come to the Sergeant's office."

Until that night, he hadn't heard a peep about what went on in her office late at night. A few of the other inmates heard what she had said to him and gave him a quick run-down on what to expect.

After hearing the war stories of sexual abuse, the killer decided he wouldn't go. Ten minutes later, the Sarge called his name over the intercom and said to come to her office immediately or disciplinary action would be taken. He hadn't wanted to go to the hole for trying to predict what was going to happen, so he went down the hallway to her office.

She had been sitting behind her desk with this sick, twisted smile on her face. "You can go ahead and close the door but keep standing up for me." The killer didn't want to close the door but thought [fuck it, it couldn't be as bad as what they said.] He would just get it over with and be on his way.

The killer close the door.

Sgt. Rodriguez had leaned back in her chair and then gave her pitch. "I have a Confidential Informant that says you have been selling drugs on my unit. Is that true?"

"No, ma'am," the killer had answered.

"Well, he said you keep them in your underwear. So, I'm going to have to perform a strip search on you." She had sat there, looking at him like she expected him to start stripping.

The killer looked around the small office like he didn't understand. "Ma'am, isn't a male officer supposed to search me if it involves me stripping?"

Anger flashed across her face, and she slammed her hands down on the desk. "I am the Sergeant on this unit, and I make the rules. Now strip, or else this will end up being one of the worst nights of your life."

The killer could have just murdered her in her office, but then he would never go home. He also could have walked out, but then he would be held accountable for whatever lies Sergeant Rodriguez decided to tell. Over his years in prison, he had been stripped search hundreds of times, if not, thousands. Nudity wasn't that big of a deal to an inmate.

The killer stripped off all his clothes. The Sarge got up and walked around him, checking him out. "My God," she said. "You are absolutely perfect. You must work out every day to have a body like this."

She stopped in front of him and ran her fingers down his chest. "I'm going to need you to do something for me tonight. If you act right, we will both experience pleasure, and this can become a normal thing for us."

Through it all, the killer just stood silently, hoping another officer would show up to put a stop to this. With his luck, it would be some homosexual men who would want to join in. Then he would have to kill them both.

Sergeant Rodriguez walked back to her seat, leaned back, and put both of her feet up on the desk with her legs slightly spread. She then unbuttoned her pants and lowered her zipper. Reaching her hand inside, she said, "Now, stroke yourself for me. And so you know, no one is coming down this hall, and both of us are staying in here until we both get off."

[Well,] thought the killer, as he watched her rubbing herself, [this image is not going to work.] Wanting to get out as fast as possible, the killer closed his eyes and thought about his ex-girlfriend from before he came to prison. Things started progressing from there, and his hand got to work.
The Sarge was moaning and groaning, and from the sound of things, she was close to climaxing. The killer still had his eyes closed until this awful smell hit his nose. He opened his eyes to see that the Sergeant had removed her shoes and pants, and her fingers were really going to town.

Her eyes were locked on his penis as she panted for him to stroke it harder and faster. She started hunching up and down and shaking, with her mouth hanging open. Then her body went rigid as she shrieked and came.

The killer's eyes started to water from the horrible smells coming out of her body. His hand kept moving, trying to finish so he could leave.

"No. Stop," said the Sarge. "Come over here and give me a hand. Or maybe a tongue."

The killer was not going to put his mouth anywhere near that cesspool she had between her legs. He decided to offer a compromise. "Listen, Sarge. This shit is not cool. Okay. So, just to get this over with, I will use my fingers on you and then I'm gone. If you don't agree with that, then I'm going to get dressed and I'll deal with whatever lies you tell."

She sat there looking at him, considering his offer. "Can I touch you while you touch me?" she asked.

He really didn't want her to touch him, but he said yes, just to close the deal.

She smiled and beckoned him over. As soon as he was in range, her hands started rubbing all over his penis. "Rub me baby. Come on. Put those strong fingers way up inside me."

He started working on her while she sat there, stroking his penis. Then she said, "Remember, you have to cum for this session to be over."

The killer knew that would be hard because, standing this close to her, while his fingers did their work, the smell was horrid. But he closed his eyes and pictured his girlfriend again, and things started looking up.

From the sounds and the smell, he could tell that she was coming again when she pulled away, and he felt her mouth on his penis. He was close enough that, with only a few thrusts, he came in her mouth.

He turned away and started dressing as she tried to talk him into coming back the next night. He agreed, just to get out of the office, but the next morning, he punched one of the bullies of the yard in his mouth, knocking four of his teeth out, so he could go to the hole.

When he got out thirty days later, they put him on a different unit.

Now, as he stood over her partially naked form, he let the rage build up. She was still under the drug's influence, so he grabbed both of her nipples and twisted as hard as he could.

Her eyes flew open in pain and surprise. Her eyes tracked him as he went over to the window and closed it, pulling the curtains shut. He walked to the foot of the bed, tore his mask off, and with a smile, asked, "Remember me?"

Sgt. Camilla Rodriguez definitely remembered him. If possible, her eyes got even bigger, and tears started streaming down her face. Her breathing picked up drastically, but because of the drug, that was all she could do.

The killer grabbed her foot and dragged her off the bed. "I'm not carrying your fat ass. I'll already have to pick you up to put you in the tub. Goddang' you stank," he said, fanning in front of his nose.

He dragged her all the way to the bathroom and then bent down, scooped her big ass up, and dumped her in the tub.

A lot of the water splashed out, but it was still about 3 inches over her head when she settled in the bottom.

The killer slowly let the water out as Camilla's eyes pleaded with him to hurry. As soon as it looked like she was right on the edge of drowning, the waterline suck below her nose, and she furiously sucked in air.

Laughing, the killer taunted, "Breathe Shamu, breathe." The image of a whale coming up to get a much-needed breath was too much for the killer. He leaned on the sink, laughing hysterically for a full five minutes.

When he finally had himself under control, he took the bag off of his back, and prepared to give the sergeant the most painful death possible.

First thing he had to do was make sure she couldn't make enough noise to alert a neighbor.

He took out a super-fast drying, extra strength, super glue, and began smearing it all over her mouth. He needed it to be hard before the drugs wear off.

He then took out a long, thin cable cord, and two metal bars, 18 inches in length. The killer looped one end of the long cord over the showerhead, then pulled out two smaller lengths of cord. He secured the metal bars to the sergeant's wrists and ankles using the two small cords. He looped the thin, long cord around the bar secured to the officer's wrists and pulled tightly until she couldn't move her arms up or down.

He stood back and admired his handiwork. He still needed to do something with her legs so she couldn't bang the metal bar into the tub.

He took out another thin cord and tied it to the metal bar in between her ankles. He then took her long hair and tied it into a knot. He pulled the cord until her legs were about a foot above the lip of the tub, and then secured the cord to the knot in her hair. This way, in order for her to lower her legs, she would have to rip all of her hair off of her head.

Right now, all the weight of her ham hock-like legs was pulling her hair, and tears of pain were streaming down her face. In a matter of minutes, she would be able to express her pain, and that's when the real show could start.

The killer sat on the sink waiting, and about five minutes later, Sgt. Rodriguez started twitching. She was fully recovered and moaning after another five minutes. She tried to be perfectly still because every time she moved, her legs would pull on her hair more. She solved this problem by folding her legs almost up to her face.

"So, Sarge, how have you been doing?" asked the killer.

Camilla mumbled and pleaded with her eyes for the killer to show mercy.

"I guess by now, you have figured out that I'm the Prison Guard Killer. And you, Sgt. Camilla Rodriguez, are a prison guard. So, I guess by definition, I have to kill you."

The Sergeant started shaking her head back-and-forth and looking around like she expected someone to jump out and save her. The killer reached in and started rubbing her breasts. "But first, we're going to have a little fun."

Being the freak, that he knew her to be, Camilla started showing signs of becoming aroused. She started hunching up and down, and her nipples got really hard. Staring the killer in his eyes, she started moaning in pleasure. Maybe she thought that this was all some sex game that she was going to survive.

The killer pulled her right nipple until it was stretched as far as it would go. Then, as the Sarge's moans got louder, fast as lightning, the killer took the razor-sharp blade that he had secretly pulled out and cut it off. While she was screaming into her own mouth, he reached over and cut her left nipple off too.

If she had the ability to open her mouth, she would have brought the whole trailer park running to help her. As it was, she was still making too much noise.

He went back to her bedroom and peeked out the window to make sure none of the neighbors had heard. Everything was quiet and dark, so he went back to work.

She was bleeding like a stuck pig, so he slathered some of the crazy glue on her breasts, so she didn't die too fast. He wanted her to stay alive and conscious for as long as possible.

Since her legs were already raised and spread, he started rubbing her between her legs. He reached under her and drained all the water out of the tub. Unbelievably, the Sarge started getting wet. She again, started moaning and hunching up and down. It was almost like she had decided to focus on the last bits of pleasure she could get if she was going to die anyway.

The killer kept going until she climaxed. The freaky slut was using her legs to pull her hair and make the climax more intense. He started rubbing her faster and harder until her eyes started to roll in her head.

Camilla seemed to be having the time of her life. Hunching and moaning like she was with a real lover. She didn't see the killer remove the stopper of liquid from the bag because her eyes were shut in pleasure. As soon as she started climaxing this time, the killer stopped rubbing and dumped the acid all over her vagina.

Her body seized from the pain. Her legs locked out so hard that it ripped the hair right off of her head. Now, the bucking and hunching was from pain instead of pleasure.

The metal bar kept her from being able to close her legs, so the killer could see how much damage the acid was causing. Smoke was coming out of her as the acid bubbled its way through her flesh.

Again, the smell of cooking bacon floated in the air. The bacon smell was a huge improvement over what she normally smelled like. It also made the killer crave a Wendy's Jr. Bacon Cheeseburger.

The acid would continue to eat away at her if it was left unchecked, but he was not done with her yet. He took out the compound to stop the effects of the acid and dumped it between her legs. It took a minute to reach all the places the acid had reached, but eventually, the Sergeant calmed down and stopped shaking.

Next, he pulled out a small box with two cords coming out of either side of it. On the end of one cord was a male plug, and on the end of the other cord was a female plug.

He reached in the tub and slapped the Sergeant in order to get her attention. "Okay Camilla. We are almost done here. This box right here is a modified step-down transformer. I am going to use it to cook your fat ass in this tub." He walked over and plugged it into the wall outlet.

The killer went on explaining. "If I tried to electrocute you straight from the wall socket, you would die in a few seconds, or the circuit breaker would trip, and nothing would happen. But I want you to suffer for as long as possible. So, I'm going to plug your hair dryer into this other end, then I'm going to fill the tub up again, and then I'll cut this box on and drop the hair dryer into the water with you. The transformer will make the current and the volts low enough to slow cook you to death." The killer smiled like he was giving her the best news in the world.

"And the best part, I can control the box with my phone. So, I'll leave you to cook for a few hours and then I'll turn it up and blow your fat ass to kingdom come."

Without another word, the killer went about every task in the order he said he would do it in. When he dropped the blow dryer in, the lights dimmed a bit and a low humming sound seemed to float in the air.

The Sarge moaned a little, but the current was low enough that it would only create an uncomfortable feeling. That is, until the water started getting hotter and hotter. Then she was trying to pull herself out using the cord tied to the showerhead.

Amazingly, using her feet on one end and pulling the cord on the other, she was able to hold herself out of the water. "Damn, that's even better," said the killer.

He did something with his phone and within 30 seconds, the water was boiling.

The steam was rising up and cooking Camilla where she hung over the tub. She was jerking and screaming until she fell back into the water.

Quickly, the killer turned everything back down and the red, blistered, tired woman slumped in the cooling water, breathing fast and erratically.

"Camilla," said the killer. "It's been fun, but I have to go now. I'll be watching you as you die and enjoying every second of your pain." He turned the current up just enough to make her moan in pain and then left.

He made it back to his car without incident and looked at the video. Camilla was once again braced above the tub. He turned the box up so that the steam engulfed her once again.

She thrashed as long as she could before falling into the tub again. The killer lowered the volts but only slightly lowered the current so that she was stuck in the water unable to move. He would hold her there until he got somewhere he could enjoy watching her slow death.

He put the phone up, turned the car on, and drove away with a smile of congratulations on his face.

CHAPTER 25

Walt kept his gun trained on the stranger as his eyes looked all over the house to make sure no one was hiding or trying to sneak up behind him.

As if reading his mind, the stranger said, "I am here by myself and I promise you, I am only here to help."

"How did you get in here?" asked Walt.

"Seeing as how I'm the one who trained the killer you've been chasing around, that wasn't hard to do."

Walt's eyes snapped back to the man who was sitting comfortably on his couch like he was just there for a friendly visit. And if he was worried about the gun Walt had pointed at his head, he didn't show it in the slightest.

Walt, not getting the tingle on the back of his neck that said danger, lowered the gun and studied the man more closely.

He was a white male, age somewhere in the mid-fifties. It was hard to tell anything else about him because he was sunk deep into the cushion of the couch.

"Stand up, take your coat off, and do a spin for me," Walt demanded. The man did it without hesitation or emotion. Now, Walt could see he was a little over six feet tall, maybe 170 pounds. He didn't have an ounce of extra fat on his body. And just from the little bit of movement, Walt could tell he was a trained soldier.

"Okay. Now put the jacket right there on the couch and go sit in the chair near the window." If the guy had put something in the couch, he wouldn't have access to it during this conversation.

"What's your name and why are you in my house?"

The soldier took his seat and got comfortable before answering. "You can call me Steve. And like I said before, I'm here to help you." Everything about the man, even his voice, screamed military.

"And how are you going to help me, exactly?" asked Walt, as he made his way over to the chair opposite the man. The chairs were not comfortable at all, but they held no hiding places and they, more or less, faced each other with the coffee table between them.

"Well, first off, I'm going to try to help you stay alive. Then, if you listen to what I have to say, I'm going to help you get your partner back."

Walt used all his skill to not show any emotion and maintain eye contact with the man. "You know how to bring people from the dead? I know the Government doesn't tell us everything, but I'm sure that would have leaked by now."

"Det. Rogers, your partner is not dead. The man you are chasing has no beef with her, therefore, he wouldn't kill her. It's that simple. I wouldn't call it a game he's playing with you, but everything he is doing has a purpose."

Walt refused to let the hope swell up in his chest. For all he knew, this was the killer's partner in crime. "What makes you an expert on what this guy will and won't do?"

The man let a small smile show for a brief second. "I am the one who recruited him into the CIA when he turned 16 years old."

The silence that followed that announcement was absolute and extended for several minutes.

Finally, with a small laugh, Walt said, "The CIA? The CIA? Come on man. Who the fuck are you and why are you fucking with me?"

The man, (Steve was definitely not his real name,) sat forward with a serious expression on his face. "If you bear with me, I will tell you a story that will blow your mind. It will have parts that are hard to believe, but if you listen to the whole story, you will know that I speak the truth."

Walt was tired, still mourning the death of his partner. But if he could get even one truthful fact out of this guy, then he owed it to Ann to listen to him.

"Do you have any form of ID? Anything to prove you are who you say you are?" asked Walt.

"Twenty years ago, you were recruited by a man named Matt Burdette. You were in Germany at the time, investigating a murder involving a soldier. You turned him down because of the loyalty you had for the Military Police. If you had accepted the offer, you would have been sent to Russia, where we would have been part of the same spy network. I was recruited ten years before you and was Matt's right-hand man."

The man paused and looked Walt in the eyes. "Is that enough proof for you?"

Walt knew that no one outside of the CIA would have those details. "Yeah, that's good enough. Please, tell me the story."

The CIA soldier settled into the hard chair and said, "I want to be clear on something before I start. The equipment that your people found while searching your home was third generation prototypes. Your killer was working on the ninth generation when he stopped. There isn't a doubt in my mind that he is either recording this conversation or listening to it live."

Both men looked around the part of the house that was visible. The man laughed and leaned forward. "The fifth generation listening device was embedded into a clear paint. One swipe of a brush in each room of this house and he can hear everything. So, with that being said, I will not tell you his name or any identifying information about him. Bottom line, I don't want him to kill me and my family."

Walt frowned. "If you're not going to tell me who he is, then why are you telling me this story?"

"To convince you to stop." Shaking his head, the man said, "To convince you that you can't win, and you are depths out of your league. To possibly get your partner back in one piece before you do something stupid that really gets her killed."

195

Walt sat looking at the man. Under all that confidence, Walt could feel the fear rolling off of the man. "One last question and then I'll leave you alone to tell your story."

When the man inclined his head for Walt to continue, he asked a simple question.

"Why?"

Walt knew the man could go several different directions with his answer, and he was curious to see which one he would take.

"I'm almost afraid for him to hear me say this, but I think that you can actually stop him. Not because you are a threat, but because I think you can breach his walls."

Hearing his answer, Walter nodded, leaned back, and said, "Let's hear it."

The man took a deep breath and then started to talk.

"We have been watching this kid since he was nine years old. That's when he graduated from high school, scoring a perfect score on every exit exam. He graduated from college at the age of twelve with a Criminal Justice degree and a degree in Computer Forensics. Again, perfect scores all around. He started playing chess at age ten. After six months of learning, he never lost a match. He actually rewrote the program for the Chessmaster computer series, which is the program most of the chess masters use to train, because he said it was too easy. The franchise paid him $40 million for the rights. By age 16, he was the best computer programmer the world had ever seen. And by rule, also the best hacker. The CIA sent me to ask him to develop a way to secure a network from any level of attack. He finished it in five days. We pulled the best hackers from the N.S.A., and they couldn't get past the first of five levels. On his own, he started developing residential and building security systems. To this day, not one building protected by his systems has ever been breached. He had begun working with us so often that we just assumed that, when he turned 18, he would join us. He went into the military instead. The Marines to be exact. He excelled on every level. Endurance. Hand to hand. Weapons. Explosives. Infiltration. Exfiltration. Tactics. And Computer Warfare. He ended up in Military Intelligence where he became their own personal 'think tank'. Almost every safeguard this country has, was developed by him. They started sending him on covert missions where he would figure out how to kill people without ever being in the same room or even the same building as them. By the time he was 23, he had over 300 confirmed kills and none of those were face to face. He is a master strategist. The top Generals would call him in and give him a goal with few parameters, then he would develop plans that, to this day, have never failed. They say he would sit for hours just thinking, and then he would lay out a strategy that was fool proof."

Walt said, "So, the Government turned him into a killer. But what made him turn on the country he is supposed to be serving?"

"Well, it might be because the country turned its back on him first," said the CIA man.

"Explain," demanded Walt.

"This kid was traveling all over the world, doing missions for us and the military. As a side hustle, he was developing top of the line spy gear for the CIA to use against our enemies. Then one day, a call comes in from the President, asking for a personal favor. It seems the governor of North Carolina, who happened to be a personal friend of the President, was having a lot of problems in his prison system. Guards and inmates getting killed, corruption all over the place. And it seemed that, no matter who they replaced, it kept getting worse and worse. So, the governor wanted a covert agent dropped in, for a max of two years to help pinpoint where the problem was. The President wanted the best, but the agent also had to be young enough to go to the youth facilities. The Director of the CIA asked Military Intelligence for a meeting with their 'golden boy'. When everything was explained to him, he agreed on the spot. He sat down with a team from both agencies and the governor, and they worked out a plan of communication that would only include the governor's office and the kid. Everything was signed off on and into the system he went. The governor's office created an identity and closed a cold case with your killer taking 26 years for the murder. Here is where things started going wrong."

"Hold on," said Walt. "You want something to drink?" The agent asked for water and Walt went to get both of them a drink.

When Walt came back, he handed the agent his water and sat, talking a sip of his own. "So, if the deal was for two years, how did he end up serving ten? Well, **if** it's the guy, Manuel Adams, that a witness says is the killer."

The agent leaned over and grabbed a coaster from the stack on the table. Leaning back after sitting his glass down, he said, "I'll get to that part, but let me fill in some of the details."

Clearing his throat, the agent continued.

"Mr. Adams, as we'll call him, did exceptional work. In the first two years, he sent out information on gangs, officers, and administrators. Everyone trusted him because he could play any role. He knew who had what, and how they were getting it. He knew which officers were bringing in contraband and which officers were having relations with the inmates. He was so good at his job that the governor talked the President and the Director of Military Intelligence into keeping him in. All of us at the lower levels were told he volunteered to stay in. Plus, none of us knew exactly what his cover was or where he was being housed. The problem was, Mr. Adams thought something was wrong because the two-year deadline passed by, and he was still in. The governor's office got a lawyer to go visit him and told Mr. Adams that the CIA and Military Intelligence agreed to keep him in as long as necessary to clean up the prison system. The governor told us that he wanted to stay in until he finished the job. The governor was playing both sides to keep our guy inside. He sent out report after report from all the prisons they were sending him to. He started asking other inmates what happened to the people that he had previously sent the governor reports on. He found that nothing had been done to any of the officers, and most of the inmates were still running free. As you can guess, he was confused and a little angry. Here he was, wasting away in prison, and all the people he reported on were still carrying on their corrupt ways. By this time, he had been inside for five years, and we had all stopped getting reports about him for a couple years before this point. None of us knew anything about it until he was released and pulled in for his debriefing."

"Hold on," interrupted Walt. "So, you knew he had went in, but you had no knowledge of the fact that he spent ten years in until he got out?"

"That is correct," answered the agent. He took another sip of water before he continued.

"You have to understand, in covert operations, we might not cross paths at all in our careers. Plus, he wasn't officially in the CIA even though he worked with us a lot. Guys would ask about him, request his help with something, and they would be told that he was busy on assignment. Anyway, if you remember, all the communication was with the governor. So, all the information everyone else was getting was second hand. Come to find out, the governor was using the information to blackmail officers and administrators, and they started using the gangs that Mr. Adams identified to funnel the contraband into the prisons to pad everyone's pocket. When the new governor came in, he picked up right where the old one left off. That's why, when you went to talk to him, he wouldn't give you the time of day. He knows exactly who the killer is because he's killing all the guards that he reported on."

The agent paused like he could sense that Walt wanted to say something.

"So, you mean to tell me that you motherfuckers have a victim's list and you're doing nothing about it? What the fuck? I know the spy world is crazy, but that is CRAZY!"

"We all have orders to follow, and our orders are to leave him alone," said the agent.

Walt was seething, but he wanted to hear all of it before the man decided to leave. "How did he eventually get out? In the record it shows that he was granted a pardon."

"Mr. Adams got his hands on a cell phone and decided to go around the governor to see if the orders he was receiving were legit. He called his boss at Military Intelligence and found out that the governor had been telling them that he wanted to stay in. His boss got to work and within a few weeks, Mr. Adams was released. Unfortunately, it wasn't before Cpt. Robert Dennis and his goons kicked his ass and put him in the hospital. He could have killed all of them on the spot, but he had been given strict orders not to harm any guards."

Walt leaned back, shaking his head. "Unbelievable. No wonder he's going around killing people. I hate to say it, but I'd be tempted to kill some people too, if I was in his position."

"I'm not done yet," said the agent, taking a deep breath. "When he was released and healed, he requested a meeting with the former governor, the new governor, his boss at Military Intelligence, and the Director of the CIA. Only they know what happened in that meeting, but I can tell you, it didn't go well. A week after the meeting, Mr. Adams was gone without a trace. One of the CIA accounts was mysteriously shut down and $40 billion disappeared. Everyone knew who it was, but they felt it was a phase and he would eventually calm down. Then people started seeing system failures on some of our networks. Then the bodies started popping up. Agents assigned to the control of physical assets were turning up dead and all traces of the inventory wiped from the system. Billions of dollars in property, gone. Because the people who knew where it was located were dead. Cars, houses, guns, cameras, listening devices." The agent paused before saying, "Prisons."

"Wait, what? What do you mean prisons?" asked Walt.

"Right before Mr. Adams went in, he had developed an underground prison system to hold people that we needed to keep off the grid. Terrorists, mobsters, anybody that if people knew where they were, their followers would be tempted to try and get to them. The prisons took eight years to complete and after they were done, all traces of them were wiped from the system. It would be a waste of time and money to build them and then leave their locations out for any half- ass decent hacker to find. All of it went exactly by the plans of Mr. Adams and only three people knew the whereabouts of the prisons…he killed the other two."

"So, the prison that Ann was held in, no one knows where it is other than the killer?" asked Walt.

"That is correct," answered the agent, "And rumor has it, there are over 500 of them in the country."

They were both quiet for a while, trying to absorb the information transfer.

Walt decided to speak first. "You have given me a lot of information and for that I am thankful. But nothing you have given me explains why you think Ann is still alive or will help me stop this guy."

"Well, I told you from the beginning that I wouldn't help you. Like I said, he **is** listening. If he thought for one minute that I would try to help you, he would kill me. About Ann…she is innocent, and she is a good cop. From what I know of him, he wouldn't kill her unless it served his purpose to do so. I know what his end game is, or at least was. If he is forced to kill to save himself, then he will kill without hesitation. But unless you are on that list, or get in the way of his kill, he won't go out of his way to hurt you."

Walt thought on that for a minute. "Alright. So, why do you think I'm the one who can stop him?"

The smile flashed on the agents face. "I won't answer that because then he would probably kill us both."

Walt looked out of the window and was surprised to see the first lighting of the sky. He glanced at his watch and was shocked at the time. "Alright, Agent Steve. Anything else before you see yourself out?"

"Yeah. Let it go."

Walt looked stunned. "Let it go? Are you insane?"

"Detective Rogers. You are an excellent cop. You are a good man, and you are extremely smart. This guy is the best of the best. I'm going to fill you in on something that goes all the way to the top. The only reason you still have a job, hell your life, is because everyone thinks you will never catch him. And even if you do, he will never see a courtroom."

He paused like he was waiting for Walt to reach a conclusion. "You don't get it, do you?" the agent asked, looking at Walt in wonder. "You haven't figured it out yet? Maybe you're not as smart as everyone thought."

"What? What haven't I figured out? What don't I get?" Walt asked, getting upset.

"They want him back, you dumb motherfucker. Not to punish him. They want him to go back to work. He is the reason this country is so far ahead in all things Military. The people who run this country are waiting for him to finish his list, and then they are hoping that he will forgive them and come back to work."

After dropping that bombshell, the agent stood up and walked to the front door. With his hand on the knob, he turned around. "You're a good guy, Walter. But these people don't play. Even if the killer decides to leave you alone, if the brass feels like you are getting in the way, they will send someone to kill you. Don't lose your life over this." Then he was gone.

Walt sat and analyzed all the information and warnings he received. He reviewed all the conversations he had had with the killer. His mind turned it over and over until a smile lit his face.

When he came back to himself, the sun was up. He jumped up and shot out of the door. Without getting any sleep, he was energized. He jumped in his car and raced away.

Detective Walter Rogers had a plan.

CHAPTER 26

The first thing Walt needed to do was become anonymous. There was no telling how far the killer had gone to keep track of him, and he needed to make certain that he was in the clear.

All the movies and shows were right when it came to going off the grid; you had to have paper money. Walt looked at his watch and saw that the bank had been open for ten minutes.

Five minutes later, he pulled into the local branch. He walked in and went straight to the bank teller.

"Good morning, sir! What can I help you with today?" She had the sunny disposition and the bright smile of a pre-school teacher.

"Hi. I would like to withdraw some funds from my account."

Walt could have gone into the office and asked for operational funds, but that would have taken too long. He needed money fast to set his plan in motion.

"Alright, sir. Just fill out this form and have your identification ready." Walt completed the form and passed it back to the teller with his police ID.

The teller looked at the amount and glanced up at Walter. "I'm sorry, sir. For this amount you will have to see one of the managers. Give me a second and I'll get one." She walked off with Walt's paperwork and ID. Within two minutes, she was flagging him over to one of the offices.

When Walt walked in, a tall, thin white man was standing up and reaching his hand out for Walt to shake. "How are you Detective Rogers? Sorry for the inconvenience. It's just policy that anything over $5000 has to be cleared by a manager."

"That's fine. I have more than enough in my account to cover the $15,000. I would like all $100 bills and I'm kind of in a hurry if you don't mind." He didn't have time for gladhanding or small talk. Every minute he spent bullshitting, the killer could be trying to figure out what he was up to.

"Certainly, Sir." The manager nodded to the teller, and she hurried off to complete the transaction.

"So, Detective. I've heard your name on the news about the investigation into that serial killer going around killing all those prison guards. I sure hope you guys catch him pretty soon." He was looking at Walt like he expected him to fill him on the whole investigation.

"Sorry sir, but it is our policy to not give out information on an ongoing investigation." Walt really didn't want to be rude, but he didn't have time for this shit. "How long is this going to take? I've counted $500,000 in drug money in the same amount of time it's taking this bank to give me $15,000."

"Oh. Um, I'm sure it won't be much…oh, here she is now." The teller came bustling back into the room with a medium sized envelope in her hand.

"If you will just sign here, you can count the money to make sure…"

Walt cut the teller off. "It's good. I don't need to count it." He signed the paper, and she gave him a receipt and the money.

He nodded at them both and headed for the office door.

The manager said, "Detective Rogers, if you need anything else…"

Walt kept going and said over his shoulder, "No, I'm good." He didn't wait around to chat anymore. He sped up to get out of there.

His next stop was the airport. He knew that his car was being tracked, so he needed to get a car without all the GPS stuff on it. There was a rental car place that had just the kind of cars he needed.

He ended up leaving his car in long term parking and walking the half mile to the rental car company.

As soon as he walked in, he got right to business to forestall any idle chit chat. "Alright listen," he said to the young woman who had smiled and looked him up and down as he came in. "I don't have a lot of time. I am a cop and I need a car without all that GPS and computer stuff in it. I would love to get that 1995 Ford Explorer you have right there in the front."

She was an extremely attractive white woman who was the spitting image of Carrie Underwood. Walt was hoping that she would sense the urgency in him and skip all the bullshit. For once, he caught a break. She switched from sultry sex goddess to businesswoman in the blink of an eye.

"Yes sir, officer. Can I see some identification?" Walt showed her his SBI ID. "Okay, how long do you need the rental and how do you wish to pay?"

"I want to pay in cash, and I'll need it for three days."

"Very well. There is a $1000 security deposit for all cash rentals, and the rate is $35 a day. So, the total will be $1105. All I need is the money and a signature, and you can be on your way."

Walt paid the money and signed all the necessary forms. She gave him the keys and his receipt with her name and phone number written on it. "If you need anything at all, please don't hesitate to call me. I'm sure I could be of service." She was very beautiful and was probably not used to men ignoring her, but Walt had a lot on his plate. Not to mention, he was all of 15 years her senior. He smiled, nodded, and was out the door.

He popped the hood to check the engine out and make sure he wasn't renting a lemon. He looked under the SUV and inspected all the tires. He climbed in and turned the Explorer on. He climbed back out and looked up under the vehicle to make sure nothing was leaking. Everything seemed to be in order, so he jumped in and drove off.

The next stop was Walmart. He went straight to the men's clothing section when he arrived. He grabbed a pair of jeans, a T-shirt, some underwear, socks, and a pair of New Balance tennis shoes. He paid cash for everything and went into the dressing room to change clothes.

It might be paranoia, but if they had paint with microchips in it, why not have something they could put on clothes that was undetectable. Anyway, he wasn't taking any chances.

He then walked to the electronics department and bought three throwaway cell phones. He didn't grab three of the same phones or take the phones from the front of the display. If the killer did track him to the store, he would expect him to buy a phone. There are ways to figure out a person's phone number if you can track the purchase of the phone. Once you have the number, it's easy to track a person's movements. Walt planned to make it as hard as possible on the killer. Every second he could stay off the radar, the better the chances his plan would succeed.

The killer was super smart, there wasn't any doubting that. The problem was, everyone was treating him like he was God. Like he saw and heard everything. It was very difficult to figure how much of that was people being paranoid and how much of it was fact. Walt knew the killer would start to wonder what he was up to. He really didn't even care if the killer tracked him. What he needed was for the killer to not focus on Denise. Or not yet anyway.

The success of the plan would really depend on how Denise played her role. And now, he needed to get Denise alone somewhere so he could tell her his plan without the killer being able to listen in. Still trying to come up with a way to reach her, he left Walmart and headed towards her neighborhood.

This part was tricky because Denise lived in a cul-de-sac. The killer could put a camera a quarter mile away and still monitor every car that entered her neighborhood. If the killer tracked Walt to the Explorer, it could jeopardize the plan if he saw it going towards her house.

Walt called Sgt. Gould of the Raleigh Police Department on one of his new phones. After a few pleasantries, Walt explained what he needed, and the Sarge readily agreed to help him. After some promises of additional help from both sides, they hung up.

He pulled out a piece of paper and wrote a detailed note to Denise on what he wanted her to do. As he was finishing, a cop car pulled up next to the SUV. Walt rolled his window down, showed the officer his ID, and handed the note to the young man. He instructed the officer on what to do and stressed how important it was to get it done as fast as possible. After Walt was sure the officer understood the plan, he sent him on his way.

The plan with Denise was simple. He needed her to stay on the grid so the killer wouldn't become suspicious of her. But he needed her to disappear for about forty-five minutes so he could tell her the plan. He needed to get her in a safe area, away from all ears and eyes, so he could make sure she understands exactly what to do. Ten minutes later, the cop drove back past and gave him the sign that everything was good.

Another ten minutes passed before Walt saw Denise's Benz drive past. He waited another two minutes before following her because he knew where she was going. Her first stop would be the Walmart that he had just left. She was to buy all new clothing but to keep the other clothes with her in a bag. She was then to drive to a local park that he used to communicate with his Confidential Informants. There was a whole section of the park that was under the canopy of trees and had no cameras.

He told her to go in the front gate so the killer would be less curious about why she was there. Walt would go in another way that was deeper in the woods, and they would meet up on a bench in the designated area.

Walt headed straight for the park because he would have to hike through the woods, whereas Denise could just walk on the open grass. Depending on how long she took, at the store, she could still beat him to the meeting spot.

When he arrived on the back road that would take him to a spot where he could hike from, he slowed down so he wouldn't miss the trail. It was very hard to spot, even in the daylight. But if he could find it, it would make the passage so much easier.

Finally, he spotted it. He drove about 100 yards past it, got out and walked back. He entered the trail and put his body on autopilot while he thought about the other aspects of the plan. He had brought one of the phones with him, but he wouldn't start anymore preparations until he knew for sure Denise would be in. This was a one-shot deal and all participants had to be fully committed.

He hiked for the better part of an hour so he could stay out of sight. He stopped when he could see the open area from the trees. Walt knew that, if the killer was there, he wouldn't see him anyway, but he still had to look. As he looked around, he spotted Denise sitting on the bench. No one else seemed to be in the vicinity.

This was certainly not the time to notice, but being a man, it was hard not to admire how stunning Denise looked. She had almost the same outfit as Walt had. White T-shirt, blue jeans, and gray shoes. But Walt could admit, it looked a hell of a lot better on her.

Walt exited the woods and made his way toward Denise. It was amazing, but the closer he got, the better she looked. She couldn't have gotten but a few hours of sleep, but she looked radiant and well rested anyway.

When she saw him, she looked around nervously, and stood up to greet him with a hug. He accepted the hug but also gave her a quick kiss on the lips.

"Good morning," she said with a smile on her beautiful lips. "So, I'm guessing something else happened last night after I left you."

"Good morning. And yes, something did happen. I had a late-night visitor sitting in my living room when I got home."

"What!" exclaimed Denise. "Was it the killer?"

"No, it wasn't the killer. But it was someone who helped train him."

"Train? So, he is some kind of soldier?"

"Yes," said Walt. "But it goes a little deeper that that. Let me give you the highlights on what I learned because we don't have much time and I still need to go over the plan with you." Walt took the next ten minutes to tell her everything of importance that Agent Steve told him.

After he finished, Denise said, "Wow. So, we have the CIA, Military Intelligence, and the governor who all have reasons to keep this quiet. Well, now we know why no one would help us with freeing Timothy Washington. Do you really think they will kill you to get you out of the way?"

Walt looked deep into her eyes. "They will kill me, you, and anyone else who they feel is an obstacle to them getting him back. That's why I wanted to talk to you in person about this plan. Bottom line, if it works, both of our lives could be in danger."

Denise stared back. "What are you waiting for? Tell me the plan. I'm in this with you until the end."

Walt broke down the plan from start to finish. Explaining the part she would play as well as the parts of the other people he hoped to involve. She readily agreed with everything. Twenty minutes after Walt arrived at the clearing, he gave Denise another hug and kiss and sent her on her way.

He slipped back into the woods and made the hour-long hike back to the rented SUV. The whole walk, his mind was going over all he would have to do to make this thing work. The sad part was that Walt could set everything up perfectly, and the killer could still beat them in so many different ways. There was no way to plug all the holes or to know how far of a reach the killer had. One misstep or mistake and a lot of people would die. He had to be very careful.

He made it back to the SUV and sat inside for another five minutes thinking before pulling out his phone and started to make calls.

Walt called Sgt. Gould again to see if he wanted in on the potential take down. "Hey Det. Rogers. Everything go okay with the officer I sent you?"

"Yes sir, it did," replied Walt. "Thank you so much for your help. Now I need to fill you in on a little plan I have been working on that will require some local help. It's a little unconventional, but I think it has a good chance of success."

"Okay," said the Sergeant. "Anything I can do to help, I'll do."

Walt told him about the visitor he had early that morning and told him to keep everything close to his chest or he could end up with a target on his back. He also filled him in on a few of the conversations that he had had with the killer. He outlined the plan that he had been trying to put together to catch the killer. Walt talked for about twenty minutes and then paused to hear the Sergeant's reaction.

"Well," said Sgt. Gould slowly. "It is a very good plan if you factor in everything you have told me. But it does rely on a lot of luck on our part."

"I know. I was hoping that you had some input to reduce the chances of this going terribly wrong," explained Walt.

"Listen. Let me talk to one of our SWAT leaders and see what he has to say. I know you guys at the SBI have your own, but our guys are more local and might have some better insight for us. I'll get back to you as soon as I can."

"This thing could end up going down tonight, so when you talk to your SWAT guy, let him know to prep his guys for a possible takedown."

"Will do. Talk to you in a bit." When the Sergeant hung up, Walt put the SUV in gear and drove back down the dirt road towards civilization.

Walt needed to talk to his boss at the SBI. The man was no kind of a field agent, but he could definitely move mountains, and be quiet while he's doing it. But the man was too arrogant and wouldn't go through all the steps to make sure he was clean. He would swear that nobody in their right mind would ever try to track a captain in the SBI. It wouldn't get you anywhere to point out that they were dealing with a psychotic, but smart, serial killer who had a God complex.

Walt decided to call one of the lab guys to go up to the captain's office and tell him to meet Walt in front of a coffee shop a couple of blocks from their headquarters.

When Walt was half a block away, he could see the captain standing on the sidewalk, looking up and down the street with a pissed off look on his face.

Captain William Graham looked like exactly what he was. An ex-jock, ex-frat boy, hopeful politician, who thought he was better than anyone else around him. He was one of those guys who would try to make Michael Jordan feel like a mediocre basketball player. He had no respect for anybody who didn't have the power to help him go further in life. Walt knew the man didn't like him, but he also knew that the captain's only hope of moving up to Director one day rested in the hands of his best Detective.

Cpt. Graham had joined the agency the same year as Walt. They were even the same age. But where Walt succeeded in the field, the captain was a wizard in the boardroom. He was a born politician with his All-American good looks and his superior personality. He always wore the proper clothes, and always said the right thing at the right time. His saving grace was that he was loyal and honest and could be trusted with any information. Walt was counting on these attributes as he pulled over to pick up his boss.

Walt wasn't in his normal car, so Cpt. Graham didn't even acknowledge the beat-up SUV. "Will, get your ass in here." The captain looked and did a double take when he saw Walt in the explorer.

Will gave the SUV a once over and then opened the door like he was afraid of catching something. "What the fuck, Walt? Where is your car? And what the hell is up with all this cloak and dagger bullshit you have going on?"

As Walt pulled away from the curb, he said, "Shut the hell up until we get to where we are going and I'll fill you in." Will wouldn't have taken this kind of talk from most people, but Walt knew the captain would take whatever he dished out.

"And where exactly are we going? I have stuff to do, you know. Some of us don't have the luxury of riding around in clunkers all day doing nothing."

Walt just gave him his most hateful look. And Will threw his hands up in defeat and stayed quiet.

He drove for about ten miles before pulling into the YMCA parking lot. By now, Cpt. Graham knew something major was going on, so he stayed quiet and got out when Walt did.

They both made their way inside and Walt flashed his credentials to be allowed access to the locker rooms. Walt put a finger up to silence his boss and pantomimed taking his clothes off. Will gave him a questioning look but did what Walt told him.

Will got down to his boxers and socks and then stopped. Walt motioned for him to remove it all. Rolling his eyes, he turned his back to give the man privacy. Walt heard a locker close and tossed Will a towel to wrap around himself. Walt then led him to the sauna. They both stepped inside the empty area.

"Now Will," began Walt. "I don't have time for your shit. I'm going to fill you in on what's going on and tell you what I need you to do. Just keep your fucking mouth closed for ten minutes and then you'll understand everything. Okay?"

Will closed his mouth and waited for Walt to continue.

Walt went on to tell his boss everything he had learned from Agent Steve. He could tell Will got excited by the possibility of Ann still being alive.

Ultimately, it had been Will's decision not to alert the media and ask the public for help in finding Ann. It hadn't been a popular decision and some of the guys on the opposing side could put a hurting on Cpt. Graham's career.

Walt finished up by telling Will about his plan and stressed the need to keep everything quiet. Walt explained that every camera or speaker could be used against them, and there was no telling what else the killer could hack or use to track them.

For once, his boss actually looked like he was willing to do whatever to help Walt. He wasn't deluding himself into thinking it was out of the kindness of his heart. No. The captain knew, if he saved Ann, and caught the Prison Guard Killer, he was shoe-in for the next Director position that opened up.

"Anything you need me to do, all you have to do is ask."

"Good. Because I need you to…" Walt went on to outline exactly what he needed his boss to do. Now, all they needed was a body and the killer to reach out to Denise. Then they would have their shot at this fucker.

Walt did take everything Agent Steve told him to heart. He believed that the killer was exactly what the agent said he was. So, Walt wasn't going to take anymore chances. As soon as the killer was in his sights, Walt was going to end his ass.

CHAPTER 27

[Well,] Denise thought, driving away from the park. Once again, she was in a prime spot to mess everything up. First, it was freeing Timothy Washington in order to save Ann. Now, Walt has come up with this crazy ass plan that relies solely on her doing everything perfectly. This time, however, if she made a mistake, a lot of people would die.

Before leaving the park, she had gone into the bathroom and changed back into the clothes she had left home in. Walt had told her in that note from the cop, to go to Walmart and buy a cheap, brand-new outfit, all the way down to the socks and shoes. She was then supposed to drive to this park, find the bathroom and change clothes.

He instructed her to put the old clothes in a bag, along with her phone, and all her jewelry, go to a certain bench, and put her bag somewhere that she could see it, but far enough away that any listening devices would be ineffective. Denise had no idea what was going on, so she did everything the way Walt wanted it.

Finding out all that stuff about the killer had been mind blowing. Child genius. Super soldier. 'Think tank' for the military. This guy was a major asset, not just to this country, but to the whole world.

Then the betrayal. To keep him locked up for ten years so the governor and his cronies could get rich sending contraband into prisons. Denise would have been ready to kill some people too. And to think, these bastards had a list of everyone who was going to die, and they were content to let the killer carry out his plan. After all of this was over, she was going to have years of reporting to 'out' everyone who was responsible for this nightmare.

Arriving back at home, it was time to start the show.

She got the mail out of the mailbox and strolled into the house. Feeling like she had eyes on her, she went about her normal routine to prepare for a Monday morning. While she was eating breakfast, she tried to call Walt on his cell phone. Of course, there was no answer, but she left a message asking if another body had popped up yet.

The killer did tell them that he was going to kill another guard, but so far, nothing had been on the news about a new death. The Wardens should have still been making all of the guards call in and report that they were okay, but as short of staff as most prisons in the state were, Denise was sure it would be easy to get sidetracked.

Next, she called her producer and asked if anything had been heard. When she received a negative, Denise told her that, unless something came up, she wasn't coming into the station today.

Denise worked out in her personal gym. Well, the room where she kept her workout equipment. After that, she soaked in a nice, hot bath and tried to call Walt again. He didn't answer again, so she left him a message, asking him to call her as soon as he was free.

About 12:00pm, she decided to go take a nap. She thought that she would just lay, staring at the ceiling, but she drifted off to sleep pretty fast.

She woke up to the beep of her phone, signaling an incoming text. Even though everything she did that morning was to push for this moment, her heart still did a somersault when she saw the text from the killer.

It was short and sweet; 'You have work to do. Do it.'

Denise sat up and grabbed the phone. She saw that a video had been attached to the message. She clicked on the video and saw a big, naked, Hispanic woman hanging in a tub of water. It appeared that the woman was being cooked alive, very slowly.

Denise hit the reply on the text and wrote back: 'Told you to find someone else. I am done being your BITCH!'

She put the phone back on the side table and laid back down. It wasn't even ten seconds later that the phone rang.

She looked at the screen and hit the button to ignore the call and laid the phone back on the table.

Just like all super-aggressive men, she knew that the killer would be pissed that Denise was ignoring him. About a minute later, a text came in.

'Last chance. You don't pick up, all today's deaths will be on you.'

She knew she was supposed to keep ignoring him, but she felt like it would be better to have the killer mad at just her instead of going after a bunch of innocent people. When the phone rang this time, she answered him.

Denise started in before the killer could talk. "You think I'm some weak woman who is scared of the big, bad boogieman? I said I'm done, and I meant it."

"Denise," said the killer. "I made a promise what I would do to you if you defied me. I really don't want to hurt you, but I definitely will if you make me."

"You know what?" asked Denise. "Walt was right about you. I know something bad had to have happened to you to turn you into this monster, but why threaten to kill other people when it's me you want?"

"Because I know that killing others that you see as innocent will hurt you more."

"But that's the point. Why do you want to hurt me?" asked Denise. "I did everything you asked me to do. I showed your snuff films. I tried to free Timothy Washington. I put out every message that you wanted out there. Now, I'm telling you, I am done!"

"Ms. McCarthy," the killer said, softly. "If you really mean that, I promise you, you will be in your own video before the night is out." He really did sound sad about that possibility.

"Well then, Mr. Adams, I can tell you now, I won't be laying down waiting for you. You sir, might have just made a promise that you can't keep." That said, Denise hung up, jumped out of bed, and started pacing back and forth in her bedroom.

She muttered to herself, "What the hell am I gonna do now?" She dialed Walt's cell phone again, and when it just rang, she said, "Come on, Walt. Pick up." He didn't answer so she left another message begging him to call her.

She threw the phone on the bed and ran to her dresser and pulled out a lock box. Even though she lived alone, she still kept her gun in a small combination lockbox. Now, she quickly put in the combination, and took out a black, American Tactical FXS 9 pistol. It was practically brand new as she had only taken it to an indoor range a few times to make sure she could handle it. She could. And she wouldn't hesitate to use it if the bastard showed up too soon.

With the gun in hand, and the safety off, she made a quick circuit of her house, checking every room and looking out every window. When she was fairly certain she wasn't in imminent danger, she returned to her room.

Denise put the gun on the bed and went to her closet to pack a bag. Denise was brave but she wasn't a fool. She was getting out of there before the killer firebombed her house and took a video of her burning body.

She packed enough for a few days and then jumped on the phone. She made one more call to her producer. "Hey," said Denise when the woman answered. "I am sending you a copy of a video I just received from the Prison Guard Killer. Since no one has reported it on air yet, I'm guessing no one has found the body of this officer. I have no idea who she is but get some people on it. I am gonna be gone for a few days, so don't do anything with the video until I get back."

"Okay, Denise," the woman said. "Is everything alright? I thought you would have been dying to go on air with something like this. I can send your crew to you if that is the problem."

"No, I'm good. I just have a few things to take care of before I can do anything with it. I might have to put another reporter on this one," said Denise.

The gasp from the producer was one of shock and outrage. "Absolutely not. If you don't do it, then I can promise you no one else at this station will do it. Go ahead and do what you have to do, and we'll talk about this when you come back. If another station breaks the news on the woman's identity, I'll get someone to cover for you until you come back. Anyway, the only way that video plays is if you report it, or you die."

"Thanks," said Denise before hanging up. She knew her producer was being serious. If Denise did die, the woman would put that video out there before the ink was dry on her death certificate.

She tried Walt one more time, but when it went to voicemail, she hung up.

She made sure she had everything she needed, checked the house to make sure everything was turned off, turned on the alarm, and was out the door.

Denise stopped once she was outside and just stared at her car. She had this horrible vision of the car exploding as soon as she turned the key. Deciding she watched too many action movies, but still trying to be smart about it, she hit the remote start button for the car. When nothing happened other than the car starting, she released the breath she didn't even realize she had been holding. She put her bag on the passenger seat, backed out of her driveway and left.

About five miles from her house, she pulled over in a gas station to fill up. The killer wasn't directly on her ass right this minute, so she took the time to make sure she was prepared to run later on.

She paid at the pump and then pulled over into the parking lot. Now all she needed was a place to stay. She dialed the number of a reporter friend of hers who had a second home in Durham that no one was using at this moment but was fully furnished.

Her friend, Ashley, picked up on the second ring. "Hello Ms. Superstar! I thought you had forgotten about us little girls."

Laughing, Denise said, "Ashley. Hello. And you know I could never forget about you."

"I heard that Channel 5 is treating you pretty good. Big money. New car. Maybe you can put in a word for me."

Ashley Kirt was a gorgeous, brown skin woman with a heart of gold and long silky hair most women would kill for. At 35, she was a little younger than Denise, but while working together at Channel 3, they had become fast friends. Ashley had a great sense of humor and a smile that was both beautiful and contagious.

"Girl, if I thought for one second you were serious, I would snatch you up today." Ashley was the co-anchor for the 6:00pm news and was probably the reason 90% of the audience watched the show. "Anyway, I need to ask you for a huge favor."

"Denise, you know anything you need, all you have to do is ask. You're my big sister."

"Ashley, I need you to understand that this is serious. To be honest with you, it could be very dangerous. For that reason, I need this to stay between us."

Ashley sobered up immediately. "What is it, Denise? If I can help, you know I will."

Denise took a deep breath. "The Prison Guard Killer is trying to force me to keep showing his videos. Last night I told him I was done because I couldn't keep promoting him or his message of violence. I told him to find someone else. He said that he would send me a video today and if I didn't go live with it, he would make me the star of the next video he makes."

"Oh my God, Denise! Do you think he was serious?" asked Ashley.

"He sent me a video this afternoon and I ignored his text and calls. He threatened to kill more people if I didn't answer, so I finally took his call. The conversation went to hell pretty fast, and he promised to kill me before the night was out."

"Oh no, Denise! What do you need?"

"I need somewhere I can go that has no connection to me, so I can hide out for a few days. I was wondering if I could use the house in Durham?"

"Of course you can, Denise. There is a false bottom on the plant hanging to the right of the steps. Turn it, and the key is inside. If you need anything at all, call me and I'll be there as soon as possible."

"Thank you so much, Ashley. I love you girl, and I promise to call if I need anything."

"I love you too, sweetie. Now get over there so you can be safe."

They both disconnected and Denise pulled away from the gas station. It was only about a twenty-minute drive, so Denise concentrated on driving safely instead of fast.

She made it to Ashley's house and found the key right where she said it would be. As far as hideouts went, this house was a massive she-shed and fit Ashley perfectly.

If this house had been in a more popular area, it would have cost millions. It was Ashley's own private sanctuary and was perfect for entertaining. It sat on five acres of open fields dotted with woodland. It contained an indoor/outdoor pool and a pool house. The inside had an open floor plan but had three different wings to separate the three suites. An outdoor kitchen and bar on the pool deck guaranteed that fun could be had outdoors as well as indoors.

No matter how many times Denise saw the home, her chest filled with pride for her friend's ability to design beautiful homes. Denise opened the door and sent up a small prayer of thanks to God for sending this small piece of Heaven down to Earth.

She made her way to one of the guest suites, which she had stayed in before, and threw her bag down on the queen-sized bed. She turned on the 60-inch T.V. and switched it to Channel 3 news. It was hours until her friend would be on, but she wanted to show Ashley and Channel 3 a little loyalty.

Denise stripped down and padded naked to the bathroom. She turned on the oversized showerhead and activated the phone Walt had given her.

She hit the speed dial button to dial the only number saved in the phone and waited for it to be answered.

"Did you get all of that?" she asked Walt when he answered the call.

"Yes, and you are doing an amazing job. I have men trying to track down the identity of the woman in the video. I'll let you know what we find. In the meantime, keep up the good work and we'll have this asshole tonight."

"Alright. You better not let this bastard get to me. If he kills me, I will haunt you for the rest of your life."

"Denise. It will be dangerous; you knew that going in. We will do everything in our power to keep you safe."

"You know, one of these days we have to have a real first date."

Walt laughed and said, "How about tomorrow night?"

"It's a date. Bye Walter." He wished her luck and they both hung up.

Denise said out loud, "Great. Now all I have to do is wait on a serial killer to come find me."

CHAPTER 28

Everything was set. The trap was baited, and now all they needed was for the killer to show his face.

Walt had been going nonstop since he dropped his boss back at the coffee shop. He picked up a lab guy and drove him out to Denise's friend, Ashley's house to set up surveillance on the property. Denise had been sure that her friend wouldn't mind, but Walt had actually talked to the woman before Denise had. He was not going to set up a full-scale operation, which might result in death, on someone's property without their permission. As soon as he explained the reasoning behind the request, she agreed to help her friend in anyway possible. Walt told her to expect a call from Denise and act as if she was surprised to hear from her. He also told Ashley that under no circumstances was she to go to the property until he called her to tell her it was safe.

Walt and the tech guy made their way to the house and got to work. They had motion sensors covering every inch of the house and grounds except for the suite that Denise was staying in and the basement. She needed her privacy and there was a chance that the killer would wait a couple of days instead of trying for Denise immediately. They also had cameras and microphones on the grounds but none inside, just in case the killer hacked their security.

Sgt. Gould and Cpt. Graham, Walt's boss, had both gone and got new clothes, rental cars, and new phones. They showed up at the house about an hour after Walt.

"So, what do you guys think?" asked Walt. "Is it doable?"

"I don't like how wide open it is," said Sgt. Gould. "Normally, it would be a good thing because we can keep eyes on the suspect. Now we have no way of hiding our guys sneaking in behind him when he arrives." The Sergeant had talked to the Raleigh SWAT unit, and they had been briefed on what was going on. Right now, they were back at the station pouring over blueprints and arial photos to plan the best way to let the killer into the kill zone, and box him in.

Cpt. Graham spoke up. "I tracked down the neighbor when you dropped me off and they have given us permission to set up in their house until it's time for us to move. It's a vacation home, so no one is staying there at the moment."

"That's all well and good if we knew it was happening tonight," said Sgt. Gould. "We can't keep twenty cops a secret for a week. These SWAT guys will end up shooting each other within two days."

"This guy is all about honor, or what he sees as honor. He told Denise he would send her a video and if she didn't go live with it, she was next. He is going to do exactly what he said. Trust me on that," said Walt.

Will Graham looked around and said, "We really don't have a lot of time. The second the killer contacts Denise and she ignores him; she will call Ms. Kirt about this house. From that moment on, we can't have any movement in this area at all. So we need to get SWAT set up next door, and Walt and I need to get set up in the house before Denise gets here. If this doesn't happen tonight, then we will have to call this off and try something else."

Walt pulled out one of his phones and said, "Oh shit. Denise just got a text from the killer. We need to move, now." Walt had given Denise a chip to put into her phone that would turn the third phone into a clone of her original phone. He was able to see any texts, hear both sides of any calls, and use the camera option to see whatever it could pick up. He had instructed her to make several calls to his real phone, which was in the center console of his car at the airport, to make it seem like she was trying to locate him.

Sgt. Gould hustled back to his car while he phoned SWAT to tell them to move their asses because time was running out. Sgt. Gould would go to the station to oversee things from that end.

Walt, Will, and the lab tech raced back to get their cars and pull them into the garage at Ms. Kirt's house. Denise still had a few steps to make before she would place the call to Ashley, but they still had a lot of work to do.

They walked through Ashley's house to get a better feel of the layout. The blueprint didn't show any furniture, so if the killer made it this far, they wanted any advantage they could get. When they arrived in the basement, they began setting up computers and other equipment to monitor all of the security around the property. They also needed radios to keep in contact with the SWAT team. When they arrived at the neighbor's house, they would need to keep in constant contact in order to box the killer in because they wouldn't have any monitoring devices to look at. More importantly, they needed to communicate to keep Denise safe.

Walt had explained to Will about the device the killer had that could take over a security system. The tech guy had brought in some hardline devices that didn't connect to any network, but Walt didn't like them. He had seen some of the drones the military used, and if the killer had one, he would be able to see the lines running over the grass. It would be better if they could bury them, but they didn't have enough time.

They compromised, and Walt only used the hardline devices right around the house. He went out and hung cameras with night vision and thermal imaging at all four corners of the house. Since the house was white, he used white tape to hide the wires running up the walls. It only took about 15 minutes, and he was back in the basement with his co-workers.

He had been monitoring the clone phone and he let the other two men listen to the recording of the killer telling Denise that he was going to get her before the night was out. They in turn, told him that the SWAT team was ready and waiting at the neighbor's house for the call for them to seal off the property.

225

They had no idea when this was going down, but Walt was sure the killer would be there to collect Denise before daylight. Wanting everyone to be as fresh as possible, they agreed to take shifts where one man would watch the monitors and the clone phone, while the other two slept. Walt took the first watch shift.

Denise arrived about 30 minutes into his two-hour shift. She knew they would have their cars in the garage, so she parked in the front and walked in. He followed her progress with the motion sensors until she was in her suite.

She wasn't even in the room five minutes before she had called him to make sure he was getting all the information, and everything was good. They chatted for a couple of minutes and then hung up.

He turned and looked at the sleeping forms of his teammates. Walt made certain they were sleep, then went upstairs to have a quick word with Denise. He approached her door slowly, not wanting to disturb his team with a creaking, hardwood floor. Opening her door carefully, she showed no surprise at seeing Walt at the door.

Denise got up from the bed and motioned him to wait as she entered the bathroom. Walt was still standing outside of the room when she came back out with a robe on. She walked past him and motioned for him to follow her.

She made her way to the master suite. When Walt followed her in, she shut the door behind him. She turned to him and launched herself into his arms. Walt wasn't sure that was a good idea, because he became aware that the robe was all she had on. She also smelled of vanilla and he became aware that his body was trying to react. He had to force himself not to.

Denise pulled back and said, "This room is soundproof, but as you can see, the whole back wall, even the bathroom, is glass. So, we can talk but we have to hurry."

Seeing Denise like this made Walt forget what he had come up to talk to her about. Seeing the admiration in his eyes,

Denise smiled and said, "Hello... earth to Walter," while waving a hand in front of his face.

He snapped back to himself and said, "Sorry, but it's your fault I can't think right now." She gave him another smile before he continued. "Anyway. I wanted you to know that we have SWAT teams at your neighbor's house, and we have surveillance equipment everywhere on the grounds. Some of it is hard lined so he won't be able to hack into it and shut it down. It's twenty-three of us total with my boss and a lab tech staying in the basement. There are also four more SWAT guys with the vehicles somewhere close."

He paused and looked around the room. "Do you know if Ms. Kirt has a safe room on the property? It wasn't on the blueprint, but they normally don't put them on paper."

Denise walked over to a closet and opened the door. She pushed all the clothes over to the side to reveal a 3' x 2' door.

"There is a switch in the nightstand you have to hit to open the door. Once inside, there is another lock that can only be opened from the inside."

"Alright," said Walt. "That is perfect. When he comes, we will be moving fast. I will knock on your door, and I want you to come in here and lock yourself in. Take the drop phone with you and don't come out until I call you." He looked deep into her eyes and said, "If I don't make it, I'll tell some guys to call you and say 'date night' as a code for you to come out. Don't trust anyone else. We still don't know if he has help."

"Okay, Walt. I understand." Denise got up on her toes and gave him a long lingering kiss before she walked back to the door. At the door, she stopped and turned. "Remember, we have a date tomorrow. So, let me give you a reason to come out of this alive." She snatched the robe off, gave a sexy little spin, opened the door, and strolled back to her room door.

Walt's eyes stayed glued to her legs and ass as she strutted across the house. At her door, she looked back over her shoulder, blew Walt a kiss, and went back into her room, shutting the door behind her.

Walt had to take a few deep breaths before he made his way back to the basement. If he had any doubts before, that had just solidified that the killer was going to die tonight.

As it was still light out, he didn't think anything would be going down yet. He spent the rest of his shift keeping his eyes on the monitors and keeping in touch with SWAT.

By 8:30pm, it was completely dark, and the team started to have problems. The SWAT team leader called and said that members of his team had started feeling sick. They were vomiting and sweating and said they were feeling weak.

Walt asked him, "Did you guys bring your own food or did any of the guys eat food from the house?"

"I asked them, and they all swore they didn't eat anything from the house. We only had protein bars and water because we are only going to be here for tonight," explained the SWAT leader.

Walt had a sudden thought. He remembered something Agent Steve told him back at his house. He said that this guy could kill people without ever being in the room with them. He hadn't thought much of it, but when healthy men just get sick for no reason, a person will start looking at every possibility.

"Ask the guys who are sick if any of them felt like they were stung or bit by something." It was unbelievable, but it was possible.

After about thirty seconds, the SWAT leader was back on the phone. "What the fuck is going on here, Detective? All of them said it felt like a bee stung them within the last thirty minutes. Are we under attack? How did you know to ask that?"

"Shit!" yelled Walt. Standing up, he said, "The son of a bitch is out there. You need to get those guys to the hospital, ASAP. The guys who are healthy, strap all the way up, and go hunting because he is already hunting…Hello? Commander?"

Cpt. Graham asked, "What happened? Why isn't he responding?"

Walt looked at him and shook his head. "We were cut off." He looked at the equipment and saw that nothing was getting a signal. "He's here, and the bastard has jammed all our signals. Somehow, he figured out we're here. We all need to get into position. I'll go tell Denise to get into the saferoom."

They had already figured a plan if the signals were cut by the killer. The tech would stay at the hardline screens because that would be the last defense they had before the killer was in the house.

Cpt. Will Graham was to cut all the lights in the house off and turn on the spotlights on the outside so none of them could be backlight for a gun battle. The thing is, all of this was supposed to happen when they had the killer in the kill zone.

Walt was supposed to stay with Denise to be her last line of defense, but since there was a saferoom, he would escort her there, make sure she was secure, and then come back to help watch the screens, responding to any attacks.

He lightly knocked on Denise's door. When she opened it, they locked eyes. "Get whatever you need and let's go to the saferoom." Denise showed him the bag that was already prepared, and they walked to the saferoom. Denise walked to the nightstand and opened the drawer. She did something and Walt heard a click in the closet. Since all the lights were out, Denise had to feel around for a bit before she was able to open it.

She stepped in and looked back at Walt. "I'm not coming out until it's you, standing at this door. Be careful, and don't worry about me. The only way he can hurt me now is if he hurts you." She blew him a kiss and then shut the steel reinforced door. Walt heard the sound of a massive lock engaging as he walked off to return to the basement.

He stepped into the finished basement and saw both Will and the lab tech watching the screens. "Anything we need to worry about yet?"

The lab tech said, "Nothing has moved around the house, and we still don't have a signal, so we have no idea what's up with the SWAT guys."

"That's a mistake that might end up causing some guys to lose their lives," said Walt.

"What?" asked Will.

"We have no way to communicate with anyone now. When he took down the hotel security, they said their cell phones still worked. I didn't think he could take out our cell phones and our internet access."

Will looked at both of the other guys and asked, "Either of you have any suggestions?"

They all stood in front of the monitors, watching the screens and thinking. The explosion that rocked the night did all the thinking for them.

Walt told the two men, who were not field agents, "Arm yourselves and stay here. All you can do up there is get in the way. Stay here." He picked up a duffle bag and ran to join the fight taking place outside.

CHAPTER 29

The killer could only laugh at how smart the police believed themselves to be. For every crime that they solved, twenty-five of them never ended in a favorable solution. But yet they still think that they are smarter than the criminals.

Some people would say that what he was doing was done for a noble cause. It wasn't. It was pure and simple retribution for the crimes against him. He didn't care about the inmates. He didn't care about the dirty correctional officers or the gangbangers. He was doing what he was doing because he could, and no one could do anything to stop him. For the Government taking ten years of his life, he was taking his payment in the form of lives lost. And today, more lives would be sacrificed to pay him his due.

Walt and Denise thought they were smarter than him. Their knowledge of tracking capabilities was so limited, they thought rental cars and new clothes was all it would take to throw him off.

Raleigh, being a major city, had cameras everywhere. Not only that, but the killer had taken over four government satellites and placed them over North Carolina years ago. With the advances that he made in facial and voice recognition, and tracking, it was impossible for anyone to "get missing."

The thing is, Sgt. Det Rogers was so stupid, he gave himself away from the start. The killer had sat and watched the conversation between 'Agent Steve' and Walter. When the agent left, the detective sat there for over an hour, deep in thought. All of a sudden, this stupid ass smile spread across his face. He jumped up and ran out the house to his car and he didn't think that would send up a flag for the killer. [Again, dumb ass cop.]

Then, the detective takes all these elaborate steps to evade the trackers, but Walter was never not on a camera somewhere. The airport. The car rental agency. Walmart. The gas station. The coffee shop that sits in downtown Raleigh. The YMCA. [Who the hell trained these guys to go off the grid?] The only time he had to use a satellite was when they went into the park.

The killer had even used the cop's body camera to read the note that Walt had sent Denise. The killer knew where they were going every step of the way.

And Walt's smart-ass boss, Cpt. Graham, had put his cell phone in the locker but Walt had carried his into the sauna with them. By that time, he had the number to all three phones and was using the camera and microphone to see and hear everything that was happening.

Walt had even called Denise's friend, Ashley, about using her house to hide Denise in. The killer had hacked into the land records and had a blueprint and the arial views of the house within minutes. He also sent one of the satellites to just stay over the property.

By then, the killer was listening to Walt, Denise, Cpt. Graham, the SWAT Commander, and monitoring anything any of them accessed online. The idiots laid out every one of their plans. Every one of their safeguards and backups. They had no idea who they were up against. He could have killed them all inside of five minutes, but he decided to have some fun with them first.

The killer made some calls of his own. He also set up a base near Ashley's house that was within a mile of the house. He literally saw the SWAT team arrive because the satellite picked them up going into the neighbor's house. Plus, he had already put cameras in the neighbor's house. And a couple of other surprises for later.

He sat, watching the satellite feed all day, making sure everyone was where they were supposed to be. By the time dark fell, he had set up a few more surprises without even leaving his hideout.

[The local SWAT guys? Really.] He didn't think most of them would make it out of the house. The ones who did, would probably still die tonight. The only person the killer wanted to survive was Det. Rogers. Everyone else was fair game.

It was a foregone conclusion that the killer would have Denise by the end of the night. If everything went as planned, she would walk right into his hands. He could only pray that a stray bullet didn't kill her before he could get his hands on her.

The killer started off the night by bringing a couple of his friends out to play. He hated that he only had two left, but he might get lucky, and they would do the trick.

On one of his assignments for the CIA, they had tasked him with killing someone who was somewhere in a forty-story building. The intel they had, said the man was never more than twenty feet from a safe room. So, any frontal assault would just warn the man that someone was coming after him.

The morons didn't even have the guy's name. All they had was a description and a recording of his voice. And there was no way for him to get inside because all the residents had lived in the building for over five years. The staff knew everyone who was supposed to be inside.

Since all the cameras were hard wired, he couldn't even hack into the security to find the guy. Everything associated with the building was confidential. No names were used on any of the records. For weeks, he thought that this would be the job that he couldn't do.

One night, he was sleeping, and the answer came to him in a dream. A bee kept following him all over a building that he was walking in. As fast as he was, he couldn't catch it, and since it didn't seem to be trying to sting him, he left it alone.

He jerked awake and called his contact to see if he could get access to a lab. They were so desperate to kill this guy, they didn't ask any questions at all. A month later, he had developed the ultimate killing machine.

It was a drone the size of a small bee. It contained a poison sack that could be used to kill fifty people. The problem was, they were as easy to kill as a small bee. One whack of a newspaper or a lucky smack in the air, and the $100,000 drone was done.

The killer had put eight cameras and a mic inside of the drone. It took him another two weeks to become an expert at flying the thing. When he perfected it, he made ten of them and took off to get his target.

It was time consuming, and excuse the pun, drone work. But eventually, he was able to spot the guy and match his voice to what they had on record. The CIA told him to kill everyone in the apartment with the man. There were fourteen people in all: the target, his wife, eight security guys, and four children, two boys and two girls. Seeing as how they were paying him $20 million; he didn't think he could quibble about the occupants. He was on the fourth drone when he started the killings and went through four of them before he stung them all.

The poison inside of the drone worked on two systems in the body. The fast-acting part contained an agent that ate away at the digestive system. The slower-acting agent attacked your nerves and made you feel like you had a fire burning inside of you. Both would kill you and both were extremely painful. The CIA commissioned him to keep working on the drones to make them cheaper and harder to kill. He made them cheaper, but it was impossible to make them tough and still be able to fly it. They were content with the $8,000 price tag and they let it go.

The killer had hundreds of them, but only had two of them with him now. He sent the first one into the neighbor's house about fifteen minutes before sunset. Everyone was gearing up, and most of them were in the empty garage. It was attached to the house by an enclosed walkway and was where the SWAT guys had stored their gear.

He got ten of them before some hillbilly-looking motherfucker swatted the drone out of the air and then stepped on it. One of the younger black guys reminded him of this officer who was only alive today because he had cancer and was slowly dying anyway. The killer stung him three times just to make sure the look-a-like died first. He got four with the second one before it too was swatted. He couldn't get to the leader because he was in the basement talking to Walt. The last drone had just been terminated when the leader was summoned to come upstairs.

The killer sat and watched as the officers, one by one, became very sick. They had no idea what was wrong with them, and the leader was just as dumbfounded. They were asking each other what they ate and if any of them had some kind of virus they were spreading to the rest of them. The killer could tell that the SWAT leader didn't like what was going on and he watched him head back to the basement to place a call.

He listened in on the call by tapping into Walt's phone. Somehow the dumb ass detective figured out that he might be using insects to infect the SWAT team. Walt told them to get the men to the hospital. [Good luck with that,] thought the killer.

First off, they would die way before the doctors could even start to guess at what was wrong with them. Second, anyone trying to leave that house would get an explosive surprise instead of salvation.

The SWAT guys were dead as soon as they went into that house. The vehicles that dropped them off were parked about five miles away with four more officers who doubled as drivers and security. The killer had also set a few traps for the vehicles that he only activated after they left. When they returned, the killer thought even Katy Perry would be impressed with the fireworks.

Anyway, he had done all he could do from the safety of his hideout. He collected a few things that he would need, pulled on his mask, and went to enjoy the up-close part of his work.

. . . .

The masked man was enjoying himself immensely. The mines that were laid out around the house had a three second delay on them, so more people could enter the kill zone before it blew. Two officers came out of the house carrying what looked like the body of a young, black man. They were quickly followed by two more guys carrying another body. They were about fifteen feet from the house when the mines that were stepped on blew up.

"Holy shit!" said the masked killer. He laughed and shook with excitement as the body parts went flying in every direction.

He was across the street from the house in a blind that some hunter had conveniently put up, ten feet inside the tree line. Although, he couldn't figure what someone would be hunting this close to the street. If he had to guess, it was probably some pervert's platform that he used to spy on the women in the houses. Both of the nearby houses had pools and hot tubs outside, and from the high vantage point, he could see both properties clearly.

Anyway, it was time to get to work. There had only been six SWAT guys left alive and four of them had just been blown to bits. That left two still roaming around in the house. He switched the view on his scope from night vision to thermal to see if he could spot the last two guys.

"Shit," the masked man murmured. The heat from the fires made it impossible to single out the heat from a person. He broke the rifle down, stored it in its case, and climbed down to go do some close quarter killing. He had to be fast because those backup vehicles would be arriving at any minute.

He ran across the street and used the path that had no mines on it. Around back, one window had been left without mines under it so, if need be, he could get in. He climbed in the window and immediately heard voices coming from the front of the house.

"How in the fuck do we get backup here to help us?" the masked man heard someone ask.

"After that explosion, every cop in the county should be on their way. But we don't have any way of warning them about the trap," he heard another man say.

They continued to talk back and forth as he crept closer to the doorway. He did a fast peek and saw both men hunched at the front windows. He stood, watching them, planning out his route to deliver two kill shots and get out of there.

The masked man looked beyond the two men and saw the SWAT team vehicles coming down the street. The two officers jumped up and started waving the vehicles off and yelling at them to turn around. Of course, the drivers couldn't hear them and roared right on down the driveway.

The two SWAT officers remaining, dropped down and covered their heads just as the four vehicles exploded in a blaze of glory. The masked killer watched the whole scene with a giddy feeling in his heart and a smile on his face. There was nothing that could compare to watching cops die. Well, other than killing them of course.

Soon as the two men stood up to view the aftermath, he walked boldly into the room and shot both of them in the back of the head with his silenced pistol. When they were down, he shot them both two more times in the head to make sure that no miracles would happen today.

He looked up and watched the hellscape in front of him. Cars and trucks burning. Body parts laying all over the lawn. This property was one fucked up mess. Since this was an SBI case, the State would be held responsible for all the damage to the place.

Job done for now, he placed his gun in the small of his back and turned to go out the same way he had come in. He laughed because, as more cops showed up, they would trigger more surprises that would lead to more deaths.

He walked back into the room containing the window that was the only safe way out the house. When he bent down to step out of the window, a massive blow to the back of his head knocked him out cold. He never saw the man hiding behind the door with the crowbar.

CHAPTER 30

"Damn, I hope I didn't kill his ass," Walt said to himself. He had been just a few seconds too late to stop the killer from murdering the last two SWAT officers. When he looked around the door frame, the killer was double tapping the two dead bodies.

He wanted to just shoot the motherfucker and get it over with, but he needed to try and get some information on Ann first. There was no way the killer was leaving this situation alive, because whether he gave up the info or not, Walt was going to kill his ass.

He stripped him of all of his weapons and most of his clothing. He handcuffed his hands behind his back and then tied his legs together from the knees down. Walt knew who he was dealing with, and he wasn't taking any chances. He snatched the mask off of the man and took pictures of him from every angle.

He couldn't send the pictures because the network was still down, but he would have them on record if by some miracle, the killer got away. Walt saved the pictures in a hidden folder on the phone and then he threw the man out of the window.

. . . .

Walt had come out of the basement of Ashley Kirt's house and ran as fast as he could across the open yard and thin line of trees. When he saw the body parts lying everywhere, he knew that there was some kind of explosive devices buried in the ground. The SWAT team must have tried to bring their guys out in case it was something in the house making them sick. He wondered how in the world the killer was able to bury mines so quickly.

Walt had frozen because there was no telling where the mines were buried. All of sudden, from his place in the trees, Walt watched a masked man climb down a tree across the street and make his way to the side of the neighbor's house.

He had taken off running so that he could follow in the footsteps of who he had to assume was the killer. By the time Walt crossed the street and recrossed at the same spot as the killer, the guy had disappeared. Walt stayed about a hundred feet from the house and slowly made his way to the back. It was too dark to try and track the bastard, but then Walt saw the open window.

Walking around, still about a hundred feet back, he lined himself up perfectly with the window and looked in with his night vision goggles. He saw movement over to the right side of the room near the door. He kept the goggles trained on the window and slowly began making his way towards the house.

About twenty feet out, he heard the sound of vehicles approaching from the front. He guessed it was the SWAT vehicles coming back, but it could have been the cops coming in response to the explosion. Then, it sounded like the world ended.

Walt didn't see a lot of combat as an MP, but if it sounded anything like what he had just heard, he understood why the trauma could stay with you forever. It sounded like a warzone. On top of that, he heard two gun shots come from the inside of the house. He ran the rest of the way and dove into the window.

He came up in a roll with his gun pointed at the door. After there was no movement for five seconds or so, he walked to the door and looked around the frame to the front of the house. That's when the killer finished off the two officers. Now, the unconscious killer was laying at his feet.

All Walt knew was that he had work to do, and the police had to be on their way after the latest explosion. Other officers knew about the sting happening tonight, so they would go to both houses looking for the officers. There was no way that the local cops were taking his prisoner, so he picked the killer up and hoisted him over his shoulder. [Glad that he was in such good shape,] he ran straight out from the house to the hundred-foot line to avoid the mines and turned towards Ashley's house.

He ran until he got to the garage and dropped the man on the driveway. He ran to the side door and pushed it open, pulling out the keys to the explorer. He hit the button to raise the door, started the SUV and pulled up next to the unconscious killer. Walt got out and threw the man in the back and pulled off.

He took a right at the end of the driveway, but he wasn't going far. He just needed a little time alone with the killer before the police found the body, and he was definitely going to be a body by the time he was found.

There was an old, abandoned cabin about two miles down the road. Walt turned into it just as, in the distance, what looked like twenty or more cop cars were on their way. He pulled behind the cabin, shutting off his lights as the cars zoomed past.

He took a deep breath to fortify himself for what he was about to do. He got out of the explorer and opened up the back. The guy was looking up at him with a smug look on his face. Walt grabbed his legs and yanked him out, letting his head hit the rocks and dirt. The killer just looked at him and laughed out loud.

"So what, you're a tough guy now?" the killer taunted him. "You going to beat me until I talk? Save us both some time and just kill me, because I'm not saying shit."

On the phone, the killer had constantly changed his voice. This wasn't the one that he used before, but the description was dead on. Six-foot black man, with a bald head and a muscular build. Skin tone was identical to the small bit of video they had from Marco's Place, the restaurant that Cpt.

Dennis' wife and daughter ate at the night they died. This was definitely the killer everyone had been searching for.

"Listen," said Walt. "You are going to die tonight by my hand and there is nothing you can do about that. Depending on how cooperative you are, it can be a bullet to the head, or a slow torture that would be good for me, but very bad for you."

The killer laughed. "So, you want me to think that you, a cop, are going to murder an unarmed, shackled man for no reason?"

"Oh, I have plenty of reason," said Walt. He dragged the man further from the SUV so as not to get incriminating blood on it. "Now, tell me where Ann is, and I can go ahead and send you to hell."

"Ann?" asked the man with a puzzled look. "Who the fuck is Ann?" The killer actually tried to sound like he was confused.

"Who the fuck is Ann? You really want to play games with me?" Walt pulled his gun and shot the man in his right knee.

"Ahhhh," yelled the wounded man. "What the fuck is wrong with you? You're a cop, man."

"Tell me where my partner is and how I can get her back."

The killer was rolling around and moaning in pain. "I don't know what you're talking about man. You have the wrong guy."

Walt stood over the man looking at him like he was crazy. "Are you serious? The wrong guy?" Walt shot the killer in his stomach.

This time, the man didn't even scream. He looked at his stomach, then at Walt and laid flat on his back. "I have nothing to say, kill me now and get it over with."

Walt laughed and said, "I was thinking the same exact thing." He then shot the killer three times in the chest and stood over him until he saw the light leave his eyes.

He already had a plan to explain how the killer's body ended up here, and why he had no choice but to kill him. Seeing as how the guy had just murdered twenty-four SWAT officers, no one would ask too many questions anyway.

Walt had no idea about how to get Ann back, and still wasn't even sure if she was alive. He had no idea why the killer would try to act like he didn't know who Ann was. Maybe, he thought Walt would keep him alive as long as he held out on the information. The criminal really didn't think Walt had it in him to end his life.

Anyway, Walt needed to get back to the scene so he could check on Denise and sell his story. He took the ties off the body, left the handcuffs on, turned him over on his stomach, and left the body right where it was. He put the killer's clothes and shoes in a pile about four feet in front of where the killer lay. He would tell anyone who asked that he had made the killer strip to make sure he didn't have any weapons. The killer had tried to run, and Walt shot him in the knee to keep him from getting away.

Walt would go on to say that the killer reached behind his back for something Walt couldn't see, and he had to assume it was a gun. After witnessing the killer brutally murder other police officers, he had no choice but to put him down for good.

After a few more small details to set the scene, Walt jumped in the SUV and drove back to the house. He had dropped the phone in Ashley's yard by the garage so no one would ask why he hadn't called for backup. He would explain that he had watched the killer come out of the window and run around Ashley's house towards a trail in the woods. For some reason, Walt had remembered seeing a run-down cabin in that direction and he had hastened to get there before the killer.

[On scene, the phones hadn't been working. So when he dropped his in the dark, he didn't take the time to find it. When he arrived behind the cabin, the killer was just coming out of the trail. Walt had told him to strip, and the line of cop cars had distracted Walt enough that he took his eyes off the killer. That's when the events happened that led to the death of the suspect.]

The story had holes, but he didn't think the investigation would last too long. When Walt got to the houses, he couldn't even count how many cop cars there were. A patrolman ran to turn him around, but he flashed his shield and was allowed access.

As he passed, the patrolman said, "They have paths that are marked with cones to show where it is safe to walk. The first ones on scene rushed in and were blown up by mines. I think five more cops died because of that. They haven't cleared the whole property yet, so just be careful where you walk."

Walt thanked the man and drove straight to Ashely's house using the same route that he used to leave.

He could admit that he had been reckless. It never occurred to him that the killer could have planted mines in Ashley's yard too. He had been so intent on extracting information on Ann that he could have gotten himself killed.

Walt pulled up to the garage and pretended to find his phone in the grass before running into the house, just in case anyone was watching him. Will was sitting in the living room and jumped up when Walt ran in.

"Where is Denise?" Walt asked Will. There were several cops just standing around drinking coffee. "And what in the hell are all of you just standing around for?"

Will put his hands up in a calming manner. "Denise is still in the safe room, as far as I know. We knew you were alive because we saw you drive away on the camera." Will led him away from everyone else and lowered his voice. "When we saw what you were up to, the lab guy stopped all the recordings for the hard lines and got rid of what he had already collected. I figured you would want to question the guy about Ann."

Walt exhaled in relief. That was the part of the plan that he couldn't have controlled. If anyone had watched the recordings of him loading the killer into the SUV, there would have been no explaining it away. "Thank you, Cap," Walt told the man, putting a hand on his shoulder. "But it was all for nothing. He wouldn't give me any information on Ann. In fact, he acted like he didn't even know who I was talking about. I had to kill him when he tried to escape. I need to get a few local guys out there to handle that scene."

"Let me take care of that," said Will. "Just tell me where it is, and then you go get Denise. She's probably going out of her mind with worry."

Walt told the man exactly where the body was and then seeing officers using their cell phones, picked up the house phone to call Denise. As the phone was ringing, Will ran off to find the detectives over the scene.

Denise answered on the third ring, "Who is this?"

"I know your mama taught you better manners than that," said Walt in an amused tone.

"Oh my God. Walt? I was so worried about you. Where the hell have you been? I heard all these explosions and then everything was quiet."

"I'm so sorry I made you worry. I had to chase the bastard down after he killed the whole SWAT team," explained Walt. "The good news is that everything is taken care of now."

"What do you mean by that?" Denise asked, in a hopeful voice.

"I got his ass."

"What! He's in custody?" asked Denise.

"No, sweetheart. He is dead. So you can come out and we can have our date night tomorrow." Denise hung up the phone without another word.

Walt had been on a cordless phone, so he was standing right at the closet door when the saferoom's lock disengaged. Denise tripped and fell in her haste to get out of the room.

Her eyes stayed locked right on his face as she righted herself and launched her body into his. She wrapped her arms and legs around him and smothered him with kisses.

He laughed and kissed her right back. "For a reception like this, I'll kill everyone who threatens you." They stood there, holding onto one another until Walt became aware that they had an audience.

Will had come into the room looking grim. "Walt, I need you to come with me, right now. You have about a hundred cops that would like a word with you."

Denise unlatched herself from Walt and looked at him questioningly. "Is everything okay?"

"Yeah," Walt reassured her. "They probably just want the details of what I saw and what happened that led to me killing the suspect."

Denise still looked worried but gave him one last kiss before saying, "I'm going to call Ashley and let her know everything is okay. Call me as soon as you are finished, but right now, I'm going to change my clothes and get to work. I have some reporting to do." She was already on her phone, probably calling in her camera crew to document the carnage.

She walked back to the saferoom door and reached in to retrieve her bag. She gave the two men a little wave, gave Walt a wink and was out the door.

Will said, "You know she will have to make a formal statement, right?"

"Yeah, and she knows it too. But that can wait until tomorrow. So, how much trouble am I in?"

"None, with the local guys. They think you are a hero. But there are some Federal boys that you're going to have to do a lot of explaining to. I just hope that you have all the details down pat because these motherfuckers are mad as hell that you killed this guy."

"Well," said Walt. "Let's get it over with. No matter what happens to me, at least we don't have to worry about that asshole ever again." With that thought, Walt went to face the music with a smile on his face.

CHAPTER 31

Will had said the FEDs were mad, but that had been a massive understatement. Walt had a feeling that, if they could knock him out and throw him in the back of an SUV, they would. But they had been unable to drill any massive holes in his story, so they had to take his word on what had led up to the death of the killer.

Walt had asked them how they had gotten to the crime scene so fast. They hadn't even identified the body yet, and the FBI and CIA were on his back asking questions about the guy. Agent Steve had told him they wanted the killer alive, but Walt didn't think they would show up so fast. It made him wonder if they had an informant in the local PD or SBI.

He thought about that for a second and then laughed. [Of course they had informants.] Probably in every police unit in the country. They had probably known all about the sting but had thought the killer would wipe the floor with them, so they let it happen. Now, they were pissed as hell that Walt came out of the encounter on top.

Walt was sitting in the medical examiner's office waiting for the body to be prepared for the autopsy. Apparently, there was a whole series of things that had to be done that the movies never showed you. He had no reason to know these steps because all he normally received was an M.E. report detailing what was found. He did know that someone would have to ID the body before they could start cutting it up. Walt was here because he wanted to see who turned up to view the body.

It might have been paranoia, but Walt also wanted to keep his eye on the body. Even though he was the one who shot him, he still had a hard time accepting that the killer was dead. It was almost like he expected this to be another layer to some devious plan the killer had already set in motion. All

Walt knew right this second was that there was only one way in or out of the room where the body was resting, and he was sitting right in front of it.

He had been sitting there for about two hours now because he had followed the body to the M.E.'s office. After the FED goons had released him at the scene, with the promise of a more serious talk later on, he had gone to the secondary scene to make sure the body was still there.

Denise had been the only media person on scene, but they wouldn't allow her camera crew to join her. Instead, she had gone live on Facetime and connected in with the station. She had gotten several of the local cops to do interviews, as well as Cpt. Graham and the lab tech who had helped them set everything up. At first, everyone wanted her to stay so they could question her. After the first hour, they were begging her to leave so they could get away from all of her questions.

Her crew had been on the outside of the perimeter taking long distance videos. They were able to get footage of the crime scene guys picking up body parts of all the blown-up cops. They also had video of the medical personnel bringing out the SWAT team's bodies from the neighbor's house.

In addition to all of that, Denise obviously had someone working on the video the killer had sent her because she aired an edited version of that as well. Walt had put that on the back burner, trying to set all this up. But, apparently, Denise had been working while she was in that safe room. Then again, the phones have been off, so maybe she had set that up earlier in the day.

Denise had reported that Sgt. Camilla Rodriguez, a 12-year veteran of Albemarle Correctional, had been found dead in her trailer early that morning. She was 35-years old and had been under investigation for years for forcing herself on inmates. From the video, it looked like the killer cooked her slowly in a bathtub. By the time she was found, the flesh of her body had been floating off of her bones. The initial report said that she was alive for most of it.

Finally, Denise had gotten all the material she could get and had gone home. She had tried to get onto the secondary site, but the FEDs had that one locked down tightly. She had tentatively hinted that the Prison Guard Killer was dead but was waiting for the body to be identified before it could be confirmed.

As all of this was running through his mind, Walt must have drifted off. Some instinct jerked his body awake and had him reaching for his gun. He was up and out of the chair with his hand on the butt of his gun when he recognized 'Agent Steve,' so he let the gun go. Then he remembered the agent telling him the CIA might send someone to kill him, so he pulled the gun out anyway.

Agent Steve put his hands up and said, "Easy there, detective. I'm not here to cause any trouble. I was sent by the brass to ID the body."

"And then what?" asked Walt. "Kill me? Cuff me? What?" Walt had his gun pointed at the agent's chest.

"None of those, Walt," said the agent. "From what I gather, they were content to let him kill a bunch of civilians, but after he took out a whole SWAT unit using CIA resources, they feel like you did them a favor by putting him down."

"So why were those guys busting my balls back at the scene? Seemed to me they were mad as hell that I smoked y'all's boy."

"Yeah, they were and still are pretty mad," confessed the agent. "But only because, with his death, they have lost all the money and assets that only he knew the locations of. The missing money is bad enough, but the locations of the prisons and other physical assets put the total loss in the hundreds of billions. They wanted to question him before he died."

"Well, by what you just said, I cost them all this money. Why would they decide to let me live anyway?" asked Walt.

"I don't think you know how these agencies work. When they feel like you owe them, they won't kill you right off. But trust me, in the near future, you will be asked to do something for your country. If I were you, I would say yes. Because the person they will send to kill you, you will never even see them coming. Then again, they might not go after you at all. It might be somebody close to you."

Walt's expression turned mean. "Fuck you and fuck them. The best guy y'all had is in there on a table because I put him there. You tell your people to leave me and mine alone or this ME is going to be very busy."

"Calm down man," said the smiling agent, still with his hands raised. "Can I drop my hands? Remember, I'm the one who risked my life to come help you."

Walt didn't like the fact that the agent thought his threat was funny, but the agent had had numerous opportunities to hurt him and hadn't. "Do you have a weapon on you?" Walt asked the man.

"Of course I do, but I don't have any intention of using it. If I did, I could have shot you just now while you were napping," the agent stated, sarcastically.

Walt lowered his gun and sat back down in his chair. When Agent Steve sat on the opposite side of the hallway, Walt asked, "I thought you were going in to ID the body?"

"I wanted to have a word with you first." The agent looked around like he expected someone to jump out and yell, "Ah-ha, I got you!"

"Well, get on with it. It's been a very long day," Walt said, showing his irritation.

"Just wanted to give you a heads up. One thing the CIA trained us to do was always wear a camera somewhere on our bodies. That way, if one of us gets killed, it can be used as a training aid to avoid future mistakes. But it is also used to view the last moments of an agent's live so his killer can be identified." He stopped talking and looked at Walt. "I don't know if they retrieved the camera because I arrived so

251

late. If they have it, and it shows you doing something illegal, they will use it to hang you."

Walt's heart skipped a beat. As much as the killer seemed to like making videos, it should have occurred to him to check for that possibility. Walt had removed most of the guy's clothes, but even a recording of the sound, would put Walt in prison. And he couldn't ask any questions about it because it would only make him look guilty.

Walt, trying to sound confident, said, "I hope they do have a recording. That way, they can see for themselves that I had no choice but to kill him."

"It also doesn't look good that your guys didn't record anything at the scene. I mean, come on. Explosives going off. Bodies everywhere. You guys had everything set up to record at the press of a button, but you just failed to do so?"

"When the explosion went off, we had already lost all of our communication abilities. I think that we just didn't think of it. We were only going to record once we had him boxed in, but with the explosions, I think everyone just panicked a little bit," explained Walt.

The agent smiled and stood up. "Don't underestimate these guys. If they come at you, it's because they already have something on you. They offer you a way to save your ass, better take it or you'll find yourself in prison, or worse."

Walt stood up with the agent, grateful for the help. "Thanks. I'll keep that in mind."

"Anyway," said Agent Steve. "Let's go in and get this ID over with."

They both turned towards the door. Walt pushed it open but let Agent Steve go in first. The body was under a cover on a steel table placed in the center of the room. It looked like every autopsy room you have ever seen on T.V. Bright lights, drain in the floor, tile and concrete walls. There were so many tools scattered around on various tables, Walt wondered why there was more to work on a dead body than on a living one.

The M.E. wasn't present at the time, but one of his assistants was sitting at a computer screen with his back to them. When they entered, he continued typing for a minute, then turned to see who had entered.

He was a middle-aged guy, with a small pouch in his mid-section and long brown hair. He had on a pair of thick glasses, and when he smiled, Walt thought the man hadn't been to a dentist in years.

"Hi! My name is Clint. You guys must be here to identify the body?" He didn't offer either of them a hand to shake, but he seemed like a nice enough guy. He did have that weird, 'I've been working with the dead' thing going on. Maybe, he had been snubbed so many times that he just quit offering to shake people's hands.

"Yeah," replied Agent Steve. "Do you have any information for me so far?"

"Well, you know we couldn't start the actual autopsy until after the body was identified, but we did take some blood and his prints. We got a positive hit on his prints, as well as his DNA."

Walt and the agent look at each other with confused looks. "What do you mean, you have a positive ID?" asked Walt. "He was in the system?"

"Oh, yeah," replied, Clint. "I was amazed the guy was still walking in the streets. He has so many convictions for violent crimes, it's insane that he's not still in prison."

"What was the name that came up when you ran him?" asked Walt.

"Let's have you guys come take a look, and then we'll see if we come up with the same name." He reached to the top of the sheet and very slowly revealed the face of the man that was shot.

Agent Steve jerked back with a shocked look on his face. "Is this the guy that was killed at the scene?" He asked Walt.

A sinking feeling settled in the pit of Walt's stomach. "Yeah. That's him. That's the guy I shot. Why do you look like that?" Walt asked the agent.

Agent Steve burst out laughing, like the greatest joke of all time had just been told. His hands were on his knees as he bent over laughing, with tears running down his face.

"What the fuck is wrong with you, man? You better give me some answers right now." Walt already knew what he was going to say but needed to hear it out of the agent's mouth.

When he was able to get himself under control, he looked at Walt and asked, "Are you sure, one hundred percent positive, that this is the guy you shot?"

"Yes," replied Walt. "Now tell me what the fuck is so funny."

"I hate to tell you this, but that is not the killer."

"That's him, man. He's the one who shot and blew up all those cops. He fits the description perfectly. How in the hell can you say it's not him?"

"Walt," the agent said patiently. "I told you that I was the one who helped recruit and train him. This man actually looks nothing like him. The same coloring and size, but the features are not at all like our guy."

Walt was so mad that he wasn't aware he had pulled his gun, until the agent's hands went up, and he started backing away. "If you're fucking with me, I swear to God, I will kill your ass right now."

"I swear to you, it's not him. I can show you his face on my phone, and you can see for yourself." Agent Steve slowly reached for his phone with Walt, once again, pointing his gun at his chest.

When he pulled the phone out, Walt said, "Hand it to me."

Agent Steve shook his head and said, "I can't give this phone to you. If anyone else but me touches it, the phone automatically deletes all of its files. I'll hold it up, and you can see the face of the real killer."

Walt allowed the agent to scroll through his phone for a few seconds before he remembered the other guy in the room. He cast a quick glance his way and saw him standing next to the body, with his hands, held high above his head. Walt's focus went back to the agent just as he turned the phone around, so the screen was facing Walt.

What he saw, was a military photo every soldier took upon graduating basic training. It could have been a fake, but Walt didn't think it was. The man in the picture really did fit the description to perfection. The dead guy had the overall same look, but the guy on the screen was their guy.

Walt lowered the gun and looked at the CIA man in disbelief. "Do you know what this means?"

"What what means?" asked Agent Steve.

"This," Walt said, motioning towards the body. "This dead body."

"No, Walt. What does it mean?"

"It means the son of a bitch planned for all of this to happen. And I fell for it, hook, line, and sinker. This was his plan the whole time, which means…"

"What?" the agent asked. "Which means what?"

"Oh my God! No! No!" shouted Walt, reaching for his burner phone.

"What is it, Walt? What's the problem?"

The phone rang and rang before going to voicemail and Walt hung up. He looked at the agent and said, "It means, all this was part of the plan to get to Denise. And she went home hours ago by herself." Walt took one more look at a dead body, and then took off running as fast as he could.

CHAPTER 32

Denise had never had so many extremes in one day in her life. It had started out bad, then got worse very fast. By the end of the night, she was sitting on cloud nine. She felt like it should disturb her to be so happy about the death of another human being, but she wasn't a fake person. To act like she wasn't ecstatic would have been a major falsehood.

She was on her way home after her most successful night ever as a reporter. The police thought they could control her, but she had ended up with the last laugh. They hadn't let her camera crew come inside of the police perimeter, but they had gotten some great overall footage to compliment her close-up work. She ended up having to use her cell phone to do the interviews, but she cornered a lot of shocked cops who might be a little upset with her tomorrow.

If she wasn't driving down the highway right now, she would do her happy dance. Her editor and her producer had come through for her on the video the killer had sent her. She had tried to call them while she was in the safe room, but until about the last ten minutes inside, her phone hadn't worked. She had given up on using it, when out of nowhere, she started getting texts, notifications for missed calls, and voicemails. It had been a tense few minutes until she got the call from Walter.

Right after their heartfelt reunion, she had jumped on the phone to her staff. She could have kissed the lot of them when her producer told her the video had been edited and was ready to air. Denise told her to have the video ready to go but keep it on standby until she called her back.

She hadn't expected her camera crew to be allowed on scene, so by the time the guys texted her, she was already set up to go live using Facetime. She had patched in with the station and had done what she was good at; gotten people to talk when they really didn't want to.

It was sad how many people had died because of this killer, but that number wouldn't be getting any higher. No matter what led him to become this killing machine, it was still his choice when it came to murdering another person. And he wasn't just killing them, he was torturing them. And in some cases, killing family members that had nothing to do with the situation. She hoped he burned in hell for all the pain he had caused.

She pulled into her driveway and a huge weight lifted off of her shoulders. It hit her that she hadn't known if she would ever see her home again. It wasn't much in size or style, but it was hers and she loved the feel of it. It was just right for a single woman on the go. It was safe because it was in a cul-de-sac and not many criminals wanted to commit crimes in a place with one way in and one way out.

Denise got out of the car and glanced at her phone. Funny, she normally had a full signal in this whole area. She didn't have a signal at all, at the moment. A sense of unease had her looking around before she dropped her head with a small laugh. The threat to her was over. She was being silly. That phone jammer the killer had used probably had a residual effect on her phone that would come and go. She had used it constantly at the crime scene, so she knew it worked. Shaking her head, she grabbed her bag out of the backseat and made her way to the house.

First things first, a hot bath was in order. She went to her bedroom and dropped the bag on the bed on her way to the bathroom. She started the water in the tub, threw in some of her favorite vanilla fragrance beads, and stripped off all her clothes. She knew there were still cameras in her house but did a quick happy dance because the bastard wasn't alive to watch them anymore.

She made up her mind to be naked for the rest of the night, so she just stood next to the tub until it was ready, and then stepped in.

"Oh, God," she moaned out loud. The hot water felt heavenly. She had been so tense for so long that the smell and the feel of the water threatened to put her to sleep. It was a dangerous thing to do, but she closed her eyes and drifted off to sleep with thoughts of a certain detective running through her head.

She had been having a steamy, erotic, love-making session with Walter when she was jerked awake. The water had long gone cold, but because of her dream, she was still hot in a few places. She stepped out of the tub and grabbed a towel to dry off. She bent over to retrieve her phone she had left on the floor.

"Shit," she said, when she saw it was almost 3:00am. She had been in the tub for well over two hours. Denise knew she would have a long day with all of her follow-up stories, so she needed to get some good sleep to look her best on camera.

It wasn't until she had picked up her clothes and returned to the bedroom that she wondered what had woken her up. She glanced at her phone again and noticed she still didn't have a signal. She walked to the living room where her landline was located and picked it up. There wasn't even a dial tone.

"What the hell," she muttered, looking around her house. She wondered if the killer had set something up earlier in the day just in case she came back to her house. She needed to get someone over there to find out what was wrong and fix it.

"Another worry for another day." She would have to worry about that later. Right now, she needed some much-earned rest. The 'Super Reporter' needed some super sleep.

She walked back to her bed and climbed in between the sheets naked. She was thinking about where Walt would want to go on their date later tonight when she drifted off into a peaceful sleep.

When she woke the next time, she thought she was having one of those false dream wakeups because she seemed to be in a small, dark place that was not her bedroom. She tried to move and found that she could, but her arms were secured behind her back, and she was laying on her side. If she didn't know any better, she would think she was in the trunk of a car. But that was impossible because the only person who would tape her hands behind her back and put her in a trunk of a car was dead. So therefore, it must be a dream.

Denise tried to will herself to wake up. She even pinched her own ass a few times to force herself to exit the dream. She could feel the slight up and down motion of the car. Could even hear the tires going over the road. Denise could also feel the sweat rolling off her body.

Her body made the leap before her mind did and started struggling to get free. That's when she became aware of the duct tape wrapping her legs from her ankles to her knees. She was in such an awkward position, she could not even work up enough force to kick out at anything.

Denise tried to reason with her body and command it to stop panicking, but it refused to listen to her. Her body kept fighting to get free. She heard a keening sound that she knew was coming from her own lips. She hadn't even realized that she had tape over her mouth and a blindfold over her eyes. The moment she did, she started hyperventilating.

The trunk was so hot and closed in that she was having a full-blown panic attack. She knew she was on the verge of passing out. For some reason, her body and her mind thought that sounded like a good idea and, within moments, she was unconscious again.

When she came to the next time, she went through the same process of discovery but was able to keep from going into a full-blown panic by sheer force of will. It helped that the car wasn't moving so the up and down motion was gone as well as the sound of the tires screaming over the asphalt. She hadn't been aware for very long, but for some reason, she felt like the car had been stationary for a while.

Once again, she started feeling around to see if she could find something in the trunk. Then she had a brilliant thought, why not remove the blindfold so she could see what she was doing.

She started dragging her head over the floor, rooting around like a pig in an effort to remove the blindfold. After about two minutes, she was able to remove it with only marginal rug burns to her face.

Denise was tightly wedged into the small space and there was absolutely no light coming in around the trunk lid. But she was still able to come to a startling revelation; she was in the trunk of her own car.

She guessed that most people would feel better about that fact, but it crushed all hope of Denise getting free. She had no tools in her trunk, not even a crowbar or a jack. All of those things were in a compartment under the car. And the reason she was so wedged in was because, what felt like her whole wardrobe had been packed into the trunk with her. She guessed that could be taken as a good sign or a bad one.

On the one hand, if the guy was going to kill her, he probably wouldn't have gone through all the trouble of taking all her clothes. Unless he was trying to make it seem like she had just run away, in which case, it was a waste of time because no one would believe that.

On the other hand, if he was bringing all of her clothes, it probably meant that he was planning on keeping her for a very long time. That would give the police more time to figure out where she was being taken to. But the more time that passed, the broader the search would have to be.

Bottom line, she was in a very bad situation, and she was in no position to help herself. At least not yet.

A million bad scenarios were running through her mind when the trunk popped open. Since her eyes were used to the dark, she quickly picked up the image of the masked man standing over the trunk.

"You see, Ms. McCarthy. I'm looking out for you even when you're being a bad girl. If I hadn't put my mask back on, I would have to kill you for seeing my face. But I figured you would take the blindfold off." He struck a few poses. "I look pretty good for a dead guy, don't I?"

Denise had suspected all along that it was the killer, but hearing his voice still sent a chill running down her spine. Walt thought the man was dead. Hell, everybody thought the man was dead. The word at the crime scene was that the dead man fit the description of the killer perfectly. Once again, he had outsmarted everyone and came up with the perfect plan to accomplish his goal.

"I'm sure, as a reporter, you have a ton of questions. Let's get you settled into your new home before we have our little talk. I will warn you though, the second you don't do exactly what I tell you, when I tell you to do it, I will hurt you. I really don't want to, but I most certainly will."

The man lifted her out of the trunk like she weighed next to nothing and stood her on her feet. This was the first time, that she was aware of, of her being this close to the killer. She took the time to size him up.

He was a tad over six feet and probably weighed in right at about two hundred pounds. He was in excellent shape. She couldn't see an extra pound anywhere it shouldn't be. She couldn't see his face, but of what she could see, there was no distinguishing marks on his arms or hands. He was dressed in all black and his clothes were very form fitting.

"I hope I passed the assessment, but now I have to put the blindfold back on for a few minutes," stated the killer.

[Shit!] She had been so locked in on measuring him up, that she hadn't even bothered to look around. The blindfold settled back over her eyes, and once again, she was in the dark.

The killer cut through the bindings on her legs and peeled the tape away. "Now, turn around one hundred and eighty degrees and walk forward until I tell you to stop." Denise did as she was instructed and walked over the rocks and dirt, hoping the killer wasn't leading her off a cliff. She was thankful that the killer had dressed her and put shoes on her feet.

She didn't have any underwear on, but the killer had put a T-shirt and sweatpants on her, as well as a pair of tennis shoes. She wanted to feel some type of way about him touching her, but he had been looking at her through those cameras for so long, it really didn't make much difference. She did wonder what kind of drug was used to keep her under while he did all these things to her.

"Stop right there," ordered the killer. She heard a series of locks being unlocked and then a door being opened. "Walk forward ten steps and then stop." At step four, she crossed over a threshold of some kind and then nothing, until she stopped.

The killer was behind her, locking everything back up. She wished she was some Kungfu expert, and she could beat the guy's ass even with her blindfold on and her hands tied behind her back. But she wasn't, so she figured the best thing to do was to follow instructions and bid her time until she could try to escape.

The masked man walked around her and then a door opened in front of her. "Walk forward," said the killer. She did, until her feet hit a metal platform that dipped a little under her weight. Denise thought it had to be an elevator. The killer told her to stop and then the doors closed, and the blindfold was ripped off of her face. Denise turned around, and she was correct, she was in an elevator, and they were going down. Way down.

When the doors finally opened, her heart sank all the way to the soles of her feet. "Step off and wait for me in the middle right there." She walked forward and stopped, waiting, and looking around in dismay. She should have taken her shot with the blindfold and taped hands because any chance at escape was now dead. She was looking at the inside of a full-scale maximum-security prison.

She started panicking all over again. Her eyes darted this way and that way, taking in the fact that there was no escape from this place. Behind her, the elevator door closed and, for no reason other than her panicking mind, she took off running through an open door to her left.

Denise ran around a circle that she wasn't aware was a circle, until she reached the end of it and saw the killer standing there looking at her. She skidded to a stop about ten feet from him and turned to run in the opposite direction.

At first, she thought her mind was playing tricks on her, or the killer was just fast as all hell. When the panic started to abate just a little, she understood that she was running around in a circle and the killer never moved.

She stopped at the furthest place from the killer and stared at him through the control booth in the center. She knew it was useless, but she made a decision not to make it easy on the guy to put her in one of those cells. She felt like if she allowed it to happen, she would die in this subterranean prison.

The killer started coming through the door to the right of the elevator, pushing her towards the door that she had initially fled through. He was very slow and deliberate. Denise wondered what he was up to. She realized that all he had to do was close one of the doors at the end of the hallway, but he had left them open.

She kept pace with the killer to keep the maximum distance between them. All of a sudden, the killer stopped, so she mirrored him. Out of nowhere, there was a muted pounding from one of the cells behind her. She wanted to look but didn't want to take her eyes off of the killer. Plus, she figured she didn't need to see anyone who had warranted being locked up in this place anyway.

The pounding grew more intense, and even sounded like someone was screaming her name. She glanced back really quickly but all she could see was dark glass. The killer slapped his own forehead like he had forgotten to do something. Denise thought he had figured out just to close the door. He did something on his phone and then looked up at her, expectantly.

Denise stared back at him when nothing happened on her end. By this time, the pounding on the glass was almost frantic, so she hazarded another look and this time the cell was revealed to her. It looked like a very expensive suite at a very expensive hotel. Definitely not the view one would expect in an underground prison. But the huge bed, the big screen T.V., or the carpet wasn't what made her legs give out and had her sinking to the floor with her mouth hanging open. It was the sight of Detective Ann Grace, standing behind the glass, alive and well, that sent Denise crashing to the floor. She didn't know if it was shock or relief, but either way, she was frozen on the floor.

The killer walked up and stood next to her. "I know all this is a shock, so your rebellion will be overlooked this one time. All I want you to do is follow instructions and you will be okay. All of this is part of a long-term plan that ends with everyone going home safe and sound. I have to hold you for a while, but I think you will be better for the experience."

It was too much. Denise had always felt like she was a strong woman, everything was just too much for her right now. She glanced from Ann to the killer and back again. For some reason, it felt like bees flying around her head. She glanced back at the killer and then everything went mercifully black. She hoped that when she woke up the next time, her brain would stop trying to torture her with these bad dreams.

CHAPTER 33

"You son of a bitch. She's a civilian. Why would you do this to her?"

"Ann, you need to calm down. I'm not going to hurt her, she's just a means to an end." Denise was laid out, face up, on some kind of hard surface. She was trying to keep her breathing nice and even so she could listen to more of the conversation going on over top of her. The killer and Ann were going at it like an old married couple.

"You know, you really are a piece of shit." Ann told the man. "Every time you pull one of these moves, it just proves how much of a coward you really are."

"Ann," said the killer, sounding agitated. "Shut the hell up for once in your life. You have no idea what's going on, and that's really what you are mad at. You fucking cops hate it when you're not the smartest person in the room. And you keep up your bullshit and you're going to be taking a trip down the hall. Now, stop talking so Denise can stop faking like she's asleep."

Denise held out through the quiet for about two more minutes, but all it did was make her feel stupid. When she opened her eyes, she was laying on the bed that she had glimpsed inside of the cell holding Ann Grace. Ann was standing on the far side of the bed and the killer was standing on the side closest to the door. They were both looking down at her.

She decided to focus on Ann first. The woman was as beautiful as ever with her long, dark hair and her perfect skin. You would think she had spent the last week in a spa instead of in an underground prison. She was even wearing designer clothes when she obviously wasn't going anywhere to show them off. For one brief minute, the thought entered her mind that Ann was working with the killer. She pushed the thought aside only because she didn't think Ann would do that to Walt.

Then she turned her focus on to the killer. Wasn't much new to look at. He had on the same clothes as when he had led her into the prison. The mask he had on hid every part of his face. It even had mesh over the eyes so you couldn't see them very well.

Glancing at them both, Denise asked, "How long have I been out?"

The killer answered, "Seven minutes, not counting the six minutes you've been laying there faking, wasting everyone's time." He actually had the nerve to sound upset.

"Well, excuse the hell out of me for not jumping up and embracing you," quipped Denise.

The killer let out a sigh. "There is a bathroom right over there beyond the doorway. Go fix yourself up, use the bathroom, hell, take a shower. Just be ready to sit down and act like an adult when you come back out that door." He looked from one woman to the other and said, "Matter of fact, I'll leave you two to talk. Hit the button when you're finished, and I'll come back." He turned and left without another word and closed the door behind him.

Denise sat up and swung her feet off the side of the bed closest to Ann and the bathroom. As soon as she stood up, Ann hugged her close and they stayed like that for a few minutes. They both cried a little bit but had their emotions under control before they separated.

Ann smiled and said, "Don't worry, everything is going to be alright. He really doesn't want to hurt us. But please, do whatever he tells you to do. Us together couldn't even make him break a sweat. I tried to fight him the first night and he kicked my ass then put me in one of the punishment cells. Trust me, you don't want to go down that road." Ann took her hand and led her to the doorway of the bathroom. "Right now, just get yourself together and I'll stay on this side so we can talk."

"Just let me use the bathroom, then come on in with me. I just don't want to be by myself." Ann nodded and Denise went in to use the toilet.

She couldn't stop the gasp from escaping with her first sight of the bathroom. The space was just as luxurious as any five-star hotel she had ever seen. And Ann was an excellent cleaning lady because everything either shined or sparkled. She quickly used the toilet to relieve the pressure on her bladder, then asked Ann to come on in.

Denise wasn't going to take a shower, but she did run some water in the sink and grabbed a rag to wash her face. Before she could say anything though, Ann told her, "Walt has just fucked himself, but I don't know anymore than that. The killer, or Manny as he's told me to call him, will explain what he wants us to know. I never know if he is listening, so it's easier to do what he says and trust him to hold up his end."

"Ann," said Denise, with a little suspicion in her voice. "What the hell is really going on with you and him? I mean, look how he has you living. We all thought you were dead, but you're down here living in a five-star room, wearing fancy clothes, and you're on a first name basis with this asshole."

"First of all, Denise," Ann responded with anger in her voice. "If you want to accuse me of something, get all your facts straight. This asshole dislocated both of my shoulders and threw me in a dark hole with a bucket. So, sue me for complying so that maybe I can get out of here alive. If you hadn't been running around out there in a panic, you would have seen that there are multiple cells like this one that he puts people in that he doesn't want to punish. Try being here for more than ten minutes before you start to pass judgement."

Ann turned to walk out but Denise said, "Ann, I'm sorry. You're right. I have no idea what you've been through and I'm sorry for jumping to conclusions. I'm just a little shocked at everything I'm seeing. Please don't go. I really am sorry." Ann had stopped at the doorway with the first apology. Now, she walked over and sat on the edge of the tub looking at Denise.

"To tell you the truth, Denise, I have no idea what is going on. He is everything we thought he was and much more. He has some kind of plan going on that involves all of us and we'll find out our part in it when he feels like telling us. I'm kind of anxious to see what he has to say. So, when you finish in here, I'm going to get him back so, maybe, he'll tell us what the hell he wants from us."

"Go ahead and call him now. I'm finished. I just needed to touch up." They both walked back to the living area and Denise looked around more closely.

There was a huge T.V. on the wall, muted, but turned to the news. Of course, the only thing anyone would be talking about for a while is the killing of the cops and the suspect. Denise wondered if the police would even admit that the suspect wasn't the PGK.

Anyway, Denise saw a gaming system, a DVR, and DVD player connected to the television. All she could do was shake her head because the killer was just too confusing of a guy. One second, he is killing a whole SWAT team for doing their job. The next, he puts a cop in a prison cell that's like a resort room for doing her job. It just didn't make sense. There was even carpet on the floor.

Ann walked to the front of the cell and pushed a button on the intercom. Immediately, the door opened, and Ann stepped back. Denise knew Ann was a very capable cop, so if she wasn't going to make the attempt to run, Denise wouldn't try it either.

The killer walked back in and told both ladies to sit down. They both sat on the bed, looking at him. He said, "I'm only going to say this once. Don't interrupt me or ask any questions until I am finished. I'm going to do something that

I never thought I would do. I'm going to reveal part of my plan."

The two women looked at each other, and remembering what the killer said, remained silent and waited to hear what he had to say.

"All my life I've relied only on myself. Because of my abilities, everyone I meet only wants to use me for their own gain. Denise, you already know about my past with the military and the CIA because Walt told you after his visit to my trainer. And I know Walt told you about what happened to me on the prison job. I'll let you tell Ann about it when I'm finished here." The killer noticed the questioning look on Denise's face, so he answered her unspoken question.

"Satellites are everywhere. Listening devices are everywhere. I knew about the plan and everything you talked about because none of you understand anything about how advanced surveillance is now. For example, Walt sent you that note. I hacked into his body camera and read it along with the cop. Nothing is secret anymore. You'll both do good to remember that." He looked at them both to let that sink in before he continued.

"Anyway, there has always been a debate about whether killers are made or if they are born. I think they are both. I think that you can put anybody into a set of circumstances that will make them kill. Not just kill, but murder. As I have proven tonight, your best friend, loved one, mentor, and great detective, Walter Rogers, just murdered an unarmed, handcuffed man, because he thought the guy was me." He paused and seemed to smile at them both. "And I have it all on video. If that video is made public, Walt will spend the rest of his life in prison. So it's safe to say that I have him by the balls."

Denise could almost feel the anger coming off of Ann with the killer's admission. Ann had said Walt was in trouble, but it was obvious she hadn't had a clue what he had done. Denise had figured Walt had killed the guy in self-defense, but deep down, she had suspected that Walt had set something up so he could get away with killing him.

"So, my plan is," the killer continued, "to turn Walt into a killer just like me. I'm really curious to see if it is possible. I never thought I could kill anyone in cold blood. Look at me now. I went from a soldier to a serial killer, at least in the eyes of the public. But I had a lot of motivation. So I am going to give Walt all the motivation he needs." Spreading his arms wide and looking back and forth between the two of them, he said, "That's where you come in. The murder video is just the icing on the cake. I really believe he would just face the punishment for that. But he will do anything to keep the both of you safe. That's what I'm counting on."

Denise didn't know if the man was crazy or not. She knew that he was super smart and capable of almost anything, but maybe he had snapped in more ways than one. The problem was, she knew that he was serious about his plan. And if Walt didn't do what he wanted him to do, there was a chance neither of them would get out of this prison.

"So, it's simple," explained the killer. "I will give Walt ten tasks to complete. After he completes task number five, one of you will be released. After all ten are complete, whoever is left will be released. The timetable depends totally on Walt. And who is released, at what time will be up to him as well. Every task will be dangerous, so if Walt dies or is caught and locked up, both of you will go free. Any questions?"

Ann raised her hand and spoke at the same time. "Why Walt?"

The killer seemed to really think about it before answering. "I think Walt is a very special guy. I also think that he is wasting his talent working as a detective. My goal is to broaden his horizon. Make him see that the world is not always black or white. Right or wrong. I want him to be open to doing whatever needs to be done. Believe it or not, I like the man a lot and I have plans to go forward with him. But at this moment, he is not ready for what will be asked of him. I just want to prepare him for what's to come so he can help me. If not, I will remove him from the board and find someone else."

Denise raised her hand and asked, "Why us? I understand the motivation aspect, but something tells me it is more than that."

The killer looked at them for almost a full minute before answering. "Neither of you have been given the full picture of who I am. Denise, you know a lot of my background from Walt, but you haven't spent time around me. Ann, you really don't know anything about me, but we have spent time together and you know what type of person I am today. Both of you have seen my crimes. Until you both talk to each other, you will only understand the worst part. One of you doesn't know why I started; the other doesn't know what I've become. I want both of you to understand me fully."

Denise was still not satisfied. "But why us? Why do you want us to understand you?"

"Suffice it to say, I can't tell you everything at this time. Eventually, I don't want either of you thinking of me as 'the killer'. I want you to think of me as a person with a plan who might need a little bit of help."

Denise let it go, but one look at Ann told her that both of them were still confused.

The killer looked at his phone and said, "I have to go and meet with Walt. He's probably found out that the guy he killed wasn't me by now. I know he is tearing up the city looking for you, Denise. You ladies have the run of the place, and I hope you have a good talk. Ann, you know how this works. The only difference is, if I don't survive, neither will either of you. Just insurance because I'll be putting myself in danger. I'll make a quick video of you both. So, maybe, I won't have any trouble out of him."

He held up his phone and used it to record a message from both women, and then he was gone. Denise looked at Ann

271

and wondered if the killer had put too much faith in what Walt was willing to do for them.

CHAPTER 34

Walter had never felt like he was bipolar, but he was beginning to think the disorder had just been lying dormant, waiting for a reason to come out. He had been racing back and forth across Raleigh for hours, trying to find a trace of where Denise could be. It seemed hopeless, but he refused to give up. That's when the bipolar had started to kick in.

He went up and down and all around. First, he was mad, then he was sad. Then, he was hopeful, then he was hopeless. He would feel determined, then he would feel defeated. He knew it was guilty thoughts playing havoc with his mind, and he felt he deserved everything he was feeling.

After going to Denise's house and finding no Denise, Walt had hurried to the airport to retrieve his car and his phone. As soon as he was in the car, he listened to his messages and made sure the killer hadn't already reached out to him. There were fifty messages, but none of them were from the killer.

Mad as hell, and mumbling to himself, Walt drove back to Denise's house to conduct a more thorough search of her house. What he found only solidified his belief that the killer had her. Her car was gone. Her phone was gone. Most of her clothes were gone also. It looked as if the killer was trying to make it seem as if Denise had just packed up and left.

Walt had phoned Ashley and the guys that served as her camera crew. No one had heard a peep out of her. He called the newsroom and talked to the manager and the producer who worked with Denise. They both said Denise had told them she was tired and was going home to take a long bath and get some sleep. Walt had hung up and raced to her master bath and found the tub bone dry. He didn't know if that meant she never took the bath, or the bath had just been so long ago.

He looked at his phone and saw that it was 8:00am. Shocked, he looked out the window and saw the blue sky and the sun shining brightly. Subconsciously, he had been aware of the light sky, but until that moment, not the passage of time. It had been ten hours since he had last laid eyes on Denise.

He did know that she hadn't left the scene to go home until after she had tried to make it onto the secondary scene and been turned away. That had been at about midnight. So, at the most, the killer had an eight-hour lead on him. With eight hours, the killer could still cover about a fourth of the country. So in short, he was gone.

One thing that was not going to happen this time around was a media blackout. He was going to alert the whole world about Denise's kidnapping. And thanks to Agent Steve, Walt had a picture in his head of the killer. He was definitely going to work with a sketch artist to get the killer's likeness out there.

Sitting on Denise's bed, Walt was just about to call Sergeant Gould at the Raleigh PD, when he got a message of an incoming video. The accompanying text said, "Watch me for instructions." Without a second thought, Walt pushed the icon to watch the video.

When it came on, it showed Denise sitting on a bed, in what could only be some kind of fancy hotel room. The relief Walt felt, was so profound, he was afraid that he would pass out. The camera was too far away for her to be doing it on her own, but he figured some bellhop was helping her out. She wasn't restrained or naked, or in any kind of obvious pain, and he started to feel stupid.

Her enemy had been killed, at least she thought so. She had done enough work last night to warrant a vacation. Walt had been about to call in the cavalry when all Denise wanted to do was surprise him with a little getaway. He knew they both had feelings for each other, but he hadn't thought she would be ready for something like this. He laughed, thinking about how good this date night was going to be. He let the joy of knowing she was okay overshadow the knowledge of the killer being alive.

The camera started to pan to the left very slowly. There was another person sitting on the bed next to Denise. When enough of the person's face was on the screen, Walt sat in shock as the beautiful, and very alive, face of Ann Grace was revealed. For the second time in two nights, Walt cried for his partner, but this time it was for both joy and sadness. Joy because they were both alive and whole and seemed to be in good health. Sadness because the killer now had everything to make him do whatever he wanted him to do. Walt knew the killer would ask something of him.

The camera zoomed out to include both women, then Denise begin to talk. "Walt, this message is from Ann and me both. Ann will not be talking, but we are both okay and don't want you to worry about us. The killer does have us, and he will be keeping us for a while. I was told to tell you that he wants to meet with you face-to-face, and he already knows where you are. He wants you to sit tight and wait for him. Walt, I need you to understand something. Me and Ann will die if he doesn't make it back to us. If you hurt or kill him or lock him up, we will both die. All he wants to do is talk and explain how you can get us back, alive."

Abruptly, the video cut off. No. Not the video. The whole phone cut off. He thought he had made a mistake and killed it because he was squeezing it so hard. Then he looked up and the killer was standing in the doorway looking at him with a mask on.

The man reached up and pulled the mask off, saying, "Old man Steve has already shown you my face, so I guess I don't need this stupid ass mask anymore."

Walt hated this motherfucker. He was too cocky. Too sure of his own abilities. Underestimated everyone around him. And was so reliant on others to do what was expected of them. Walt stood up, pulled his gun out, pointed it at the killer, and pulled the trigger.

The explosion was deafening in the enclosed area, but neither man seemed to notice. The bullet passed about two inches from the killer's head, and the asshole never even flinched. The bastard did smile and shake his head though.

"Please tell me that you're a better shot than that," taunted the killer. "You might need more training than I thought."

"Training?" asked Walt, putting his gun back in the holster. Both of them knew that, with the women's lives on the line, he wasn't about to shoot the guy.

"Yes, training," said the killer, walking around Walt and laying down on Denise's bed.

"Damn, this bed is the shit. I have to get me one of these purple mattresses."

Walt's eyes followed the man, and he didn't even try to hide his feelings. He wanted the man to understand that he would kill him if he had to. He had just proved it by killing the guy he thought was the killer.

The killer laid there with a smile on his face, dressed in all black, like he didn't have a care in the world. Walt's heart was pounding as adrenaline flooded his system. He might not be able to kill the motherfucker, but he could definitely kick his ass.

The man jumped up off the bed, and said, "Well, this is what you've been asking for. Me and you. Man-to-man. I promise not to hurt you too bad, but I think I do need to teach you some manners." At the flip of some internal switch, the killer's whole disposition changed. Walt had been around enough killers to recognize that he was standing in front of a very dangerous man. If Walt was in his right mind, he might have paused and thought about his actions. But the anger had him in its grip, and Walt went on the attack.

Walt was no slouch when it came to fighting. Along with his training as a soldier and a cop, he was also a black belt in multiple martial arts. He delivered punches and kicks with the viciousness and ferocity of an MMA fighter. He didn't give the killer a chance to respond as he kept the man on defense. Walt didn't see the man move in any threatening way, but the next thing he knew, he was trying to get up off the floor. Only now did he feel the blow to his left temple.

He had been aware, subconsciously, that none of his attacks were effective against the killer's defense. The man was too strong and too fast, not to mention, too well trained. Walt was in excellent shape and was bigger than the other man. But, while Walt was on his knees, barely able to breath, the killer was perfectly composed and not breathing hard at all. Walt came to the conclusion that nothing short of a bullet would put the other man down.

Reading him like a book, the killer kicked him in the stomach and disarmed him of both of his guns and a hidden knife. The man took the weapons into the bathroom and came back, shutting the door behind him. "This course of action will get you killed, as well as those two beautiful ladies. I actually want you to get them back. To save them, all you have to do is follow orders, and all of you will be free."

Walt had made it to the bed and used it to pull himself up, then sat down. The killer just stood there staring at him, maybe waiting for a reply to his statement. "Let's cut the bullshit, man. Just tell me what you want so I can have my life back."

The killer laughed and said, "Walt, I hate to be the one to tell you this, but your life as you know it, is over. You want to get to the point and cut out all the bullshit? Fine. I left you your phone, look at the new message."

Walt pulled his phone out and brought up his messages. There was a new video and he wondered when the killer had time to send it. He clicked on it and watched what looked like bodycam footage. All of a sudden, a group of men came out of a house. It took a few seconds, but Walt recognized the house that the SWAT team had been staying in. Six men in total came out with two of the men being carried. About twenty feet from the house, the six bodies disintegrated as explosions ripped them apart.

Walt heard a voice say, "Holy shit!" And at that point, he understood what the killer meant when he said his life was over. Walt skipped along in the video and saw himself standing over top of the downed man. Even through the tiny speakers of the phone, the shots sounded loud. Walt skipped to the very end and saw the real killer, with his mask in place, take the body camera off of the body and melt back into the night. The killer had him at his mercy in every aspect of his life.

"What do you want?" asked Walt, with his head hanging down.

"I'll make this short and sweet so you can make your decision and I can be on my way. In this envelope," he said, throwing an envelope on the bed, "is a list of instructions. Ten very detailed sets of instructions, that you will follow, at least if you want the girls back. Every one of them will end in a death or some other illegal activity. You do them, there will be rewards, with the ultimate one being, both women returned to you unharmed. If at any point, you want to quit or you just refuse to do any part of the list, follow the instructions for quitting and I will kill both women and turn the video over to the FEDs. There's no point in acting like I won't be watching, and for some of it, I will be joining you. But for the times you are by yourself, if you get any bright ideas, the women will be punished, and I'll send you a video of it. Bottom line, you have a decision to make, and I'll know what you chose by watching the news. I have already set up everything for your first task. All that's needed is for you to be present and follow the instructions. One word of warning. I'm sure you know that once you start, you will be one of the most sought-after fugitives in the world. The only way for Denise and Ann to live is for you to complete all ten tasks. I will help you if you need it, but it's going to be up to you to finish each task. Some of them will push you to do things that you will have to put your morals aside in order to do. To be honest, I could give a fuck how you feel, just do what you're told."

The killer walked to the bedroom door and stopped. "I have faith in you, Walt. I know you don't understand why I am doing this, but you will. Good luck." With that last statement, he walked out without a backwards glance.

Walt sat there with the early morning sun streaming into the bedroom. He was not one to feel sorry for himself, but he felt drained and worthless. He reached over and picked up the envelope. It was thick with papers that Walt knew would lead to his destruction. Only because he knew that he would do whatever it took to free those innocent women that he loved.

He knew that he was procrastinating because, once he opened the envelope, all of his choices would disappear. Sitting up straight with a look of utter determination, he tore open the envelope and started to read.

EPILOGUE

"What a beautiful day to be vindicated." Captain Robert Dennis was waiting inside of the courthouse for his press conference to begin. He was standing in the middle of his sea of lawyers, waiting to be escorted to the top of the steps where he would preside over his own press conference.

After months of being locked up and humiliated on a daily basis, he couldn't wait to rub it in everyone's face that the D.A. had to drop all the charges. The D.A. didn't really have a choice once his lawyers got ahold of the evidence the police had been holding back. It was going to be the highlight of his life to tell the whole world to kiss his ass.

Looking out of the courthouse doors, he was kind of disappointed in the turnout. There were only five reporters waiting for him to emerge. The worst part, that black bitch reporter, and that nigger detective were nowhere in sight. He had been watching the news every day on the inside, so he consoled himself with the knowledge that the reporter was missing.

It had been two weeks since that Prison Guard Killer had murdered all those cops, and everyone had thought Det. Rogers had killed him. Turns out, the guy who was killed was an ex-con who the FBI is saying was an accomplice. So, the consensus was, the killer had retaliated by killing the reporter. Cpt. Dennis just wished he could have killed her himself.

At his lawyer's signal, he knew it was showtime. He put everything else out of his mind and focused on putting confidence in his step as he walked to the podium with a smile on his face.

"I want to start off by saying, everyone who thought I was guilty of killing my own wife and daughter, fuck you. All you media types who never once gave me time to grieve for my family, fuck you. And to the cops, the DA, and the judge, who all conspired to keep me locked up when they had the evidence to free me this whole time, fuck you. And finally, to the man who killed my family, and set it up to make me look guilty, fuck you!"

Robert had wanted to come out and smile and act like the world couldn't faze him, and his prison time had been nothing. The reality was, he was mad as hell, and he was going to use this time to express himself to all the people who had doubted him.

"It's amazing to me how easy it is for people in this Nation to turn against you. I've been serving this country my whole life. First in the military, then keeping these animals off of the streets of civilized America. I've put my life on the line so that you people can walk these streets without fear of being kidnapped, or raped, or murdered. But when I needed someone to believe in me, no one wanted to help the fat redneck."

He was really working his way up to a massive explosion. Robert heard his lawyers saying something to him, but he was too far gone to pay them any attention. "Why? I don't deserve help from the country I helped defend? Huh? Is it because I use the word Nigger? Is it because I'm part of the KKK? Well, fuck all of you sons of bitches."

His lawyers were actively trying to pull him away from the microphones, but his near four hundred pounds were going nowhere he didn't want them to go. A reporter shouted out a question. "Did you ask the killer to get rid of your family for the money?"

"What!" shouted Cpt. Dennis. "You motherfucker. I loved my family. Why would you even ask me that? Haven't you been listening to what I've said? Even after everything that's been revealed to exonerate me, you people still won't give me my due. I'll tell you all this, the money I'm getting from my family is nothing compared to the money I'm going to get when I sue all of your stations and the city for slander."

The same reporter asked, "What about your son-in-law? What are you going to do about him?"

"Fuck that nigger," Robert exploded. "He is not my son-in-law. Just because he was fucking my daughter, you think that makes us family? I'll never acknowledge that black bastard."

While he had been in jail, his daughter's husband had come out of the woodworks trying to drum up some sympathy for himself. He had also publicly condemned Robert, saying that he was sure he had something to do with his family's death. The good thing was the man had money. So Robert was adding him to the list of people he was going to sue.

Cpt. Dennis spread his arms wide and laughed at the stunned faces staring at him. "I don't need any of you pieces of shit. Once I get done with this city, I'll be filthy rich. And I'm going to stay right here in Greenville to rub it in all of your stuck-up, ugly faces. You see, nothing can stop me from being great. Nothing or no one can keep me down. No matter how much you idiots hate me, I'll always come out on top."

With his last word, his head exploded in a shower of red mist. As the body fell backwards, a hush fell over the small gathering. No one heard the shot, so no one moved for about three seconds. Then, everyone but the cameramen were running and trying to find cover.

The cameramen were turning in every direction, trying to catch sight of the shooter. They all knew the networks wouldn't allow the actual shooting on T.V., but the internet was a whole different story. The murder of one man had just made the lives of the cameramen and reporters better. At least the ones who could get over the carnage that they had just witnessed.

It was sad, but even in death, not one person made a move to help the redneck, who only wanted someone to believe in him.

• •

In the parking garage of the hospital, about a half mile away, a phone call was being made.

"Did you like the show?" the man asked when his call was answered.

"Don't get cocky," admonished the man on the other end of the call. "You still have a lot of work to do."

"Just wanted to make sure everything was good before I started on task number two."

"Everything was perfect," replied the killer. "See, I knew I could bring the best out of you."

"As you said, I have a lot of work to do. No time to chit chat." Walt hung up the phone and stowed the rifle in its case and closed the back door of the van.

He wondered if after he finished all of these tasks, he would even have a heart to share with the women he was trying to save. He drove off and easily blended in with the hospital traffic, who had no idea what had just happened.

More people were going to die, and even more would wish for death. The killer had an agenda, but so did Walt. It was going to be an amazing journey to see which one of them comes out on top.

L. A. BURCH

Available Now

L. A. BURCH

About The Author

Leon A. Burch was born in Philadelphia, PA; and now
resides in North Carolina. He attended Temple University.
To contact him with questions or comments,
you can reach him at
authorlaburch@gmail.com

www.ingramcontent.com/pod-product-compliance
Lightning Source LLC
Chambersburg PA
CBHW030347020726
47493CB00003B/731